THE
NEGOTIATOR

THE
NEGOTIATOR

A NOVEL OF SUSPENSE

BRENDAN
DUBOIS

MIDNIGHT INK
WOODBURY, MINNESOTA

FIRST EDITION
First Printing, 2018

Book format by Bob Gaul
Cover design by Kevin R. Brown
Editing by Nicole Nugent

Midnight Ink, an imprint of Llewellyn Worldwide Ltd.

Library of Congress Cataloging-in-Publication Data
Names: DuBois, Brendan, author.
Title: The negotiator: a novel of suspense / Brendan DuBois.
Description: Woodbury, Minnesota: Midnight Ink, [2018]
Identifiers: LCCN 2018007504 (print) | LCCN 2018011425 (ebook) | ISBN
    9780738755830 () | ISBN 9780738754017 (softcover: acid-free paper)
Subjects: LCSH: Murder—Investigation—Fiction. | GSAFD: Suspense fiction. |
    Mystery fiction.
Classification: LCC PS3554.U2564 (ebook) | LCC PS3554.U2564 N44 2018
(print)
    | DDC 813/.54—dc23
LC record available at https://lccn.loc.gov/2018007504

Midnight Ink
Llewellyn Worldwide Ltd.
2143 Wooddale Drive
Woodbury, MN 55125-2989
www.midnightinkbooks.com

Printed in the United States of America

This novel is dedicated to my brother Dennis,
world traveler and the finest real negotiator I know.

ACKNOWLEDGMENTS

The author wishes to extend his thanks and appreciation to his fantastic editor, Terri Bischoff, as well as other members of the Midnight Ink publishing team. Thanks, too, to my wife and first reader, Mona Pinette, as well as to dedicated fans Ken Sullivan and Edmond D. Smith for their assistance.

ONE

I'M A NEGOTIATOR, THE best in the world.

You won't see my face or read about my successful work in *The Wall Street Journal, Fortune, Barron's* or the Business section of *The New York Times.*

That's not how I roll.

For years I've been conducting successful negotiations with a variety of dark characters and shadowy companies in all corners of the world. I was once flown by a private Gulfstream jet to Monaco, where I stayed at a penthouse suite in one of the famed casino hotels on Place du Casino, hammering out the sale of stolen bearer bonds from Serbian thieves to eager buyers from Indonesia. I once conducted another successful business deal near the corner of Woodward and West Robinwood Street in a burnt-out section of Detroit, where the lampposts were dark and feral dogs ran among the shadows, getting to a successful resolution of a deal involving rare motor parts for an even more rare demonstration model of a Ford sports car that never reached market back in 1959.

I got paid fairly well both times. That's how my business model works.

Years ago I found—through a series of lucky accidents—that I had a gift of being able to instantly place an accurate market value on a wide variety of objects, from Ming dynasty vases of the fifteenth century to limited production line editions of Air Jordan sneakers. Somehow, I was born with a funky memory and the cognitive ability to make intuitive leaps to negotiate deals that would leave both parties happy when the wheeling and dealing was over.

These particular talents served me well before I went out independent on my own. Oh. What did I do before I went independent?

Perhaps I was one of those $500 an hour Wall Street lawyers working for a hedge fund, going line by line through financial documents, yawning desperately in an attempt not to toss myself out of a twentieth-floor window. Or maybe I was the best Toyota car salesman in Southern California, with a wall of plaques and a shelf full of trophies denoting the same, complete with my own private parking space and a host of envious fellow car salesmen who wished they could dine on my liver. Or maybe I was a Special Forces soldier, with a love of firearms and the canny ability to be dropped into whatever Third World hellhole was making the news that month, and being able to reach an agreement between tribes that have been at war since the time of Charlemagne over a stolen goat.

Take your pick. All I know is that when I went out on my own, I knew I could end up on one of the PBS shows that appraise various bits of attic junk for supposedly unsuspecting middle-Americans, or I could give in to the seductive dark side and see the world and meet interesting people.

I chose the dark path, with open eyes, a new suit, and a fine collection from the best that Beretta, Colt, Remington, and Sig-Sauer had to offer.

But there's rules. There's always rules, otherwise you don't thrive and you don't live.

The big three, if you please: no drugs. A real nonstarter. Not necessarily because it's inherently evil, but because it attracts an entire class of people who are dopey, dangerous, deranged, and any other word beginning with *d* that suits your fancy. If they feel insulted or dissed or if you step on their $700 Manolo Blahnick shoes, they'll slit your throat without bothering to put down a plastic tarp beforehand to contain the mess. Drug dealing also attracts a good collection of bottom-feeders who will turn you in or hurt you or kill you if they're bored or feel out-of-sorts. Not that I'm particularly concerned about those bottom-feeders, but I figure, why waste time, energy, and mental health over who they are, and also, the time it takes to dispose of their bodies if it comes to that?

The second rule is no human beings, which definitely crosses the border into evil. Nope, no people, not even those who have unfortunately been kidnapped, either child or adult. Way too many emotions involved, sometimes you're not too sure who the good guys or bad guys are, and speaking of attractions, it can easily attract a high number of law enforcement agencies. Who needs the hassle? And don't get me started on anything to do with the trafficking of women. Not going to happen.

And last rule, and not the least, is I won't do anything I feel would be against the best interests of the United States of America. That means random bits of technology that could end up in the hands of those nations or organizations that have bugs up their collective asses about the Land of the Free, Home of the Brave. Not that I believe the current administration is doing much of anything to prevent those rogue nations from getting what they need in the forbidden weapons realm, but I figure, what the heck, why make it easy for them?

Besides, for all its faults—and I don't lie awake at night worrying about them—it's still a fine place to live, be an entrepreneur, and enjoy the very best BBQ in the world.

————

On this early afternoon in May, I was in a motel on the outskirts of Lawrence, a crumbling and depressing city in northeastern Massachusetts. Decades ago it was a thriving city with a prosperous downtown and plenty of busy mills that had been built along the Merrimack River. Then the mills closed, lots of businesses shuttered as well, and now the city is trying each year to rebuild, a true and hopeful American story. Alas, the last time it tried to rebuild, its not-so-bright citizens elected a man for mayor who was later under a number of investigations for various charges of political corruption, including illegally shipping a garbage truck to the Dominican Republican, to impress some relatives there.

A trash truck!

Makes one long for the expansive days of Tammany Hall.

The motel room I was in was small, made even more small by the four other men sharing it with me. There were two single beds—each sagging in the middle—a countertop bearing a television airing Univision and a window with its shades drawn that overlooked the parking lot, and another closed door no doubt leading to the bathroom. The light green carpet was worn, stained, and had several cigarette burns. Besides Univision, airing an early repeat of *Sabado*

Gigante, the only other real noise was the constant hum of traffic from nearby I-495.

The four men were Hispanic and heavily armed. Two sat on each bed. All four wore baseball caps turned around, leather jackets, white tank top shirts (I refuse to use that dreadful description "wife-beater"), jeans, and black sneakers. Two had highly illegal sawed-off shotguns in their laps, and the other two had semiautomatic pistols. At various times during my brief stay, the four would play with their weapons, slapping the stocks, pretending to aim at things through the sights, little macho games like that.

I think they were trying to psych me out. Good luck with that.

I had on clean pressed jeans, black sneakers, a checked flannel shirt, and short leather jacket. I dressed the best I could to blend in, while managing my own style. I've done other negotiations wearing my black-tie evening wear, and twice, wearing just a bathing suit. Whatever works is fine by me.

I was sitting in one of the two uncomfortable wooden chairs in the room. The other chair was empty, and the chair and I were patiently waiting for my assistant and factor, who was currently outside making sure the other negotiating party was coming in on time and moving into an adjacent room.

But my clients were nervous, were jumpy, and I just sat there and maintained an expression of disinterested cool, which, truth be told, wasn't hard to project. I was armed as well, a Sig-Sauer Model P226 semiautomatic pistol tucked in a side holster under my coat, but I was depending on my attitude to keep things calm and on an even strain.

Hard to believe from my vantage point—since I consider myself a sweet guy who doesn't mind walking little old ladies or men across a crosswalk—but I guess I have a look around my eyes and face when I get exasperated. A few years back I had dated an assistant bank manager in Sun Valley, Idaho, a single attractive mom with a young son and daughter. One night I was involved in a disturbance in a combination pub/restaurant when a German skier made nasty comments about my friend's bosom. Later, when I was washing the skier's blood off my hands, she had gently kissed me and told me she couldn't see me again, ever.

"No offense, darling, but when you got angry, you had the look of 'I am death, fuck with me not' on your face, and that scares me," she had said.

So there you go.

I still send her a Christmas card each year, so you can tell I'm not one to keep a grudge.

The lead man in the group, called Ramon, spoke up and said, "Yo, so what happens if the buyers don't show up?"

"Then I leave and you guys have to go somewhere else."

"Don't like it," he said.

"Not my problem," I said. "I'm here to negotiate, not to babysit."

His three fellow *amigos* muttered darkly among themselves and that was all right by me.

You see, the way it works, you have Party A that has something of value they want to sell to Party B. But maybe Party A's not too sure what they have, or what its value might be. And they don't trust Party B to offer a fair deal because they don't know Party B's background.

That's where I step in. I look at what the object is, evaluate it, and determine the fair price. If the two parties agree, I make the exchange and I get a 5 percent fee tacked on top of the price, paid by the buyer because a) the buyer has the cash and b), the buyer obviously has an incentive to make sure that none of the dealings ever get passed on to any authorities. And then I move on, more often than not, never to see them again.

There are additional rules, of course. The negotiations have an end date: one meeting, and one meeting only. I'm not interested in spending hours or days dickering around. This isn't a Bravo reality show about whiny young real estate agents who wouldn't know hard times if it kicked them in their shiny teeth and gave them atomic wedgies with their Calvin Klein underwear. Both parties have to show up on time, though being a reasonable fellow, I give them five minutes' grace time. If someone doesn't show up, then I'm gone, never to come back. You have one chance with me, and only one.

The door to the motel room opened up. A tall, broad man who looked like he'd be at ease on a rugby field or a state prison exercise yard came in, seemingly taking up every formerly empty square inch of space. He had on a dull-looking two-piece tan suit, white shirt, and brown loafers. The coat was baggy on purpose, to disguise whatever weaponry he was carrying. He had a strong chin, bald head, and a bristly gray and white moustache that looked liked it was trimmed with a chunk of pumice.

"Our visitors are here," he announced in a firm voice. "They're getting settled. Should be ready in five minutes."

"Great," I said. "Have a seat."

He did, and the chair creaked ominously, like he was going to break it. Clarence Briggs folded his large scarred hands and waited.

"Your clients don't look happy," he observed.

"They're just worried about the deal."

"They hired you," Clarence said. "You'd think that would give them some comfort."

"Yeah, but no accounting for taste," I said.

Ramon glowered at me. "Hey. Shut the fuck up, will you?"

I just stared right back at him, and then he looked away. To Clarence I said, "You were gone for a while."

"I was."

"How did you pass the time?"

"There were two working women at the end unit," he said. "They made me an offer, I made a counteroffer, and a deal was reached."

"Clarence…"

"Hey, you should be honored," he said. "I've learned to make deals from the very best."

"And what did you learn?"

"To expand upon an original offer, to see if we could reach an agreement that would address both of our interests."

"I know what their interests are: to make money," I said. "I'm not sure I want to know what yours was."

He flicked his thumbs together. "Pretty vanilla. I just wanted to be in their room, looking out the window, and to pass the time, I asked them to kiss each other."

"For real?"

"Sure," Clarence said. "I didn't even ask them to take their clothes off. Just sit on the edge of the bed and make out."

"Well."

"Hey," Clarence said. "For me, the sight of two women kissing is the most erotic thing in the world. So I paid them well, I sat there, they started kissing, and then the other party showed up."

"You plan on visiting them when we're done?"

"No," he said. "I need to take my ex and my boys to a Little League game later on tonight. Then we got an awards ceremony a couple of days later, want to make a good impression."

Ramon said something in Spanish, one of his mates did the same thing, and there was a knock at the door.

Clarence stood up, and so did I.

"Be back in a bit," I said to Ramon. "Don't fret."

The other room was identical, but there were only two men inside, both sitting on the chairs. The television set was off. They had on black suits, neckties, and white shirts. One was in his sixties, the other in his thirties. Both wore black fedoras and had long black beards. The younger one, who had knocked on the door and led us over, said, "Are you ready?"

"Very ready," I said.

The older man said, "Well. So you're the famous negotiator. Eh?"

"That's what it says on my business card."

With surprise, the younger man said, "You have a business card?"

"No," I said. "I was just messing with you. I'll be back shortly."

The older man waved a hand, like he was dismissing a craftsmen or contractor, and I let the insult slide and let him live.

Back through door number one, I said, "All right, Ramon, let's see the merchandise."

From his coat pocket he took out a black velvet string bag, dumped a handful of cut diamonds on the countertop, which was smeared with furniture polish and old fingerprints. From my own pockets, I took out a pair of tweezers and a jeweler's loupe, 10x magnification, and went to work, closely examining each of the six stones.

I know, I know, it's a particularly grim and criminal occupation, but without us folks working in the shadows, the insurance companies would fold up and all those widows and orphans depending on stock dividend payouts from said insurance companies would either starve or have to eat Alpo. Besides, in most cases when it comes to theft like this, it's not an insult to blame the victim. Sometimes folks will have thousand dollar locks on their front door and a hook-and-eye securing the rear screen door. Or maybe a Nigerian prince, or a Venezuelan generalissimo or a Boston City councilor scams them.

I slowly examined one stone after another. One man in the rear, belligerent with a shotgun, yelled out, "See? See? That's good shit. It's good shit, isn't it?"

Ramon snapped at him. "Shut up, Tomas. Let him work!"

And work is what I did. I took my time with each stone, knowing that these four bozos were getting more and more excited, and more and more concerned. Excited at the payout they were thinking about getting, and concerned about me, I'm sure. For how could they trust me in reaching a fair price?

Decent question, and my only answer is my reputation of service. I have a nice long record of providing fair and equitable negotiations among many different kinds of customers, and it's that word of mouth that keeps additional business coming in. I know the minute I screw someone over, my phone calls and email messages will dry out.

I looked once more at the rocks, put my tweezers and jeweler's loupe away.

"Be right back," I said.

"Hey!" Tomas yelled, standing up with his shotgun. "What bullshit is this? You tell us what it's worth now! Don't you fucking walk away from us."

I didn't say a word, but Clarence said, "Appreciate your concern, *amigo*. But walking away is what we're going to do."

Clarence has worked for me—or with me, depending on your point of view—for three years. He's my factor, adviser, and extra firepower if the circumstances demand it. I hired him after a negotiation went sideways when the sale of eleven rare books got stuck in a rut. Clarence was a member of the first party, who wanted to sell the books, and during a quick break in the negotiations, in a barn outside of Albany, New York, he took me aside and said, "Word to the wise, my boss intends to kidnap you when this is done."

"Why?" I asked. "He doesn't like my necktie?"

"He doesn't like anything," Clarence said. "He wants me to kidnap you and torture you, so you'd give up where you stash your cash at your home. He's not one for taking the long view, building a business relationship."

"Gee, thanks for the information. Not sure what to do with it, though."

Clarence looked over at his boss, a jumpy kid who dressed in all black, and whom I gathered had stolen the rare books from his grandfather, and he said, "Tell you what. I like your style, your approach. I'd like to work for you."

"I've always worked alone."

"That should change," Clarence said. "Next time you might not meet up with someone as thoughtful as me."

"Good point," I said. "Can I hire you now, or is there going to be a waiting period?"

His boss yelled from across the room. "Hey! Clarence, get over here! Stop fucking around, okay?"

Clarence said, "I can go with you now."

"That'd be great."

Clarence walked across the barn floor, took out his Beretta, put it to the side of the kid's head, and served his termination notice. Because I was expecting it, I didn't flinch much at the noise.

———————

Back to the second room, and after a single knock, we went in. "So?" the older man asked.

"They have six stones, round brilliant," I said. "Color G, very slightly included, four carats per, nice lot. I put a price on the whole haul of one hundred thousand dollars. With my fee, that's a payout of one hundred five thousand."

The older man looked at the younger man, and said, "Well. I think I'd like to take a look at them myself."

"Clarence?"

"On my way."

Clarence left and came back within a minute, accompanied by a glowering Tomas. At least Tomas had his weapon hidden.

The older man examined the stones with his own tweezers and loupe, spreading them out on a briefcase cover balanced on his lap, and nodded. They went back into the black bag, were handed back to Clarence, who walked back outside with Tomas. The door shut with a gentle *click*.

The younger man said, "Papa?"

A weary shrug. "Oh, what are we, a charity?"

"Not an answer," I said. "One hundred five thousand dollars."

"No," he said. "Eighty, perhaps eighty-five."

A knock at the door. Clarence came back in, sat down.

I said, "Not going to happen. That's a fair price and you know it. After I get paid, they're getting one hundred thousand dollars, after doing their … work, which could have put any of them into prison if they had been caught for a very long time, indeed. After you clean and set those stones, you'll do very well. It's an equitable price."

"Eighty-five. Go and tell them eighty-five."

I stood up. "Tell you what. I'm going to walk out with my associate here, poke my head into their room, and tell the crew in there that I'm done. Then you're free to negotiate with the four of them, all of whom are heavily armed and aren't in a happy mood. And while you try to negotiate with them, my friend and I will go out for some ice cream."

The younger man said, "Wait. Please." He leaned over and there was a harsh exchange of whispers. I made a point of looking at my watch. Clarence looked bored. The younger man said, "Papa agrees, one hundred thousand dollars. Plus five thousand dollars for your view."

"I want to hear it from him. No offense, but that's the agreement that was arranged for this meeting. I negotiate with him, and nobody else."

Another heavy, world-weary sigh, as he flipped up a few fingers. "One hundred thousand."

"Plus the five thousand."

A shrug. "I assumed that was understood."

A sharp look from me. "Please don't assume anything on my behalf."

He looked away. His son looked frightened.

Good.

———

Back to the first room, and Clarence said, "Ice cream? Really?"

"What, you don't like ice cream?"

"I do," he said. "But that's an after-dinner treat."

We both sat down in the room's wooden chairs. "All right. Lunch, and then ice cream later."

He smiled. "Great."

Tomas yelled out, "Hey! Stop that yip-yap! What's going on?"

I nodded. "Good news. You four … gentlemen did quite well. Those diamonds are the real deal, they're valuable, and the man next door wants to make an offer. One hundred thousand dollars."

Ramon didn't say anything, but the other two guys in his entourage looked at each other with big smiles, but Tomas seemed to have seller's remorse.

"No!" he shouted. "That's *mentira!* No! That's too little!"

Ramon yelled back. "Shut up, Tomas! Shut up!"

I guess Tomas needed to work on his employee-management skills, because he came forward, slammed his hip into Ramon, and pointed his shotgun at me. "No! No way! Those rocks are worth a hell of a lot more! A hell of a lot more!"

Clarence quietly said, "How are you doing?"

"Oh, I'm good. You?"

"Hanging in there," Clarence said. "Just waiting on you."

"Thanks."

Ramon said, "Tomas, be quiet!"

Tomas waved the shotgun back and forth. "No, no, the stones are worth … two hundred thousand." He grinned. "That's right. Two hundred thousand dollars!" Then he looked at me again, pointed the shotgun at my head. "You go out there and you talk to that thief next door, and you tell him, two hundred thousand dollars. Not a fucking penny less!"

Ramon caught my attention. "Well?" he asked.

I said, "That's a nonsense number, pulled out of your friend's perky bottom. I'm not going to go out there and present such a number in an unprofessional manner. It has no basis in reality."

Tomas came closer, the barrel of the shotgun under my chin. He pushed up, trying to lift my chin. He might have even succeeded for a millimeter or two. "No ... this is reality ... you go out there and say two hundred thousand, or I'll take your head off and do the same to your slow friend. Then I'll go out there and seal the deal myself, *hombre*."

Clarence sighed. "Dear me," he said.

I cleared my throat. "Hold on for a second. Ramon ... if I may?"

"Yes." He looked frustrated, angry, and embarrassed—an unpleasant combination.

"Ramon, when we made this arrangement, the agreement was with you, me, and the buyer. Isn't that true?"

"Yes."

I held my hands up and open, in a very nonthreatening move. "Then let's keep to the agreement. One hundred thousand dollars. That means twenty-five thousand dollars apiece, for you and your three companions, for what was probably just a couple hours of work. Am I right?"

A pause in the action. The other two men came closer from their sitting positions on the two beds. Tomas's breathing had quickened. I looked straight at Ramon. "You and these three other men will receive the payout, in less than ten minutes. Cash money, untraceable, right in your hands. But it's up to you how many associates are eligible for a payday. You're the man in charge. *El jefe*. Do you understand what I'm saying?"

Ramon's eyes flashed. He understood. He yelled something quickly in Spanish. The other two men jumped Tomas, dragged him

15

back, tugged the shotgun out of his hands. They threw him on the near bed. Ramon went to the television, turned it up louder. The two men had Tomas stretched out on the bed, a pillow on his head. Ramon went over, pushed the muzzle end of his pistol against the pillow, shot twice. Tomas's legs quivered, and the other two men stepped away.

Ramon turned to me. "The terms are acceptable. I agree."

TWO

OUT IN THE PARKING lot, Clarence and I met up with the younger bearded man, who opened up the trunk of a black Audi 6000. Inside was a black satchel. He unzipped it and reached inside, taking out a couple of bundles of cash, which he put into his pants pocket. Clarence went forward, counted the banded packs of one-hundred-dollar bills that remained in the satchel, removed five of them and put three in my hand, and kept two for himself. We both slipped our bundles into our coat pockets.

The younger man said, "Did I hear two gunshots back then?"

"Must have been the television," I said.

Ramon was watching us from the open door of his room. Clarence went over with the athletic bag, Ramon passed over the bag of diamonds, and Clarence then came back, put the bag into the young man's hand. The bag went into another pants pocket.

Exchange complete.

The younger man said, "Look ... ask you question?"

I said, "No."

The younger man's face flushed, and then he scampered back to the motel room. Clarence raised a bushy eyebrow. "That was cold."

"That's what's to be expected. Hungry?"

"Starved."

"How about Billingsgate?"

"Why not?"

Then Clarence and I went our separate ways. He went to a black Lincoln Navigator with Massachusetts license plates, and I took my black Lexus with Maine license plates, and off we went.

We met up about thirty minutes later in the remote New Hampshire town of East Kingston. The town has some light industry, a golf course, farms, and a rabbit-breeding facility. Billingsgate was a restaurant made from a converted cider mill, and the owner thought its name was something British and veddy upper class. In actuality, the name comes from an area in London known for its sale of fish, and the cry of the fishmongers was so foul and nasty that the term "Billingsgate" was used for offensive or obscene language. But there was nothing foul with this building. Lots of old stone and exposed beams and a fast-moving stream in the rear that helped propel a water wheel back in the day.

The owner was a nice cheery guy with a premature receding black hairline that made his exposed forehead look like a shiny bowling ball, and I never bothered to correct his misunderstanding of his restaurant's name. Life was too short and why shatter the poor guy's illusions? Clarence and I took a corner booth where we could sit with our backs against the wall and examine both the menus and the front door.

I went with a lobster and scallop dish, while Clarence took the good ol' Amurrican route of steak and baked potato. While we ate, we never once talked business. I stuck to the weather, politics, and my new favorite show on PBS examining the history of the Bible. Clarence talked about his ex-wife and his sons, the Little League players—who were being honored at an awards banquet next week—and how spoiled his boys were, for each year they expected a Red Sox team that would make the playoffs.

"My dad," Clarence pointed out, "died a month after the Sox nailed their first World Series in nearly a hundred years, and he was the happiest I'd ever seen him. Ever since the Impossible Dream of '67, he always prayed for next year. Today's fans … don't get me fucking started."

During our first post-work meal nearly three years ago, Clarence had gently and insistently pressed me on my background, where I had been born and raised, what my career choices had been, and other life-bonding information like that. I kept on deflecting his questions, like an ace hockey goalie playing against a grade schooler on ice for only the second time in his or her life. But he hadn't given up the pokes and probes. Finally I had excused myself and gone to use the restroom, and from there I departed—after picking his pocket and sticking him with the bill.

He never asked me a personal question again.

When we were finished and got to the cups of coffee stage, I asked him if he was up for some ice cream, and he shook his head. "Nope. My gullet is full."

"Then we'll take care of it next time."

He wiped his face with a crisp white napkin. "Anything in the pipeline?"

"Not as of yet," I said. "But in a retrenching economy like this one, you can bet something will come up soon enough."

An attractive young waitress came by, all smiles, and dropped off the check. I picked it up and without using our new gains of one-hundred-dollar bills, I paid in cash with my daily supply, left a hefty tip, and then we headed out. A cheery wave and he went off to Massachusetts, and I stayed in New Hampshire and headed north, making sure to stay off the toll roads, with their cameras and monitors and snoopy State Police troopers in parked cruisers.

———

Outside of Manchester, the state's largest city, I pulled into a Super Wal-Mart, stepped out, and went over to a five-year-old dull green Honda Pilot. I got into that vehicle and really started to go home. That Wal-Mart has its own surveillance cameras, but they didn't cover the far end of the lot, which I used from time to time as my own personal staging area. Neither the Lexus nor the Pilot have one of those GPS systems, and I've made sure the little black boxes in the engines that measure speed, distance traveled, mileage, and other interesting bits of information have been disabled.

I live in what's cheerfully called a bedroom community outside of Manchester, a sweet town called Litchfield that I had chosen carefully. It's close enough to the highways and the airport out of Manchester for easy travel, and it still has a small-town feel that meant it stayed out of the news most times. Plus it had one heck of a volunteer fire department, which made for a comfortable sleep at night.

It was nearing dusk as I made my way down Route 3 and then took a right into a neighborhood called Merrimack Banks. It's built near the Merrimack River, and I like it because the homes aren't

McMansions and the lots aren't huge. Some time ago, in puzzling through where I wanted to live as I embarked on my new career, I thought that the clichéd stereotype of the master criminal living in a penthouse apartment or a remote, secluded Fortress of Solitude— complete with guard dogs, lights, a high fence, and command-detonation mines—wasn't going to work. For one thing, penthouse apartments are pricey, indeed, and are subject to a lot of curiosity from your downstairs neighbors. Plus, being high up in a penthouse, you were trapped even before anybody took violent notice of you.

So, why not the aforementioned remote compound? That wasn't wise, either, for setting up such a place was like setting off fireworks every Saturday night, begging somebody out there to pay attention. Building such a large, guarded compound in a rural area meant lots of tongues wagging, and texts being exchanged among the curious. Plus, being a one-man show—this was before I met Clarence—it would mean a lot of angst and anxiety over safety: if you're on a re-mote hundred-acre strip of land, accessible by a mile-long dirt driveway, then the bad guys could come in with an M252 81mm mortar system and reduce hearth and home to broken rubble and burning beams with no one noticing.

Not that I believe there are a horde of bad guys out there in the shadows, gunning for me, but I always try to act accordingly.

I pulled into the driveway of my home, a quiet-looking country house, stained dark brown, with a two-car garage and farmer's porch. My neighbors were across the street and in homes adjacent to me, about a hundred feet or so in either direction. Enough space for privacy, but close enough so that if a black-clad platoon of Jihadi warriors decided to trot down the road and into my driveway, some of my neighbors would take notice and call the cops.

I got out and left the Pilot in the driveway, walked over to my mailbox and pulled out that day's thin offering—a bunch of fliers and two preapproved credit card applications—and then I went to the porch steps. Some low shrubbery separated me on the left from the Smith family, a young couple with two girls—ages six and four— and a yellow German Shepherd that was friendly enough, but had a cold spot in her eyes that said clearly that if you did any harm to the two young girls, her teeth would instantly sink into your throat.

To the right was Clem Houston, a retired American Airlines pilot who was a nice guy to chat with—especially if you wanted to kill an hour discussing the sorry state of politics—and he was in his front yard, trimming some juniper bushes. I gave him a wave, got up on the porch, unlocked the very pricey and secure lock to the front door, and walked in.

———

The front and rear doors are expensive, solid, and dependable, with deadbolts. There's no keypad, no alarm system, no stickers on the windows or little signs stuck in the lawn to warn anyone passing by that this little suburban house has something to hide.

That's attention I don't want. Which is why when I'm not working, I'm the perfect quiet little suburban bachelor. I tell everyone who asks that I'm writing a textbook concerning macroeconomics—which should be finished in three or four years—and which makes most people's eyes roll back in their heads. I'm of a certain age that companionship of some sort is expected, so if I'm asked, I tell the questioner that I'm a widower who had the love affair of a lifetime. Then I make a sad face, and the subject quickly gets changed.

I give out candy during Halloween, help the elderly couple across the street shovel out their driveway, and twice a year, when the street is closed off for a block party, I volunteer to make my world-famous cheeseburgers.

Occasionally I invite my neighbors in for dinner. My house is clean and unimpressive. Bookshelves, shiny kitchen, nice furniture, and a wall-mounted plasma television. No gun cases, no mounted heads of killed animals on the wall, and certainly no *Guns & Ammo* magazines scattered around the coffee table. And when my neighbors are eating, there's no discussion of politics or anything else on my part that would make me memorable down the road.

I proudly give them tours of my house, if requested, and I even take them down to the cellar, which has a workbench with a collection of tools, an oil tank and furnace, and a spare freezer.

All plain, vanilla, and boring.

Which works perfectly.

———

I went inside my home, dropped the mail off on the kitchen counter for later inspection and disposal, and made a quick wandering around the rooms, no set pattern, just random, but I was checking all my windows, making sure the little telltale signs I left there— small lengths of toothpicks—had remained in place. Very simple and very effective.

All seemed secure.

I got into the basement, went to the workbench, manipulated the racks holding the hammers and a yardstick. The pegboard swung back, revealing my large, foundation-based safe, and I worked the combination and slid the day's earnings inside.

In another minute, I closed everything up, and I had a quick memory of a tour six months ago, when a newly moved-in architect up the street took interest in my house, started lecturing me on its style and shape, and in the basement, started talking about the special foundation and how it was made from local stone.

He got pretty close to my hidden safe.

Lucky for him, pretty close wasn't in the zone where I would have had to have snapped his neck and waste part of an evening finding a place for his body.

———

Sounds like a boring life, eh? But I love it. Get up when I want to, eat whatever suits me, read lots of books, watch a lot of movies, and sometimes take continuing education lessons at the local state university.

But work is always out there, and I'm always ready for it.

———

After coming back from a midmorning bicycle ride nearly a week later, I went into the kitchen via the one-car garage and heard a slight *hum*, followed by a pause, and then another *hum*. It was my latest iPhone, telling me a message had come in.

Goody. I was getting bored.

I took a swig of orange juice from my refrigerator, put the container back in, and checked the iPhone, clicking through a variety of screens until I got to a very valuable and unique app that I was promised years ago would take the efforts of the National Security Agency to track and maybe—maybe—crack.

I thumbed through, saw two invites for an upcoming negotiation. The messages were sent via text through an email system based in Finland, which went through a series of anonymous email forwarding systems before coming to me.

This forwarding system was also made by the same woman who made the unique app for my iPhone. I met her once, years ago in Perth, and had never communicated with her, ever again. And it took me nearly six months to earn back the money I had paid her, but it had been worth every penny. Or rand. Or yen. Or Bitcoin.

The date was set for tomorrow at two p.m., at a private residence in eastern Vermont, where the buyer lived. A drive, then, and reasonably local. Okay. And the item in question was a rare painting. Okay again. And the buyer was flying in tonight to Boston from Tokyo, and would arrive tomorrow at the same time.

I sent back my affirmative reply, made sure to copy Clarence, and then went upstairs to take a shower. The shower felt good, and when I was done, I pulled the shower curtain open and left it there.

When I came back downstairs—shaved, dressed, and teeth fully brushed—I checked my iPhone again and saw a reply from Clarence, setting up a rendezvous point and time. I quickly acknowledged that, shut off my iPhone, and then read up for the rest of the day about rare paintings.

———

Twenty-four hours later, I was with Clarence as he drove us to the small village of Chester, about ten or so miles away from the Connecticut River, splitting Vermont and New Hampshire into two almost identical halves.

As we got closer, Clarence said once again, "I thought you didn't like private homes."

"I don't."

"So why the exception?"

"An additional five percent, that's why."

"Oh."

"And if it's a very rare painting, that could mean a very fine payday for us both."

"Oh."

"And I was thinking that additional money would be helpful for you, your ex, and your boys, and whatever interests you have."

He smoothly navigated his Lincoln Navigator along the narrow country lanes outside of Chester. He said, "Appreciate that, boss, but you don't have to worry."

"I can't believe you just said that."

"What? That you don't have to worry?"

"No," I said. "That you called me boss. You feeling under the weather?"

He sighed, ran a hand across his bald head.

"No, feeling fine," Clarence said. "It's just that ... yeah, I'm worried about the future. Always worry about the future. You think this will be a good payday?"

"Rare paintings don't get bought for a hundred bucks and Starbucks coupons," I pointed out.

He grunted in appreciation, looked at the hand-printed directions. I don't trust having printed-out directions from computers, because they always leave a trace. The land was mostly farms, with a few homes scattered in, ranging from mobile homes that were no longer mobile, to suburban-style Cape Code homes, to houses just a bit bigger and better. We turned on a road called Timberswamp, and went on for another mile.

"Okay, this looks like the place," he said.

Clarence slowed and turned right. There was a nicely paved driveway, with flanking stonewalls going off to the left and right. A simple granite post had the numeral 19 carved in, painted black. There were a few birch trees and oak trees, and a nicely trimmed lawn. The driveway widened into a two-space lot before a two-car garage. No other vehicles were visible.

The home was old, made in the simple late 1700's or early 1800's Colonial style. Two story, with a peaked roof and shrubbery around the foundation. Clarence turned and backed in, so that the front of his Lincoln was facing out. He put the SUV in park, switched off the Lincoln's big engine.

"You ready?"

"I was going to say I was born ready, but I don't want to raise expectations."

"Glad to hear it." He unbuckled his seatbelt, leaving his dangling set of keys with a scratched round plastic Red Sox logo hanging from the ignition. That way, no matter what happened, we always had the ability to get the hell out of Dodge if the bad guys showed up, hitchin' to do us harm, without worrying who had the keys.

Clarence got out first, and I followed him.

"Nice place," he said.

"I like it, too."

The door opened and an older couple bustled out. Both wore baggy khakis, and the gentleman wore a light blue pullover sweater while the lady wore a bright red cardigan. They were smiling and their faces were tanned and slightly worn, like salt-of-the-earth Vermonters who were just so happy to make your acquaintance.

"So glad you're here," the man said, stepping forward, extending a hand. "Did you have a problem finding the place?"

"No, not at all," I said.

"George," the woman said. "Invite them in. They must be tired for driving in all the way from Massachusetts."

I instantly felt a flare of suspicion at her statement—how the heck would this grandma know about us coming from Massachusetts?—and then that flare was extinguished by embarrassment. The way Clarence had parked his Navigator, the red-and-white plate for the fair Commonwealth was quite visible to anybody looking on from the house.

"Sure, Beth, that sounds fine," George said, waving us forward. "Come along, now."

Clarence followed George and Beth into their house, and I kept a step behind him. I had on black shoes, gray slacks, white shirt, and blue blazer. Clarence had a two-part gray suit, also with white shirt and no necktie, and it was its usual baggy style. We were trying for up-scale country fashionable, and not to be modest, I think we both nailed it.

Inside was a small foyer, with a narrow plain wooden staircase leading upstairs. To the right was a kitchen and dining room, and to the left, a living room with built-in bookshelves crowded with books that I was instantly envious of.

Clarence and I halted, and George waved a hand to the stairway. "Come this way, up to my office," he said. "Beth? Could you bring us some refreshments?"

"Absolutely, dear," and she went off to the kitchen, and George led us up the narrow stairway. The walls were plain yellow plaster, with small-framed etchings of New England landscapes. Our footsteps were loud on the wooden risers. At the top an open door to the right led to a master bedroom, and we went to the left, to a book-lined office.

George led the way, sat behind a wide mahogany desk. There were two plain wooden captain's chairs, which Clarence and I took. Behind George were two windows overlooking the rear yard and woods, and behind the two of us were similar windows. I spared a glance as I sat down. I could make out Clarence's Navigator, parked in the driveway.

"I appreciate you coming here," George said. "Would you like to take a look at the painting now?"

"Certainly," I said, looking at my watch. It was five minutes until two p.m. "Your buyers have ten minutes to get here. Have you heard from them?"

"That I have, that I have," George said. A sound of footsteps and Beth came in, holding a wooden tray with three ceramic mugs of lemonade and a plate of sugar cookies. The cookies had an elaborate swirl of sugar on the top, looking like maple leaves. We each took a mug and then Beth left. George munched on a cookie and sighed. "Damn, that woman makes the best cookies. Fresh out of the oven today." He wiped his hands with a paper napkin and stood up. "May I?"

"Go ahead."

George got up from his chair, went to a near bookcase. One of those large black zippered carrying cases for artwork was leaning up against the case. He picked it up with both hands and brought it over to the desk, pushed aside the plate of cookies, and put the case down, zipping it open. I went over as he flipped the case open. It was large, just over five feet square.

I looked down, looked back up at George, and then down again.

"What?" he asked. "Is there a problem?"

29

I couldn't talk, couldn't move, could hardly breathe. It was a large framed painting, filling up almost the entire carrying case. It was old, depicting a dramatic seascape. A small fishing boat with a tall mast was in danger of being swamped in a storm. Men at the bow of the boat were shown struggling with lines of rope coming down from the mast. At the stern, almost being washed away, another group of frightened men were gathered around a bearded man in robes. The colors were white and blue and black, and I couldn't believe they were within my reach.

George leaned over. "Is there something wrong?"

Lots of questions were bouncing around in my mind, but I remembered another rule of mine, which is never, ever inquire as to how a certain item got into someone's possession. Just accept the fact of possession, and move on.

"No," I said. "Nothing wrong. I'd like to take a closer look."

He gestured with his right hand. "Go right ahead."

I managed to pick the painting up and looked at the back. No fresh paper or canvas was visible, which is always a sign of a forger trying to hide something. I gently put the painting back down on the desk. I took out my jeweler's loupe from the previous job and gave a quick scan of the painting. The brushstrokes looked old, and they looked legitimate. The color of the paints used was also the right time period—nothing like cerulean blue, which wasn't invented until the nineteenth century. The condition of the signature was good, too, with no bleeding or other signs that it had been added on after the painting was completed. The craquelure—the pattern of small cracks that develop on a painting over time—also seemed to be in the right locations and in the right amount.

"Well?" George asked. I ignored him, still letting the impact of the painting just overwhelm me. It was rare during a negotiation that I become intoxicated with reviewing the item for sale, and this was definitely one of those times.

I shook myself free. Clarence was still standing, cookie in one large hand. "Do you know what you have here?" I finally asked.

"A very old painting, I hope," he said, sitting down in his chair. I took one more glance at the artwork and went back to my own chair, picked up my mug of lemonade, took a quick sip.

"Anything else?"

"Well ... I saw this on the Internet. It looks like it could be what's-his-name, the Dutch guy. Rembrandt. That's what I thought the signature said."

I nodded. "You're correct. Rembrandt van Rijn is the painter. This ... this piece of art is called 'The Storm on the Sea of Galilee,' and was painted in 1633. It's considered quite rare and valuable, since it's the only seascape Rembrandt ever painted. It shows the Apostles fishing on the Sea of Galilee, when a storm rises up, threatening to drown them. You can see Christ at the stern, with the apostles begging for his intervention."

Next to me Clarence said, "Holy shit. For real?"

"For real," I said. "And it's been missing since 1990 ... where it was stolen from the Isabelle Stewart Gardner Museum in Boston, along with a number of other valuable artworks."

George's eyes grew wide at that. "How much is it worth?"

I pondered that. "A lot. But because of its current provenance, the size of the offer is going to depend on the buyer, and what he or she is prepared to offer. It's a stolen piece of artwork. Very hot, very attractive to law enforcement. Just so you know, your buyer is going to have to be a special person, indeed."

George picked up his lemonade mug. "He's a Japanese collector and businessman. In fact, he should be here right about now."

And he tilted his wrist to look at his watch, spilling lemonade all over his desk.

"Oh, damn it," he said, standing up. "Beth!" he yelled. "Could you bring up some paper towels? I've spilt the damn lemonade on my desk."

I heard a cheery voice, "Coming, George!"

He smiled and shook his head. "What a mess."

He lowered his hand, opened a desk drawer, pulled out a pistol, and shot Clarence in the throat.

THREE

THE SOUND OF THE gunshot was deafening, and the next sounds came from Clarence, gasping and gurgling, grabbing at his throat, and another shot from George's pistol blew off a chunk of Clarence's head, spraying me with blood and brain matter.

Between the first and second shot, I tossed my mug at George and fell to one knee, slipping out my Sig-Sauer Model P226, rapidly firing off two shots. He dropped behind his desk. I got up, replaced my Sig-Sauer to my waist holster, snapped it shut, and grabbed the wooden captain's chair and blasted it through the near window, and then I followed it out to the ground, two stories below.

It was a sloppy escape. I landed in the juniper bushes, slamming my shoulder against the chair, and rolled to the lawn and kissed a good chunk of dirt and grass, hands cut from the broken glass and branches.

But my plan was to get out of the house, that killing zone, and in that way, the plan was working.

I got up, retrieved my Sig-Sauer, and raced to Clarence's Lincoln Navigator.

All four tires were flat.

I went around the front of the Navigator as the door to the house flew open.

Beth came out, wearing a Kevlar vest over her red cardigan sweater, expertly holding an H&K MP5 submachine gun in her hands. She brought it up to her shoulder, but I was quicker—maybe a touch of arthritis in her joints—and I fired off three rounds, knocking her back into the house.

I opened the door to the Navigator.

Keys were there.

Brief miracle.

I started up the Navigator and got the hell out of that driveway.

I drove a couple of miles away from the house on the Navigator's flat tires, found a dirt road, backed in the Navigator, switched off the engine.

My hands started shaking.

The right side of my head was wet. I put my hand up there, gave it a touch, brought my hand down.

Blood and bits of gray-white tissue.

From Clarence.

I reached over, opened up the glove compartment, took out a fistful of napkins and a moist towelette. I cleaned myself up as best I could. I got out of the Navigator, took more towelettes out, and wiped down any place I could have touched. I took a series of deep breaths.

Lots of thoughts rattling and racing through my mind right then, but I focused on just one.

Get out safely.

I stepped away from the Navigator, taking the keys with me, out of habit, I guess. If I was a smoking man, with matches or lighters, I'd be tempted to set the Navigator ablaze.

But despite what you see in the movies, setting a car or an SUV on fire is a tough job, needing lots of gas and experience. I had the experience, but not the gas, and definitely not the time to try to experiment.

I'd have to leave Clarence's vehicle behind.

I walked deeper into the woods.

———

Two days later I was back home. It had been a long, disruptive, and disquieting journey from Vermont to New Hampshire, by walking and using taxicabs and buses. Food was spotty and the weather was rainy, and the trip gave me lots of time to think and brood. First things first, there was obviously no other party in the negotiation, no Japanese. My job had been to verify the painting as the real deal, and once that had taken place, my job was over. Clarence and I were witnesses to be disposed of.

That's it.

I could see it was a wise decision on George's part, even though it killed Clarence and had nearly killed me.

I slowly made my way through the line of woods that bordered my rear yard, went past a cleared area where I stored my canoe for the occasional paddle on the Merrimack, and sat down against an oak tree to look at my house.

Everything seemed normal.

Sure.

Just like that house back in Vermont.

Once upon a time, folks working for the White House came up with a very weaselly phrase that admitted things were screwed up without assigning blame. "Mistakes were made." Not, "The President has a poor grasp of political reality and really boffed it." Or, "The Chief of Staff got hammered last night at Le Cirque, and at the early morning briefing, forgot the difference between Iraq and Iran."

Nope, mistakes were made. Nameless, faceless, bodyless folks screwed the pooch, nothing more to see here, let's move on.

But not for me.

I had screwed up, and Clarence was dead.

Mistakes? Let's begin: I was seduced by the promise of a very big payday, and I wasn't my usual suspicious self. I was also seduced by the charming couple in a charming house in a small town in Vermont. What could possibly go wrong with people like that?

And when I saw the Rembrandt, I should have asked for a private talking with Clarence out on the front lawn, and then gotten the hell out. The Rembrandt had been missing for a quarter-century, and a couple of years ago, the FBI leaked a story that some organized crime outfit from Philadelphia had been responsible for robbing the Isabelle Stewart Gardner. Lots of impressive headlines, breathless television reports, and then, just when most everyone expected the paintings were about to be recovered, nothing. Zilch.

So if the tale had been true, how in hell would one of those paintings have ended up with an older couple in rural Vermont?

My suspicion meter should have pegged off the scale, because it certainly looked like somebody had robbed the mobsters and used me to make sure they had the real deal.

Mistakes, all right, and all of them were mine.

But George—if that was his real name—had also made a big mistake, back there in Vermont.

He had shot Clarence first, which made sense. Clarence was the muscle, Clarence carried lots of weapons, he was a threat that had to be eliminated first.

His next shot should have been me, to either wound or kill. But his first shot hadn't done the job, and so he had to shoot Clarence one more time.

Which gave me a chance to escape, to live, and to start thinking of what I was going to do next.

For a while now I had been watching my house, and nothing had happened. The Smith girls were loudly at play in their back yard, with their happy German Shepherd, bouncing around, yapping.

Clem, my other next-door neighbor, was in the rear of his own yard, trimming a rhododendron bush that looked big enough to swallow a person.

But nothing was happening around my house. There were no black, window-tinted vehicles parked in my driveway, and no white van sitting on the road.

Everything seemed normal.

I still didn't like it.

It started getting dark. I stretched my legs, got up, and casually walked to the rear of my house, like the quiet, normal, and law-abiding citizen I was striving to become one of these days.

———

The house search took twice as long as my usual style, and I wasn't complaining, not at all. Sig-Sauer in hand, I cleared every room, every closet, every cabinet to make sure I was alone. Tiny attic, and then down to the cellar, and then back upstairs.

Clear.

I stripped off all of my clothes, took a half-hour shower, and after drying off and getting dressed, I took my old clothes and went downstairs. In my living room, I piled up some kindling and wood in my fireplace, and lit it. When the fire was burning merrily along, I fed in each piece of clothing, stirring it around with a poker, making sure it burned to ashes.

Then I sat there for a while, staring at the fire, until hunger got me up and into the kitchen, where dinner was a defrosted container of chicken stew I had made last month and a half bottle of an Australian pinot noir.

Bed time, where I slept deeply and for almost twelve hours.

———

The next day I called a local taxi service and met the driver at the intersection of Route 3 and the entrance to Merrimack Banks Road. The driver was a woman with steel-gray bouffant hair and glasses shaped in the style of cat's eyes. She dropped me off at the Super Wal-Mart in Manchester, where I wandered around the aisles for about thirty minutes or so. Then I went to the parking lot, found my Honda Pilot, and dropped a couple of quarters on the ground. I knelt and checked the under carriage, and, not seeing any suspicious objects, I got in the Pilot, started it up, and got on my way.

I left my Lexus behind. It was too fine and stood out too much.

———

I drove to Milford, a small town about a half hour southwest of Manchester, and spent a productive number of minutes on one of the computers at the Wadleigh Memorial Library, going to the website for the town of Chester, Vermont, and other places.

Interesting fact number one, outweighing every other interesting fact I was probably going to learn today: No news reports of any shooting in Chester, of a man from Massachusetts being murdered, or that any chaos had erupted at that sweet old house in the rural countryside of the Green Mountain State.

That was search number one. And when search number two was done, I learned the home at 19 Timberswamp Road was not owned by anyone named George or Beth, or anybody else for that matter.

It belonged to a real estate company called O'Halloran & Son, of Bellows Falls, Vermont, and once I got their phone number, I went outside to the library's parking lot and made a phone call, where I eventually spoke to one of the agents, a pleasant-sounding lady named Tracy Zahn. I told her that I was retired to the area and was driving around rural roads in Chester, whereupon I saw this lovely home on 19 Timberswamp Road.

"Could you tell me who owns it?" I asked. "I know I'm being forward, but it really called to me. Is there any chance it's for sale? "Well," she said in a chipper voice. "We manage it. It's held in trust for a family here in Vermont and New Hampshire. Ever since their mother passed on two years back, they've been fighting over what to do with it. In the meantime, we pay the utilities, do the landscaping. But if you are interested in purchasing it, I could start making some inquiries."

"Oh, I see," I said. "Is it being rented, then?"

"No, not at all."

"For real? I thought I saw a vehicle in the driveway when I went by the other day."

The real estate agent laughed. "Then you must be mistaken. Nobody's living there."

That got my attention. Beyond the library were the flowing waters of the Souhegan River, and lots of thoughts were bouncing around in my mind, like an old-style popcorn machine.

"Sir?"

"Yes?"

"Would you be interested in looking at the house?"

"Absolutely," I said. "How about if I meet you there?"

"Hold on, let me check my schedule," she said. "Mmm ... yes, I can see you there. How long will it take you?"

"About ninety minutes."

"See you then ... oh, I didn't catch your name."

"Ninety minutes it is," I said, and I switched off the phone.

Then I took a casual stroll down to the flowing water, took out the SIM card, and tossed it into the roaring waters, followed by the phone.

I walked quickly back to my Pilot.

———

Ninety minutes later I was back on Timberswamp Road, my senses all jingling and jangling. I stopped for a moment at the dirt road where I had abandoned Clarence's Lincoln, and walked up, Sig-Sauer in my hand.

The Lincoln was gone.

I checked the grass and dirt. I didn't see any heavy tire marks, which meant the Lincoln wasn't towed away. It meant someone—or several someones—had come in, re-inflated the tires, got the engine started, and drove it off.

Pretty damn impressive.

I went back to my Pilot, pistol still in hand.

I drove by 19 Timberswamp Road twice. Nothing in the driveway, nothing going on, nothing making sense.

I returned and decided not to park in the driveway, so I pulled over on the side of the road. I kept the engine running, kept my pistol in my lap, waited.

Ninety minutes came and went.

At minute ninety-three, a light green Volvo stationwagon with Vermont license plates came down the road, flashed its headlights at me, and then turned into the driveway. The driver seemed to be on her cellphone, talking away. I got out, holstered my pistol, and stood at the end of the driveway, waited. A woman in her mid-forties came out, holding a file folder, and offering a dazzling smile. She had brunette hair pulled back in a ponytail, khaki skirt above tanned shins and knees, and low-scooped yellow blouse.

"Hello, I'm Tracy Zahn," she said, extending her hand, which I shook. Her fingernails and toenails—visible through her open-toed shoes—were painted a bright red.

"Thanks so much for making the time," I said. "My, what a beautiful house."

"It certainly is, ah, mister ... "

"Built in the early 1800s?"

"Actually, in 1795 ... so close enough," she said, laughing. It was a genuine, pleasing laugh. "Want to take a look around the property first?"

"Sure."

I went to the front lawn, tilted my head back. The window I had blown through three days ago was hale and hardy, like nothing had happened. I poked around the juniper bushes. None of the branches appeared damaged, but they had all been trimmed back. No bits of glass, or broken road, and gee, not even a shattered wooden captain's chair.

But the house still didn't look like an old, inviting antique anymore.

"Ready to take a look inside?" Tracy asked.

The house now looked like a place of evil, where gunshots and cries and the gurgling sound of death would never be heard by faraway neighbors.

"Sounds fine," I said.

She unlocked the door and started her real estate agent spiel. I half listened as I went through the rooms downstairs, noticing a smell I couldn't quite place, until I realized it was some sort of apple-cinnamon mix that probably came from a number of burning candles, lit to hide the smells of burnt gunpowder, spilt blood, and other bodily fluids.

Something about the smell tickled at me, and I filed that away for later. I followed her upstairs, admiring the sway of her tight skirt, and we ducked into the bedroom—where her smile seemed wider and her breathing seemed quicker—and then into the upstairs study.

"This looks ... charming," I said.

True enough, but I stayed in one spot, not bothering to tour the familiar and deadly room. The window had been expertly repaired and then dirtied up and dinged to make it look like the same age of the other windows. The carpet had also been cleaned, and both captain's chairs were relatively new, and definitely not the ones Clarence and I had been sitting in two days ago.

Dear Tracy was going on about well water, perk tests, the efficiency of the oil burner in the basement, and I then moved around the office. I had shot at George twice, yet there was no evidence of any bullet damage to the area around where he had been sitting.

I idly looked over the desk, opened a couple of drawers. All empty.

I realized something was off.

Then I got it.

Tracy had stopped talking.

"I'm terribly sorry, Tracy," I said. "Sometimes I get lost in my train of thought, and most times, it leaves the track and dumps itself in a ravine."

That earned me a sweet smile, and she was standing on the other side of the desk, with the two new chairs behind her. She was twirling a loose piece of hair in one finger, and her legs were slightly spread, so they pushed against the outlines of her khaki skirt.

"Apology accepted," she said. "Do you see anything you like?"

I smiled back, took the highway exit to Being A Gentleman. "Yes, this place is fascinating … and I was wondering, I plan to be in Vermont for the rest of the day. Do you know of a good place around here for dinner?"

"A few," she said, still twirling her hair.

"Since I'm a stranger around here, would you be willing to give me directions?"

"Of course."

"And would you join me?"

Her smile grew wider. "That's the price of the directions, so I don't see why not."

———————

I went out first and she followed me, locked the door, and when she got to her car, she suggested I meet her at her offices in Bellows Falls, and I said that would be fine. She got into her car and before starting it up, she laughed.

"You know, you still haven't told me your name."

I said, "You like mysterious men?"

"Very much so," she said, the driver's door still open.

"Then why spoil the moment?" I gently closed the door and she drove off with a honk and a wave, and I went back to my Pilot, got in, and thought.

The smell inside the house bothered me.

Why?

It was obvious that after Clarence got shot and I successfully escaped, George and his team—it was quite clear from all the work that had been done that George wasn't just working with Beth—had gone into overtime to put the house back into some semblance of normalcy, including lighting scented candles to mask what violence had happened there earlier.

So why were the smells bothering me?

I tapped the steering wheel, whistled the opening theme from Kevin Costner's "Robin Hood," and looked back at the house. It seemed to mock me, like it was challenging me to go back inside, where it could guarantee that the third time around, I'd be trapped.

I flipped the house my middle finger, remembered going in with Clarence, chit-chatting with George and Beth, not smelling much of anything, going up to the office, more chit-chat, and George saying this: *Damn, that woman makes the best cookies. Fresh out of the oven today.*

There was no smell of baking when Clarence and I arrived.

Nothing.

I started up the Pilot and began driving.

———————

Less than a half hour later, I stopped at a little store/gas station/ bakery on the other side of Chester, called Devitt's Gas & Go & Baked Goods. There were a couple of small businesses across the road—a florist, small engine repair, beautician—and farther up the street, a one-story motel. I parked to the side of the sagging wood building, which had a flat roof and painted red clapboards. I went up a small porch, opened the door, a little bell ringing as I did so. Before me were long display cases, and there were doughnuts, pies, cakes, and cookies. Molasses cookies, chocolate chip cookies, and sugar cookies.

With elaborate sugar swirls on top, like maple leaves.

Just like the ones Beth had served us.

A thickset woman came from behind, wearing a soiled chest-high white apron, blue striped blouse, and a sweet smile. Her hands were chapped and soiled with flour.

"Can I help you?"

"Gee, I hope so," I said, pointing to the sugar cookies. "Could I buy one of those cookies, as a sample?"

"A sample?" she said. "Heck, I think this little enterprise can spring for a freebie."

She took a wax piece of paper from a box, reached into the counter, grabbed a cookie, and passed it over.

I took a good bite, rolled my eyes, and said, "Yes, that's it … I'll take a dozen, please."

She was happy at that order and as she was packing it up, I said, "Ma'am, you know, the other day I was at this potluck dinner, and this couple came in, bringing these cookies. I couldn't believe how good they were, and they told me where to find you."

"Well, I'm right glad they did," she said.

I looked into the case again. "Your apple pie … do you make that with cinnamon?"

Her eyes twinkled. "I certainly do. Would you like a piece as well?"

"Why not the whole pie?"

She laughed, reached behind her, took down a white piece of cardboard and in a few quick motions, made it into a pie box. She put the apple pie in and then quickly taped shut the three sides of the box.

"So those cookies," I said. "This is going to sound funny, but I wanted to thank that nice couple who brought them to that potluck dinner. Do you remember them? Older man with white hair, nice smile … his wife was about the same age, but her hair was gray."

She started ringing up my purchase. "You know, I believe I do remember them coming in, maybe three or four days ago."

"I think their names were George and Beth."

She nodded and said, "Seven fifty, please. You might be right."

I passed over a ten-dollar bill. "Do you know them?"

"Can't say that I do, sorry."

The change came back into my hand and I dropped it all into a glass tip jar near the register. That got her attention and I said, "So they're not from around here, are they."

"Oh, I can guarantee that," she said.

"Why?"

She pointed out a window overlooking the road. "When they left, I saw them drive over to the Chester Motel, get out, and check in."

FOUR

WITH MY PURCHASES SAFELY secured, I was in the parking lot of the Chester Motel. It was a typical off-the-major-highway motel—an office and tiny swimming pool at one end, a long row of one-story units stretching out to the left. You parked in front of your unit, where management had thoughtfully left out white plastic chairs to sit in.

The nice lady from Devitt's Gas & Go & Baked Goods told me that her sweet murderous customers had been driving a light gray car—"Maybe a BMW or Mercedes, they all look the same to me"—but no car in the lot matched her description. Some sad-looking four-door sedans, two pick-up trucks, and a dented red minivan that had a bumper sticker claiming MY SPRINGER SPANIEL IS SMARTER THAN YOUR HONOR STUDENT.

I munched on a cookie, considered my options, and then stepped outside. I squatted down on the ground, wiped some dust on my fingers, and then rubbed my fingers in my eyes and went to the little place with a red-lit sign that said OFFICE.

This door didn't jingle-jangle, but it did give out a steady buzz as I came in. There were three hard orange plastic chairs on the scuffed tile, a waist-high counter, and a wooden stand with a collection of brochures promoting the historical sites and areas for happy visitors to the Green Mountain State.

A young woman came through an open door, nodded to me. She had black hair cut high on the sides, some sort of stud through her lower lip, and both bare arms were covered with intricate tattoos. She was wearing a simple black shift that was high around her throat and seemed to go to the floor. I had caught a flash of pink when she entered the room and I think she was wearing pink sneakers.

Based on her appearance, I was expecting a sullen greeting, coming in here as an ambassador from the alleged Real World, interrupting her time in the back office where she might be studying poetry by H. P. Lovecraft or the collected writings of Kate Millett, but she gave me a cheery good afternoon and asked if I wanted a room.

I wiped at my reddened eyes. "No ... sorry ... this is going to sound awkward, but I'm hoping you can help. I'm looking for mom and dad ... they drove off a few days ago and my sister and I, we're frantic looking for them."

"Wow," she said. "I'm so sorry to hear that. What happened?"

I wiped again at my watery eyes. "You see, they're both getting along in age, and Dad ... well, he's slipping. He's forgetting more and more, and my sister and I ... we've tried to make sure he doesn't drive any more, but he won't let us take the car keys. And Mom ... she's slipping, too, and tells me and my sister to mind our own business."

I took a breath. "Every now and then, they'll go out for a drive, like they're going for lunch or something, and then we don't hear from them for days! I mean, last month, they said they were driving to Maine to visit an aunt, and they ended up in Troy, New York. But this time, we knew they were heading for Vermont, and sis and I have been trying to track them down. The cops won't help, because they're both adults … have you seen them in the past couple of days? Older man and woman, driving a gray … "

"Sure!" she said, her face brightening up. "A gray Audi. They were here, three days ago."

"Really? Do you know when they left?"

She went to a filing box, flipped through, took out a card. "You know, it says here they haven't checked out." She leaned over the counter. "But I don't see their Audi there."

"Maybe Dad went to get some groceries for the trip home. Can you tell me what room they're in?"

"Unit 14," she said. "Do you want me to come along?"

I smiled, took out a handkerchief, and blew my nose. "No," I said. "I don't want to embarrass them. But thank you."

———————

I took my time, going down the narrow concrete walkway leading its way to all of the motel's rooms. At one of the units one of those carts housecleaning uses in the morning was parked, with folded sheets, towels, various soaps and sundries. I passed the open door and saw a grandmotherly type woman in white slacks and a black smock, tossing a sheet around like she was an exiled and expert bullfighter.

At Unit 14 there was a surprise: a Do Not Disturb sign hanging off the doorknob. There was one wide window to the left, with the blinds down.

How to get in, then?

I checked the parking lot again. None of the earlier vehicles had moved, and nothing new had rolled in. I supposed I could go through the window—after all, I did have experience—but I didn't like the thought of going in blind. Besides, the only furniture available was those white plastic chairs. I could pick the lock, but that would certainly look suspicious if someone were to wander by.

A bit of whistling from Unit 12. I checked out the housekeeping cart and saw something delightful: a lengthy key chain dangling from one of its corners.

I moved as quickly as I could to the cart and to Unit 14, then back to the cart. I had carefully unlocked the door without opening it, and with the nice housekeeping lady otherwise occupied, now was the time. Sig-Sauer in my right hand, I grabbed the doorknob with my left hand, spun it quick, and propelled myself into the room.

It was cold.

Not a good sign.

There was a dead woman on the room's only bed.

Good or bad, she would have to wait.

I closed the door behind me and got to work.

Clearing the room took about thirty seconds. The only other space was the bathroom, empty. A small closet near the door. Also empty. I made a quick check under the bed. Nothing.

Time to check the dead woman.

It was Beth, the woman who served Clarence and I the sugar cookies three days back, and the one I had shot at three times before getting the hell out.

But it didn't look like it was my fault she was dead.

Because her throat had been slit, ear-to-ear, gushing out blood and soaking her pillow and the floral bedspread.

So not my fault.

Not that I would have felt any guilt.

Beth still had on the nice outfit from before—complete with the Kevlar vest—but her hair was short and brown. A wig, then, when I had last seen her. Beth was younger than she had appeared, but with being dead for some time, her face swollen and grayed out, it was hard to tell her real age.

A heavy knock at the door.

"Housekeeping!"

Well.

Another heavy knock. "Housekeeping!"

The sound of keys jangling was quite loud. I moved to the door and lowered my voice, "Hey, can you give me five minutes, please?"

She said, "Buddy, c'mon, you're one of the last ones to do, I've been waiting long enough."

The doorknob vibrated from the housekeeping key sliding in. I went over quickly and grabbed the doorknob and said, "Please … ma'am … I'll make it worth your while. I'll leave a nice tip."

"Really?" Her voice was full of suspicion.

"Honest."

"This ain't the kind of place where people leave tips."

"Then it'll be a nice surprise for you, won't it."

My hand was still tight on the doorknob. She said, "You promise?"

"Tell you what," I said. "I'll tip you right now. Look under the door."

I made the gamble to free my right hand from the doorknob, and I still moved quick, taking a twenty-dollar bill out of my wallet and sliding it out to the outdoors. I was fortunate that the twenty was crisp and clean. It slid through with no problem.

There was huffing and puffing from outside the door. A slight chortle.

"Mister? You can stay for exactly sixty-four minutes."

"Thanks," I said. "But why sixty-four minutes?"

"'Cause I punch out in two hours, and that'll leave me enough time to clean up after you."

Another chortle, and she went down the walkway.

And I went back to work.

———

I gave the room a quick scan, checking the drawers, under the drawers, and under the bed. Nothing, save for an empty Trojan condom wrapper I found lodged in a corner under the bed.

The room's cooling system was rattling along, and I recognized the tradecraft: cooling down this room would help screw up determining an exact time of death.

I stood over the dead woman, whoever she was. Looking closer and at the sorry condition of her face, I noted her make-up was cracking and falling to pieces. She was definitely younger than she looked when I had first met her, and the wig had helped as well.

I lifted my left leg, reached underneath my pants leg, withdrew a Ka-Bar combat knife from a scabbard strapped to my shin. I went to the dead woman, spotted the three pockmarks in her bulletproof vest where I had successfully shot her and knocked her down.

"Nice shootin', Tex," I whispered as I used the knife to pry out my 9mm bullets, which were deformed and squashed but could still be used down the road as evidence. I didn't want to go down that road or be a passenger on it. It took a good while to dig the slugs out, and once I had to walk away when the woman's body shuddered and released some decomposition gases, causing me to breathe through my mouth. But eventually I got all three slugs out, and pocketed them in my jacket.

The woman was still there, was still dead. I figured out what must have happened back on the day. She had been retrieved by George and whoever else was in on the ambush, and she was brought back here. My three slugs had probably broken some ribs, maybe her sternum. She had been in a lot of pain. Maybe raising a fuss. Yelling. Loud noises that could attract unwanted attention.

A quick and brutal decision. She was left behind, ensuring she also wouldn't talk.

One more look around the room. Nothing.

Just one dead woman who wasn't going to say anything.

I went to the door.

Stopped.

Went back to the bathroom, where I located a paper-wrapped drinking glass. Holding it by the rim, I went back to the bedroom, and slowly and carefully pressed her fingertips on the glass.

I replaced the glass into the paper, casually held it in my hand, and then walked out the door.

My friendly housekeeper was now two rooms down. I closed the door, went to my Honda Pilot, and drove out of the parking lot.

Ten minutes later, the unexpected presence of a conscience decided to flutter down and rest on my shoulder, whispering into my ear.

I wasted a minute or two ignoring the voice—I blame my twelve years of Catholic school education, if you're looking for an excuse—then I pulled over to the side. I went into the glovebox, took out one of my disposable cellphones, and dialed 911.

When the police dispatcher answered—local, country, state, I didn't care—I spoke clearly and calmly:

"There's a dead woman in Unit 14, the Chester Motel."

I disconnected the call, removed the SIM card, broke it in half. I resumed driving and when I came across a bridge spanning a small stream, I tossed it in. There. My good deed for the day. I didn't want that nice grandmotherly housekeeper unlocking the door to Unit 14 and opening it up to find that charnel house.

I checked my watch. If I drove straight and well, I'd make it just in time for my dinner date.

After a brief visit at her office, I followed the Volvo station wagon for a ten-minute drive. Tracy Zahn had chosen a French restaurant outside of Bellows Falls, and we split a ten-year-old bottle of Bordeaux. She had a vegetable quiche and a salad, and I had some sort of roast pork dish that probably had way too much fat, and I really didn't care. She had freshened up and put on a black knit dress that fit her snugly and well. She had on new make-up and had done something to her hair that made it fluff out some, like she had caught a passing charge of static electricity.

We talked about weather, travel, business, politics, and Hollywood, and there was a lot of laughter and smiles.

When we got to the coffee stage, she said, "Tell me about Brass Cannon Systems."

"It's a holding company, has its fingers in this and that," I said. "Real estate, a couple of software companies, that sort of thing."

"And what do you do for Brass Cannon Systems?"

"This and that," I said. "Run errands. Check out companies for sales. Promising properties." I lifted up my coffee cup to her in a toast. "You're thorough," I added. "Did a license plate check on me, did you?"

"You know it," she said.

"Probably when you arrived at the house," I said, recalling her being on her cellphone as she pulled in earlier today.

"Correct again, my friend."

I sipped from my coffee cup. "You also stayed a good distance from me during the tour. You let me take the lead. But you were always ten or so feet away from me. What were you carrying in your purse? Revolver? Pistol?"

She smiled. A good look for her. "No. If I make a mistake and ventilate an over-amorous client, you can't make it up by knocking another five percent off the selling price. Nope, I have a Taser." She dabbed at her lips with a napkin. "That way, if I make a mistake, after he's done convulsing and wetting his pants, I can try to make it right."

"You're one smart lady," I said.

"Bet your ass," she said. "I wasn't raised to be a victim, and I refuse to be one. Too many stories are spread around meetings and conferences about real estate agents going out to show a listing and being found bound and raped the next day. Or showing up in a shallow grave a couple years later."

"But here you are, having dinner with me," I said.

"So?"

"Still haven't told you my name."

A waitress came over and dropped off the check, which I quickly called my own.

"I like your eyes," she said.

"That good enough?"

A shrug. "I get the feeling if you told me your name, it wouldn't be your real one. So why go through the pretense?"

I smiled at her. "I like your eyes, too."

Tracy leaned over the table. The zipper holding the front of her knit dress looked quite strained. I decided I liked the look. She said, "What's it really like? What you do."

"I do this and that. Run errands. Check out properties."

"Lie, lie, and lie," she said. "Don't forget, part of my business is the human factor. I can tell when someone's lying, when someone says they want to think about a nice two-bedroom house on the lake, when in fact you know they'll be calling you later that night to make an offer."

"Nicely done," I said.

"I have the feeling you're armed. But not with a Taser."

"Your talents are being wasted in real estate."

Her smile grew wider. "So I've been told. But I like the area, I like putting families into nice homes, and I like pretty much being my own boss."

I examined the check, pulled out my wallet, and extracted enough bills to cover the meal and to add a 20 percent tip.

"Me, too."

"Ah, but I thought you worked for something called Brass Cannon Systems?"

"It's more of a consulting gig than a permanent position."

"Permanent with a gun?"

"Sounds like a hairstyle," I said.

"You're quick," she said. "I like that, too."

"Thanks," I said.

The waitress asked if we wanted more coffee, and we both declined. Then she asked us one more time if we wanted dessert, even having paid the bill.

"Nope," Tracy said. "I'm stuffed."

"Me, too."

The waitress picked up the check and went to the other side of the dining room, and Tracy's eyes twinkled at me. "What do you want to do now?"

I said, "I have a fresh apple pie in my car. But no utensils."

"I have plenty of utensils back at my condo."

"You up for apple pie?"

"I'm starving," she said.

"Me, too."

FIVE

THE NEXT MORNING I got up before Tracy and put on some clothes before going downstairs. I padded around the condo for a bit, just checking it out. I hadn't seen much of it when we had both arrived last night. There was a nice kitchen area right off the front door, which expanded into a living room. Upstairs was a bathroom, the bedroom, and another bedroom converted into an office.

I poked around the kitchen and at some point Tracy came down, yawning. She had on a nice thigh-length shiny red robe with a dragon emblazoned on the back, like it was made for hot samurai warriors.

"You're up early," she said. "I'm not sure if I like you anymore."

"I made breakfast," I said.

"All right," she said. "You've got a reprieve."

Along with coffee and orange juice, there were fresh blueberry pancakes and bacon. Both the bacon and the blueberries had been frozen but I had adapted and overcome those particular challenges. There was a breakfast nook off the kitchen with a nice view of the condominium's common forest. She sat down and said, "This is a pleasant change."

"Thanks."

She poured some maple syrup on her pancakes. "In more ways than one." Tracy looked up at me, winked. "Last night ... well done, sir."

"Gosh, I think I'm blushing."

"You should, you brute. And another thing ... breakfast. Most men I've dated in the past have all lied about their professions."

"Really?"

"Oh, yes," she said. "They told me they were lawyers or salesmen or doctors ... and when their sweet O had passed on, they all transformed themselves into farmers."

"How did they do that?"

"They all said they had to leave right away because they had to get up early the next day."

"Then they missed seeing you in the morning, and sharing the most important meal of the day."

"Very funny," she said, and we both continued to break our morning fast. But when she moved around in her seat, the robe opened some, and opened some more, and then I took her hand, led her into the living room and decided to make a close inspection of the couch.

———

Tracy was on her side, catching her breath, the robe still on but failing in its duty to cover her curvy body. I brought over our breakfast beverages and she eagerly drank the orange juice, and then lay back down on the couch with a sigh, holding a coffee cup.

I sat across from her on a round padded footstool, also holding a coffee cup.

"I'm going to be late for work."

"I thought you worked for yourself," I said.

"I do. And my boss is a bitch on wheels."

I smiled at her, put the coffee cup down on a—wait for it—coffee table. "I need to check something out with you."

"What, lunch plans?"

"No, not that. I need to know who was in that house three days ago, the one on Timberswamp Road."

"Sorry, I don't understand," Tracy said. "Nobody was in that house three days ago."

"Correction," I said. "I was there. With a coworker. Meeting with a man and a woman. The man shot my coworker and killed him. An upstairs window was also destroyed, bullets were discharged in the second-floor office, and a body was left there was well."

Tracy's face paled with fear and she quickly rearranged her robe, covering her impressive breasts. "I don't know what you're talking about."

"Perhaps," I said. "And I don't mean to threaten you, but I'd like to point out that you're about three feet away from me, and I don't see a Taser or firearm in sight."

She shot back, "And all I see is a naked, well-muscled man sitting across from me with some interesting scars."

"I'm not armed in the usual sense," I said. "Keep that in mind."

"Did you call the police three days ago?"

"No."

"Why the hell not? Jesus Christ, if something like that had happened to me, dialing 911 would have been the first thing I would have done."

"If I had done that, the second thing that would have been done would be me getting arrested. And number three would be me dying in a holding cell, by something made to look like suicide."

"I've heard enough," Tracy said, voice light. "I'd like for you to leave."

"You got it," I said. "You never have to fear me, at any time."

She sat up on the couch. "What the hell do you mean by that?"

I stood up, picked up my coffee cup. "I mean that something happened at that house. Gunfire, body removed, window replaced, house tidied up. Somebody chose that house for its purpose that day. That means someone did some research, located the house, found out it was uninhabited, and got keys for the place. This same someone also did a quick and efficient repair in under a day, to put everything back in its place, so it looked untouched."

I went to the breakfast nook, picked up our breakfast dishes. "That means money being exchanged, work being done, somebody eventually noticing. Maybe somebody in the neighborhood, or somebody in your real estate company. In any event, did you tell anybody about our meeting?"

"Just Patrick, the office manager," she said. "I told him I was meeting a potential buyer for the property."

"Did you tell anybody afterwards?"

"No."

"Good," I said. "Keep it that way. You tell Patrick that the license plate you ran yesterday was a mistake, it was some dumb lost tourist. The buyer never showed up. Do the usual bitching and moaning."

"You're scaring me," she said from the couch.

"Good," I said. "So be careful out there."

———

Five minutes later, after getting dressed, I quickly went back downstairs to the kitchen. Tracy was washing the dishes, robe carefully put back into place, and I helped with the drying. She kept quiet and I did the same, but her face seemed calm, not that set face with a permanent frown indicating You Are In The Doghouse.

When the dishes were put away and the wash towels hung up, she turned around and leaned back against the near counter.

"Here it is," she said. "This has been … an interesting encounter, my nameless friend."

"Same here."

"You were telling the truth back there, about the gunshots and your dead friend?"

"Coworker," I said. "Yes, that was the truth."

"What kind of work do you do?"

"The stuff that takes place in the shadows, between the cracks, outside of the normal arena."

"Is it dangerous?"

"Sometimes. But it's also well paying."

I waited, seeing how she would respond. Then she crossed her arms. "What's it like? Meaning … ninety-nine percent of guys are out there every morning, doing the same stuff, day after day, working out of cubicles and going to budget planning meetings, passing papers back and forth, on the phone, selling or buying. Being a lawyer or a doctor or a manager. Part of the huge cogs that run this gorgeous society."

"I get to set my own hours, for one," I said. Then I smiled. "And I meet the most interesting people."

"And do you kill them?"

It seemed a serious question.

"Only when they've been bad and hurt my feelings."

"And you're after someone because they killed your friend?"

"No. A coworker."

"I'm sorry, I don't understand. If he's just a coworker, why not go to the police?"

"Because then I couldn't be what I want to be. If the police ever got interested in me, then my work would be over."

"But still ... a coworker ... if he's not your friend, why are you making the effort to find the killer alone?"

I said, "You ever see that old movie *The Maltese Falcon*, with Humphrey Bogart?"

"Sure, a long time ago. Sam Spade. The fat guy. Black and white movie. The black falcon."

"His partner got killed at the very beginning of the movie. Later on, Sam Spade explains it all, why he goes after the killer. I don't know it by heart, but watch it again. You'll understand."

She crossed her arms, kept a hand tight around the collar of her robe. "I'll be back at work today," she said. "At some point ... you're right, word might get around. About a window being repaired, some quick work being done at a house. Something being seen on Timberwsamp Road. If I hear that, I want to tell you."

"No, you don't," I said.

"No one's told me what to do since I divorced the misbegotten man that was my husband for a number of miserable years," she said. "Give me an email address, a phone number, something so I can safely pass along what I might find out."

From the refrigerator and among the various magnets and knickknacks was an attached pad of paper. At the top of it said GROCERY LIST. She had written *milk OJ eggs carrot stix.*

I tore off the sheet, grabbed a pen, and wrote down the number of one of my burner phones reserved for incoming calls that weren't part of my normal—or what passed for my normal—day-to-day business.

"There you go," I said.

"Thanks," she said.

"Why do you want to help me out?"

She smiled back. "Part of what I like in the real estate business is also meeting interesting people." With that, she folded up the piece of memo paper and set it on the counter. "You need to leave now?"

"Well, I was thinking of it," I said. "Those fields won't plow themselves."

Tracy's smile grew naughtier as she undid the top of her robe. "Funny you should mention plowing."

———

Just over an hour later I was back home in Litchfield, having had a quiet drive from Vermont to New Hampshire. I was feeling relaxed, loosey-goosey, and I was happy at what I had achieved. True, it would have been nice to have stormed that motel and settled accounts with George and Beth, but I had some potential leads. My account with Beth was now settled, and I hoped her fingerprints would lead me to George, or at least someone who had hired the two of them, and whoever else was helping them.

In addition, I had an ally back there in enemy territory, willing to be a listening post for me, and by now, the Vermont State Police were no doubt crawling all over the crime scene back at the Chester Motel. If luck swung my way, maybe they could uncover some strands of Beth's life and make it public, which could lead me to George and a very interesting and final meeting.

I pulled into my driveway, got out, and waved once more to my neighbor Clem Houston, who was diligently trimming the grass around the base of a granite lamppost set up at the end of his own driveway.

I unlocked the door, got in, and after checking all my telltale signs and determining no one or nothing had made its way into my house, I went upstairs to take a shower.

———————

In my bedroom I stripped off my clothes, carefully removed the water glass from the Chester Motel, and put my Sig-Sauer pistol and its accompanying leather holster on top of the bedroom bureau. I switched on the television to the History Channel—sometimes I like background noise in my home and occasionally, the History Channel will stun me and air a program that has something to do with history instead of UFOs and pawn stars—and strolled into the bathroom.

At the sink I retrieved my toothbrush and Colgate toothpaste, and glanced up at the mirror. I saw a tired yet handsome face—prejudiced, I know—that needed a good shave. I also saw the shower curtain behind me.

The closed shower curtain.

After I finished brushing my teeth and spitting into the sink, I said, "You standing in the bathtub. If you wanted me dead, you would have shot me by now. So let's stop playing around, and we can talk."

I turned and waited, and the curtain suddenly flew open, revealing an attractive slim blond woman, several years younger than me, wearing black slacks, a black jacket, and a plain ivory-buttoned blouse. She had a thin gold chain around her neck, and her face was very serious, indeed. I couldn't see what she had on her feet, but her fingernails were done in a nice bright red polish, nicely offsetting the metallic black of the pistol she was pointing at me, a 9mm Glock.

"You're naked," she said.

"You're quite observant," I said. "Look, this must be some sort of mistake. If you were hired to jump out of my tub and sing 'Happy Birthday to You' while stripping out of that nice up-and-coming business exec suit, then you've got the wrong house and the wrong man. My birthday's not for another three months."

"I have the right person," she said, voice cold. "Up with your hands."

"For sure?" I asked, lifting up my hands.

"For sure."

"All right, my hands are up. What now?"

She said, "You know Clarence Briggs?"

"I know lots of people."

"Don't fuck with me, bud," she said. "I'm with the FBI, Boston field office."

"May I have some identification please?" I asked.

"You'll get it when I'm good and ready."

"You've got one heck of an attitude."

68

She said, "I haven't even started. Now let's get back to why I'm here. You know Clarence Briggs?"

"I think you already know the answer to that question. Otherwise you wouldn't be here."

"Humor me."

I kept quiet, arms still up, still naked, and the FBI woman still in my bathtub. I've had some interesting experiences in my life as an independent contractor, but this one was definitely among the top five.

I kept my mouth shut. She was impatient. "All right, humor me and the fact I'm pointing a pistol at you."

"Yes, I know Clarence Briggs."

"Do you know where he is?"

"No, I don't."

"When was the last time you saw him?"

I said, "Ma'am … if I may, I'm getting cold. You might notice a certain appendage of mine is shrinking. Could we adjourn for a moment or two while I get dressed?"

"No."

"Ma'am, even though you've not yet told me your name, I promise that I will answer all of your questions if you allow me to get dressed. Or do you plan to put a bag over my head and send me on a plane to Gitmo?"

"It's a thought," she said. The pistol still didn't waver.

I stayed still.

"All right," she said. "This is how we're going to do it. You're going to keep your arms up. You're going to slowly back away. I'm going to be right in front of you. Anything funny happens while you wrap a towel around you, I'll shoot. I promise I'll do my best to shoot you in a leg or arm. But don't count on it. Did I make myself clear?"

"As clear as glass," I said.

"Okay." A motion with the pistol. "Get moving."

I slowly rotated so I could back out without hitting the bathroom sink and vanity, and started backing toward the door. I moved slowly and deliberately, and I also moved to the right so I would be out of the FBI agent's view.

As expected, she didn't like that, and started to step out of the tub. When her left foot was lifted up and she started to move over the side of the tub, that's when I leapt forward and shoved her. Off balance, her right foot popped up and she fell back with an emphatic *oof!* In the tangle and tussle, I grabbed her pistol, stepped away, and for good measure, turned on the shower.

She shrieked as the water struck her. I grabbed a towel and secured it around my waist, and then examined her pistol. It was a Glock all right. I popped the magazine, worked the action, ejected the shell, and scooped it up from the bathroom floor. I replaced the cartridge into the magazine and slipped it back into the Glock.

The FBI agent got to her feet and turned off the shower. She glared at me, her blond hair a tangled mess around her face, her clothes sopping wet.

"You're a fucking asshole," she said.

"In some circumstances, yes," I said. I went to the bathroom closet, opened it up, retrieved a light blue terrycloth robe. I draped it over the bathroom vanity.

"I'm going out to get dressed," I said. "Feel free to dry yourself off and put on the robe, and then we'll have a nice open talk. Like two reasonable adults should. How does that sound?"

"Considering you've got my fucking gun pointing at me, it doesn't sound like I have much of a choice."

I put her pistol on top of the robe, then retrieved my own Sig-Sauer. "There you go. See? No hard feelings."

That caused her to pause. She rubbed at her soaked arms. "Why the hell are you doing this?"

"Because as one, I admire a bullshit artist. I'll see you downstairs."

I got dressed in my adjacent bedroom, putting on blue jeans, a light gray UNH sweatshirt—not that I ever attended, but it's nice to fit in with the neighborhood—and then went downstairs. I moved around the kitchen some and then my FBI agent came down, hair somewhat dry, wearing my robe, and also wearing one pissed-off expression. She had her pistol in her right hand, and I got the faintest whisper that maybe I had just been too trusting, but she came into the kitchen and made a prominent point of putting the pistol into the right pocket of the robe.

It made that side of the robe sag, but I decided not to comment on this obvious fashion faux pas. As she came in, eyes cold and hard, I said, "It's past noon, and my body is telling me it's time for lunch. I have fresh pastrami and sliced turkey, the usual additions if you're interested in a sandwich. If not, I have a container of fresh soup with tomato, veggies, and noodles. It's the best I've ever had."

"Did you make it?"

"I've many skills, but soup making isn't one of them. No, I got a couple of containers from the nice French-Canadian couple next door, the one with the white German shepherd on the front lawn."

"Why?" she said, sitting down on a wooden kitchen stool. "You shoot coyotes in their back yard?"

"No," I said. "Two years ago, the missus over there went into labor on the proverbial dark and stormy night. Instead of waiting for an ambulance to arrive, I drove her and her husband to the hospital, about twenty minutes before their daughter entered the world."

"You think doing things like that balances out the other shit you do?"

"I can only hope," I said. "You ready to place your lunch order?

"No," she said.

"Okay, let's try this. You took a mighty tumble back there in my tub. How's your head and back? You need an Ibuprofen or something?"

"I didn't take a mighty tumble, you pushed me."

"Not to sound like we're both back in grade school, but if you recall, you started it," I said.

She glared at me. "I want to know what you said back there, about knowing I was a bullshit artist. What the fuck did you mean by that?"

I opened the refrigerator, double-checked my lunch supplies. "It's obvious, isn't it?"

"Enlighten me," she said.

I closed the refrigerator door. "Oh, come now. FBI agents never go out on their own to conduct an interview with a possibly dangerous suspect. It's against procedure. It's just not done."

"Did I say you were dangerous?"

"You were in my bathroom, pointing a weapon at me. That's a pretty good indication of what you were thinking. Plus you were waiting for me there, behind the shower curtain, because if I'm in the bathroom, I'm going to be vulnerable. I'm going to be taking a shower or using the toilet, which gives you a clear advantage. Which meant you planned to come in here by yourself, without backup. So who the hell are you?"

"I'm FBI."

"Oh, please."

"My ID's upstairs, in my slacks, hanging over a shower rod."

"All right, then. I will admit you're skilled." I leaned over my center kitchen counter. "You got in here without me noticing any of my telltales being disturbed. Not bad."

"It was pretty simple," she said. "I got in through the front door."

"Your lock picking skills are pretty good," I said. "That particular lock was designed by a locksmith who said it was nearly unpickable."

"And my research into you and the locksmith you used four years back are even better," she said. "It's amazing what information and what keys will be made when certain pressures are applied, especially if you've invited the IRS to join in the fun."

That got my attention. I hadn't thought about that happening, and I don't like being surprised.

"I try not to be cynical, but ma'am, you are doing your part to keep me cynical," I said. "Now. Care to tell me your name, even without showing me your ID?"

"Carla Pope," she said.

"Nice to meet you."

"Hunh," she said. "Care to tell me your name?"

"Why should we get into that? You've obviously done your research."

"True," she said. "Which means you've slid through life using a half dozen or so different names. Impressive."

"Thanks, Carla. Or should I say Special Agent Pope?"

"Call me anything you like, but answer my damn question. Where is Clarence Briggs?"

"And where's your warrant?"

"Somewhere."

"I return to my earlier bullshit artist observation. You're off the reservation for some reason. No warrant, acting on your own, not even letting the local police forces in on your little break-in. So what's going on?"

"I'm looking for Clarence Briggs. Do you know where he is?"

"No."

"When was the last time you saw him?"

That made me pause for a moment. What kind of game was she playing? I wasn't sure, but I knew I was currently playing a deadly game out there with George, the partner of the now-dead Beth.

Maybe it was time to expand the playing field.

"Three days ago, in Chester, Vermont."

She perked up at that.

"What were the two of you doing there?"

"My job."

"Yeah, your job. You're some sort of go-between, or negotiator, or some sort of slimy slug that helps people get rid of stolen goods."

"Fair enough," I said.

"And how did the job go there, in Chester?"

"Lousy," I said.

"Why?"

"Because it ended up getting Clarence Briggs shot and killed."

Carla froze after I said that.

Something worked in her face, and she sighed. "Tell me again your lunch options?" the FBI woman said.

SIX

SHE ENDED UP GOING with the soup. I microwaved the container and as it was heating up, I took out a frozen French baguette, tossed that on top of the closed soup container, and got that defrosted as well. I offered her a nice five-year-old Bordeaux and I was surprised when she took me up on the offer. In about fifteen minutes or so we were eating the soup from thick ceramic bowls, with sliced warm pieces of bread smeared with butter, and some slices of Cabot cheddar cheese. Cabot offers a variety of cheddar cheeses, and I always purchase the Seriously Sharp, which has a nice checked pattern on its wrapper. If you're not used to it, it can make your eyeballs sweat and your lips pucker up like you're chewing on a lemon.

Carla halfheartedly took a sip from the soup, and then took another one, and another, and she looked up after the third spoonful. "This soup … it's great. What's it called? Tomato vegetable?"

"No, it's not," I said. "It's got chicken pieces and broth inside it as well, plus some pastas. My French-Canadian neighbors call it 'Mimi soup.' I guess Mimi was their grandmother and the soup was a family recipe."

We didn't say much after that, and I was surprised again when Carla took a second glass of Bordeaux. When lunch was done, I said, "Look, while I admire you doing your job while sitting in that robe, why don't you go upstairs, retrieve your clothing, and if it's fit for a dryer, I'll toss it in and we can continue whatever it is we're doing here."

A quick nod. "All right. But just so there's no misunderstanding … I'm sitting here, in your bathrobe and nothing else. But I'm armed. And if you try to fuck with me or fuck me, I'll shoot you dead."

"I wouldn't have it any other way."

So a few minutes passed, when she went upstairs and came back with her wet clothing, all of it was suitable to be dried at low heat, and I went to my dryer downstairs and came back and she was sitting on my living room couch. I didn't want her to be threatened at all, so I sat across from her and said, "What now?"

"Now I try to find out who killed Clarence Briggs."

"Funny, that's what I've been doing, too."

"Do you know who did it?"

"A man who told me his name was George. And he was assisted by a woman who called herself Beth."

"And how did you come to visit them?"

I sipped from my wineglass. From this vantage point, Carla Pope had a smooth set of long legs. "Please. Am I going to see a warrant?"

"Apparently not."

"Identification?"

From the bathrobe pocket that wasn't holding a 9mm Glock, she took out a thin leather wallet. She walked over, flashed it open to me.

I saw the badge and her photo and her name, and nodded with satisfaction. She returned to the couch, but she walked backward slowly, making sure she hadn't turned her back on me.

"How did you meet up with that couple in Vermont?"

"Trade secret," I said.

"Oh, come on…."

"No, it's true," I said. "Trade secret. Through my own ingenuity and other technical means, a way is available where one party seeks out another party, and in turn, they contact me."

"What was being sold three days ago?"

I gave her a steady, pleasant yet unyielding glance. "Special Agent Pope," I finally said, "before I proceed, you and I are going to need to come to some sort of an arrangement regarding any and all information I pass on."

"Like immunity?"

"That's a thought."

"Sorry," she said. "I don't have time or interest to scurry to the US Attorney in Concord and spent a week hammering out some sort of immunity deal with you. Not going to happen."

"Then why should I continue?"

"Because we both are seeking the killer of Clarence Briggs. Right?"

I thought about that. "All right. How about this? You give me your word that I won't be investigated, prosecuted, or otherwise bothered by the full force and fury of law enforcement for anything I let loose from this point forward."

"That's unenforceable."

"Of course it is," I said. "But you are one hundred percent correct—I want to find out who killed Clarence. So I agree to cooperate. And that's binding on you, and nobody else."

Her pretty eyes narrowed at what I said. "That's a pretty big damn blank check you've just sent my way. You know I can't make any guarantees."

"Ah, but I hope you'll make an unofficial guarantee. That you'd do your best to help me if your supervisors come knocking on my door, ready to express some serious unpleasantness."

She sipped from her wine, crossed and recrossed her legs—not sure if that's an FBI training move but I was definitely distracted—and Carla said, "Deal. Whatever you say or show to me won't be used against you, to the best of my ability."

"Agreed."

Then, instead of basking in the afterglow of our hard-negotiated deal, Carla went right to it: "What was being sold in Chester?"

"One of the stolen paintings from the Isabelle Stewart Gardner Museum."

Her pretty eyes narrowed so much it was like they were hard slits. "Which one?"

"The nautical Rembrandt. 'Storm on the Sea of Galilee.'"

"Impossible," she said. "We have a pretty good idea that all of the Isabelle Stewart Gardner paintings are in the Philadelphia area. Not Vermont."

"Well, I saw it in Vermont."

"You sure it wasn't a fake?"

"Positive."

"Why? You have a degree in art history or something?"

"Or something," I said crossly, finishing off my wine. "I have a degree in the worldwide university of travel, experience, and hard knocks. You show me your jewelry, I can appraise it within a hundred dollars. The same with those shoes of yours, now drying off. Or if you cared to show me what kind of government-issued vehicle you used to come here and bother me."

Carla didn't say anything. I added, "I gave it a thorough exam, using the best tools possible, which were my eyes, brain, and hands. The look of the paint, the canvas, the frame and its condition and cracking all led me to believe that it was the real deal. Then something else happened that confirmed it."

"Which is what?"

"Once I said it was for real, the man called George took out a pistol and shot Clarence. I don't think he would have done that if he were playing games with a fake Rembrandt."

"But what about the other customer?"

"There was no other customer. The whole setup was a lie. That man and his companion wanted me to verify that the painting was for real, was worth millions. When my job was completed was when the pistol came out and the shooting started. That was the job. Verification. Not negotiation."

Her eyes closed for a second. "Where was he shot?"

"Twice," I said. "Once in the throat, once in the head. It was … fairly instant."

"And you? What did you do?"

"I returned fire and got the hell out."

"Why weren't you stopped by the woman … Beth, right?"

"That was her supposed name, correct," I said. "After Clarence was shot, I wasn't sure who else might be in the house. I fired back twice and George ducked behind his desk. I threw a chair through the window and defenestrated myself from the second floor."

"Fancy word," she said.

"Sometimes I'm a fancy guy. I hit some juniper bushes, got up, and started running. The woman called Beth came out with a semi-auto Heckler & Koch, and I put three into her chest. She was wearing a Kevlar vest so she just fell back, and then I got into Clarence's vehicle and drove away."

"You didn't go back to help? Or to check on him?"

"He was dead."

"How could you be sure?"

The questions were beginning to bug me, but I tried to let that pass. She was from the government, after all, and I knew I had to take that into consideration. "I saw him take a bullet to the throat and one to the head. When I had a moment to clean myself, his blood and brains were on my right arm and shoulder. Going back to the house would have been a suicide mission, and would have doubled my stupidity quotient for the day."

"What happened to Beth after you shot her?"

"She's dead."

"Did you kill her?"

"No, I didn't."

That seemed to confuse matters so I told her about my return trip to Chester, about going through the house, tracking down the bakery and then the motel, and then finding Beth's body. Being somewhat of a gentleman, I left out details of most of the time I spent with the lovely and talented Tracy Zahn. I felt by then we had both entered the "don't ask, don't tell" zone.

"All right," she said. "You located Beth, found her dead. Did you call the cops then?"

"Yes. Anonymously, of course." I checked my watch. "It's been over a day. If you contact whichever law enforcement agency that responded to the Chester Motel yesterday, you might get a lead on who this Beth was and who she was working with, along with anything else that might come up."

A frown traveled about her face and she said, "Yeah, well, I'll give it a try. Turf battles, you probably know how it is."

Now, this was probably not the right thing to do, but I was getting into the spirit of cooperating with the federal government, so I said, "I can offer you some help there, if you'd like."

"Which is what?"

"I've got fingerprints," I said. "Just before I left the motel room, I took a fresh water glass and put her fingers on it."

"That's pretty ... imaginative of you."

"The room had been swept clean, save for the body. I didn't want her to go to waste."

"Where's the glass now?"

"Upstairs."

She nodded. "I'll take it when I leave. Now. Do you know who the other party supposedly was?"

"A concern that I once did business with, three years ago, in Tokyo. That's in Japan, you know."

"Their name?"

I shook my head. "No. You're not getting that. Client confidentiality, don't you know."

"Don't fuck with me."

"And don't try to intimidate me with your potty mouth. The name has nothing to do with it. My best guess is that George did some impressive research, determined my connection with this Japanese interest, and then used the name as bait for me. Plus ... "

I hesitated. I so dislike being made to look like a fool, especially in front of a stranger, especially in front of a Federal stranger.

"Go on," Carla said.

"Plus I was stupid," I said crossly. "It was bait, but it was stupid bait. I should have known better. The thing is, with stolen paintings like the ones from the Gardner, they're incredibly valuable, and incredibly hot. Where can you sell such a thing? So stories start, rumors get passed, that some of this multimillion dollar artwork ends up in the hands of some rich collector, either from Japan or Saudi Arabia. That's the only real market available … but those stories are nonsense. They never pan out. It's like a James Bond movie, about some secret organization or Doctor Evil who pulls strings to get things done. It's pure fiction."

"But the Japanese name got your attention."

"It sure did."

"Why not a Saudi name?"

"I don't do business with the Saudis."

"Why? Their money is just as green as anybody else's."

I said, "Because I don't like their driving laws."

"Oh," Carla said. "Is that supposed to make me feel better? That you're standing up for women? The oppressed sisterhood?"

"You didn't look so oppressed back there, pointing that pistol at me."

Carla said, "I've learned a lot."

She emptied her wineglass, ran a finger around the edge. I was going to offer her another glass, but thought I was pushing things by having her drink two, especially since she was still armed and in a foul mood.

"All right," she said. "Let's go back to the painting. You're sure it was real?"

"As real as it gets."

"So George … or somebody who was paying George … gets you and your muscle up to Chester. They say they want you to broker a deal between him and a nonexistent buyer. And after you verify that yes, the painting is genuine, they try to kill you both. Pretty fair assessment?"

"Very fair assessment," I said. "They taught you well at Quantico."

"Gee, I'm so grateful to hear that," she said, but her tone of voice was saying something else. "But why kill you both? Why not drag some guy in from a local Japanese restaurant to pretend to be Mister Moto or whatever?"

"Because they didn't want to pay me, that's why."

"Oh," she said. "That makes sense. So what's the going rate for creeps who help criminals move stolen goods?"

"I have no idea, but my rate is five percent of the object's value, that payment coming from the buyer."

"Mmm," she said. "So if the painting was worth, say, a hundred million dollars, that's one hell of a payday coming your way. But not if you were breathing long enough to receive it. But still … pretty dangerous, taking over a house like that, setting up a buy that was going to go wrong from the start. All because they want a stolen painting verified. That make sense to you?"

No, it didn't, for a number of reasons, but I wasn't going to give her that piece of information today.

"Only if the owners were desperate," I said. "What kind of info do you have on how that painting might have gotten up to Vermont?"

"What makes you think I know anything about the painting?"

"You're FBI."

"Oh, so I'm tied into everything, then?"

"It was a thought," I said.

"Let me make this plain once more," she said. "I know nothing of the stolen painting, how it got here, or your involvement in this whole mess. I was looking for the whereabouts of Clarence Briggs."

"Why?"

She leaned forward slightly. "For reasons of national security."

"You're kidding."

"I kid thee not."

"I've worked with Clarence for some time," I said. "The thought of him entering the arena of national security ... I find that hard to believe."

"He's been dead now for how long?"

"Three days."

"You try to contact his family, tell him he's dead? Or at least missing?"

A dull dagger of stone seemed to strike my chest. "I did not."

"Why? You were business partners, right? Why wouldn't you do that?"

"Because I've been busy, trying to find out who shot him."

"What, you couldn't spare ten, fifteen minutes?"

"I was busy."

"Fifteen minutes worth of busy?" she asked. "Or did you hate the thought of having to tell his ex-wife how you got him killed?"

I wished I had another glass of wine to sip from. "Probably."

"Probably? I'd say exactly. You were cowardly, not telling her what had happened."

"So says you," I said. "But when I do talk to her, I want to be able to tell her what I had done, in finding the man called George." I paused. "His body ... has it been located?"

"No."

"And his ex-wife?"

"All she knows is that he's missing."

"And his vehicle?"

"Where did you last see it?" she asked.

"I parked it off a road in Chester. It's not there now."

"I see." She got up and said, "This is how we're going to do this. You're going to go down to the cellar, check on my clothes. If they're dry, then you'll go upstairs and get that glass with the woman's fingerprints. While you're doing that, I'll get dressed, and you'll come back and hand me the glass."

"My, you seem to have that well-planned."

"Trying to earn my taxpayer's salary."

"And what happens after you leave?"

She tightened the sash to her borrowed robe. "I'll poke around, ask some questions. If I need some additional information from you, I may contact you. But don't be surprised if I don't."

"Can I contact you?"

"No," she said. "I'll reach out to you when I need to."

I shrugged. "Do what you want, it doesn't matter to me."

I turned to go to the cellar and she said, "Wait a sec. What do you mean by that?"

"Exactly what I said. What you're doing doesn't impact me at all."

"Hold on," she said. "Just what the hell are you going to be doing while I'm conducting this investigation?"

I walked to the door leading to the cellar. "Doing what you're doing, I suppose. Looking for this George character. But there'll be one key difference between you and I."

"Which is what?"

I opened the door, switched on the light to the cellar. "You intend to find him and arrest him. I intend to find him and kill him."

"Don't do that. You hear me? Don't do that."

"Loud and clear," I said.

SEVEN

Eventually Special Agent Carla Pope got dressed—in private, of course, since she wasn't that kind of girl—got the room service glass, and exited my home after telling me in so many words to be a good boy. I said I would, while keeping one hand behind my back with the fingers crossed.

After cleaning up the kitchen, I took my old Raleigh ten-speed and went out for a mind-clearing ride in the neighborhood. Litchfield is near the Merrimack River so it's pretty much flatland, which makes biking easier for me. I admire the guys and gals who get all dressed up in multi-colored spandex gear and go for long rides on bicycles whose frames were inspired by NASA technology, but I'm a bit old-fashioned. I just throw on comfortable clothes, sneakers and helmet, and a fanny pack with some water, a granola bar, and my Sig-Sauer.

I also stay away from Route 3, a state highway that cuts right through the center of Litchfield. For one thing, it's a busy road. And for another thing ... well, it's a busy road. It would be easy for some distracted motorist to swerve over and catapult me into some trees, where my bike helmet would only be good in keeping my shattered skull and leaking brain matter in one place.

Oh, and I always think it would also be easy for an undistracted motorist, maybe somebody from my checkered past, to run me down on purpose and claim it was an accident.

The afternoon bike ride went well, all along flat roads, most of them back roads with cute suburban homes and farms, and then I got home and put the bike away, checked all the telltales, and made it a point to also check the shower.

When all was clear, I showered and got changed, and right about then, one of my phones rang, and I was soon driving back to Vermont.

————

Tracy Zahn met me at a diner outside of Bellows Falls on Route 5, where she had the pot roast and I had the traditional Thanksgiving dinner of turkey breast, gravy, mashed potatoes, stuffing, and corn. As we ate Tracy eyed my plate and said, "I see you're a breast man."

"That's an old joke and unworthy of you," I said. "But still, I like the directions your mind works."

When we were finished and plates were cleared away, I said, "Go on and tell me more."

She looked around. I had made it a point of taking a corner booth, to give us some bit of privacy. Her hair was still looking pretty good, as was she. She had on a tight white turtleneck blouse with some sort of red and black Norwegian sweater that didn't button up front.

Tracy said, "I've been keeping my ears open, that's what I've been doing."

I interrupted her. "But you've been careful, correct?"

"Except for having an endless taste for nameless, naughty men, I'm quite careful, indeed."

"I like your tastes," I said. "Then go on."

She wiped her fingers with a white paper napkin. "Last night I was at a Chamber of Commerce function. You know, the kind of thing where the supposed business is to meet up with fellow business people, trade tips and leads, do some community work. Okay, we do that, but most of the time, it's just a chance to have a few drinks and socialize."

"I bet you were the center of attention."

She gently kicked me under the table. "I bet you say that to all the girls."

"Not even close."

"You're distracting me," she said, which I hoped made sense, because after she had kicked me, I had slipped off my right shoe and was running my foot up and down her lower leg.

"Thanks. Do go on."

Tracy took a breath. "So. Nat Fuller, he owns a construction firm, he was laughing about how Eddie Century had finally paid him for an excavation bill from last year, when a septic tank had to be replaced. He said something about how the dumb shit—excuse my French—had finally come into some money. And somebody said, hunh, what did he do, get a winning scratch-off ticket, and Nat said, hell, no, Eddie's too dumb to use a scratch ticket. But Nat said that Eddie told him he had some kind of rush construction job to do, putting up a window, plastering, and that's why he had the money to pay the old bill."

I said, "If I had a Spidey sense, it would be tingling right now. That sounds pretty good."

"It gets better," she said. Then her eyes widened and she whispered, "Oh," as my foot slid between her legs and went a tad higher.

"Tracy?"

"Ah, yes ... it does get better. Just a bit more pressure ... mmm ... yes, well, as I was saying, there was a bit more conversation, and I didn't catch all of it, but somebody asked something more to Nat about how dumb Eddie was, and Nat said Eddie only complained that the hardest thing to do was to get the blood out."

I quickly removed my foot, pushed it back into my shoe.

"What can you tell me about Eddie Century?"

"Brute ... "

"Tracy ... "

She made a point of taking a deep breath and fanning herself with her right hand. "Local guy. What some would call a townie. Barely made it out of high school. Survives out in a rural area with some woman that's probably his common-law wife and a couple of kids. Lives in a homemade shack with a couple of tar-paper additions. Makes money by staying on welfare, doing some snow plowing, lawn mowing, probably dealing marijuana and crystal meth if he's lucky. And home contractor stuff, though I wouldn't trust him to repair a birdhouse."

"Why do you think he was picked to do the repairs on the Chester house?"

"Because he's dumb and probably promised to keep his mouth shut."

"Can you tell me how to get to his place?"

This time I sat back with a funny expression on my face, as her black-stocking enclosed foot slid up my thigh and rested in a favorite spot of mine.

"I really don't want to."

"Why?"

"Because Eddie … he's dumb, he's a leech, but he is mean to the bone and beyond. I know for a fact a couple of police departments in the area have outstanding warrants on him, but they don't want to arrest him. They figure it doesn't make much sense to get him for some misdemeanor and end up with two or three cops in the hospital with bruises, broken bones, and bloody lips. Nobody around here wants to get on his bad side."

"Maybe I'll just be looking for his good side."

"Not sure if it's there to be found." Her foot pressed against me with some sweet emphasis. "You've got a nice, rugged face. It looks like you've spent some time outdoors, in cold winds, hot days, bright suns. I don't want to see that face messed up."

I reached under the table, gently caressed her foot. "I'll be fine."

"I'm sure … but Eddie … "

"When did it happen?"

"What?"

"When did he do something to you?"

She gently removed her foot. "All through high school."

"All four years?"

"Well, yeah, I wasn't smart enough to finish it in three, and I didn't stay back. But he made those years miserable, he did."

Her right hand gently brushed against her white turtleneck blouse. "My girls came in at a young age. They were big. Most boys teased me but got over it. But not Eddie. He didn't see me as a girl who got undressed at night and cried over the sore parts of her skin where the bra straps had cut in. Nope, Eddie Century thought I was put on this earth to tease him with my mammaries, and he never stopped. Not ever. He snapped my rear bra strap, called me Guernsey, and much more. I complained to my teachers, to the principal … my mom did the same, bless her. And it might improve for a couple of days, and then he'd come right back and do it again."

"I see."

Her eyes flashed something at me, and she said, "You planning on seeing him tonight?"

"Yes."

"Can I come along and watch?"

"No."

"Please? I'll be your best friend forever." The harsh look in her eyes was gone, replaced by a cheery gaze.

"That's quite the offer, but I still don't want you in the area."

"All right." She made a pouting gesture with her pretty full lips, and I laughed as she got a pen out of her purse, along with a pad of paper. She wrote for a moment and then slipped the piece of paper across the tabletop.

"Here you go," she said. "When you're done visiting with him, what next?"

"Haven't thought about it much."

"Then think about this. The back door of my condo will be unlocked."

I picked up the piece of paper.

"You know, that's an invitation for a bad man to slip in for a visit."

She smiled, arched her back. "I'm counting on it."

———

Tracy's directions were precise and to the point, and it still took almost a half hour to locate Eddie Century's property. It was on a remote rural road that had old stones lining each side. There were well-constructed and maintained farms, with recently planted fields, the occasional Cape Cod home, and the very occasional McMansion with recent stonewalls and gated entryways. And scattered among these expensive homes, like distant cousins who won't go home when a family wedding reception is trying to wrap up, were the homes of the townies.

This particular home was as Tracy had described. A trailer that had once been white and was sagging in the center. Three tarpaper shack additions on each end and to the rear. The driveway was muddy dirt, and there was a barbed wire enclosure to the left with about a dozen chickens milling about. A dented and rusting Chevy Tahoe pickup truck was parked in front, next to a rusting and dented Toyota Corolla. Pine and oak trees were scattered around the property, and smoke was easing its way up from a round chimney pipe. As I pulled to the side of the road, a German shepherd on a chain emerged from a battered doghouse and started barking. Nice early warning system.

On both sides of the driveway were two good-sized boulders, and I walked up to the wooden porch that was barely attached to the trailer. Up the stained wooden steps, I knocked once, twice, and then three times on the door.

It opened up, barely. I saw a grim-looking woman, long grayish hair, wearing a gray sweatshirt, stained on the front, and black stretch pants. Her feet were bare. There was a rose tattooed on her right ankle, and she said, "What?" Her teeth were brown and a number were missing.

"I'm looking for Eddie Century."

"He's not here." She started to close the door, and I deftly slid my foot in to keep it from closing.

"Oh," I said. "That's too bad. I'm looking for some construction work to be done, and he came recommended." I took out my wallet, slipped out a hundred-dollar bill, and tore it in half. I passed the torn half to the woman.

"If Eddie suddenly appears, I'll be waiting for him at the end of the driveway." I turned and then headed out.

I sat on top of one of the rocks and didn't have long to wait. The door slammed open and Eddie Century barreled out, coming off the porch and down the driveway, moving like there was a free beer keg waiting for him on the road. I stood up and he glared at me, though I guess he was happy to see the torn half of the Ben Franklin I had produced.

"What the fuck is this?" he said as he got closer. He had on dirty black Wellington boots that went up near his knees, and gray sweatpants. His light blue T-shirt advertising the Boston Red Sox didn't do a good job covering his flabby, hairy belly, which flopped over his sweatpants, and he had on a dungaree vest. His hands were red and rough, and his face was pudgy, with a bulging nose that looked like it had run into a number of fists or doorjambs over the years. His hair was thick, black, and oily looking, like the younger Elvis used to wear, and he had a black beard that looked to be a week or so old.

"This is the start of a business relationship, I hope," I said. I held out the other half of the hundred-dollar bill. He snatched it from my hand and, with suspicion in his eyes, held up the original piece, to make sure they matched.

"Your wife didn't think you were home," I said.

Ignoring me and staring at the torn bill, he said, "That fat cow isn't my wife. It's my step-daughter. And she's as dumb as shit." He lowered the torn bills and they disappeared into the right pocket of his vest.

"So whaddya want?"

If there was a cliché of a dumb country bumpkin who couldn't pour piss out of a boot even if the instructions were printed on the heel, Eddie Century fit the bill and then some. But I wasn't underestimating him. For one thing, under all that blubber were firm muscles that were used to being used hard, and in bloody practice. And his eyes were intelligent. He was good at sizing someone up, at looking at the situation, and I knew that's what he was doing right now.

I slowly got my wallet out, took out another hundred-dollar bill, passed it over to him. "I need some construction work done, and done quickly. I understand you're the man to see in Chester."

"Who told you that?" There was denial in his voice, but I could see pleasure in his eyes, that his talents were being noted.

"Somebody in the same business that I'm in," I said, giving him another hundred-dollar bill, which he quickly snapped away. "The ... extra-legal contract and trade business. Do you know what I mean?"

"No," is what he said, but as before, his eyes betrayed him. "What did you say your name was?"

"I didn't."

"Hey ... "

"Eddie, you and I, we're men of the world, we're out on the edges of life … why should we get caught up in names?"

I held up another Ben Franklin. "You were called in a few days ago to do quick repairs at an old residence on 19 Timberswamp Road. There was a broken window on the second floor, at least three if not more bullet holes, and some bloodstains. You did such a good job that anyone visiting it wouldn't notice a difference at all, unless they were forensic scientists."

I took out one more Ben Franklin and kept it right out of reach. I sat down on one rock and after some apparent deep thinking, Eddie sat down on the other rock, splaying out his legs. His sweatpants rode up so I could make out his hairy and fish-white shins.

"I don't know," he said.

"Eddie … don't you have pride in your work? Don't you?"

He grinned, leaned over, and I joined him halfway and he snapped the bill out of my hand. "Maybe now I'm remembering it."

"Good."

"So what if I did that work, hunh? I know the building inspector in town and you ain't it."

I said, "It's very good work. Would you be open to doing some more?"

Another grin. "You figure on shootin' somebody soon?"

"My business, isn't it." Another hundred-dollar bill made its way across the muddy driveway. "And my business is very complicated, so I'd rather not get into it right now. So how did you get the repair job?"

He folded his bulky arms, causing his old T-shirt to ride up more on his flabby and hairy belly, which definitely didn't improve his appearance. "Why do you want to know?"

"Private and personal," I said, holding up three more hundred-dollar bills. "Come along. You did a great job, did it quickly. Aren't you happy with that?"

"You better fuckin' believe it, pal." He got up and ambled over to me, and I pulled the money back.

"Glad to hear it, but let's reach an agreement. I want to know how and why they contacted you."

His cockiness evaporated, as he sat back down heavily on the rock. "I … I don't think I should."

I made it a point to look surprised. "Really? Did they threaten you, Eddie? Did they? You mean to tell me some flatlanders from away came and pushed you around? Told you to keep your mouth shut? Made you their bitch?"

His nostrils flared, his faced colored. "Nobody make's Eddie Century their bitch, pal."

I gave him the money. He took it as quickly as a snapping turtle grabbing a baby duckling. "Two guys came up to the house, driving a rental. White Buick. You see things, you know that the only white Buicks in this fucking state are rentals."

I thought about George and said, "Was one of them an older guy, white hair, well-dressed, cheery-looking fellow who looks like a car dealer who wants to repossess your truck?"

"Fuck, yes."

"And the other guy."

"Large, wide. Dark hair. Dark skinned. Kept his mouth shut. He was the one that drove the guy in. I guess he was the muscle."

"All right. What then?"

He unfolded his arms, scratched at his baggy crotch. "Pretty simple. Offered me some bucks to repair a house. No questions allowed to be asked from me. Just report to the house and get it done in a day, a bonus if I got it done quicker."

"How much did they pay you?"

"You from the IRS?"

"Not hardly."

"Then fuck you, pal." He paused. "No offense."

"None taken."

He scratched at his crotch again, like a sleepy bear looking for some satisfaction. I produced five more Ben Franklins. "All right, Eddie. Final Jeopardy."

"Hunh?"

"You need to watch more than *Duck Dynasty*. My final question." I waved the bills around in the air. "You tell me something, anything, about how to find these guys, this packet comes your way."

"Man ... "

"Come along, Eddie. Something. Anything. I'm not looking for their darn cellphone number or Twitter account. Something that can lead me to them. The older guy. Did the younger guy call him something?"

"Mister ... something. Once. And the older guy nearly punched him out ... like the younger guy had made a mistake."

"Last name, then."

"Sickerly, Sinclair, something like that."

"No first name?"

Eddie shook his head. "The guy wasn't the kind of guy you called by his first name, okay?"

"Fair enough. What else."

His eyes looked hungrily at my hand. "Whaddya mean, what else? Isn't that enough?"

"I'm sure if you think really, really, hard something will come up. Any idea of the license plate?"

"A Vermont plate, that's it."

"Anything else?"

His legs crossed and recrossed. "I'm trying!"

I waved the bills once again. "Try harder. Was there anything in their car? Luggage with an airline sticker on the handle? Sandwich bag? Shopping bag?"

He grinned, snapped his fingers. "Parking stub."

"Explain."

Eddie talked fast, like he was trying to get everything out before I changed my mind. "On the dashboard. An orange parking sticker for that new hotel outside of Bellows Falls ... the Green Mountain ... Hotel, Inn, that sort of thing."

"Very good," I said. "That's very impressive. Did they give you an idea of how long they might be staying in the area?"

"Not a fuckin' word."

"Fair enough."

I stood up and he stood up, and I brandished the five one-hundred-dollar bills, and he looked happy indeed at the money that was coming his way, but a split-second later, he was definitely not happy in how I delivered it. I spun on my feet and drew back, and then propelled myself forward, using all of my body weight to be behind my clenched right fist as I punched him hard in the throat. I'm sure that at any other time, Eddie would have anticipated the coming punch, or at least try to deflect it, but greed had colored his mind.

And as I punched him, I made note of long-ago training I had received. Most folks, if they're not sociopaths, are always reluctant to throw the first punch, unless drastically provoked. This doesn't work if a first punch needs to be thrown, because the output tends to be weak and flabby. But if you pretend your target really isn't a person, and you pretend that you're trying to smash a housefly buzzing in the air about three inches behind his head, then your blow will hit him with righteous fury.

Eddie took the punch pretty well, gagging and coughing, and he stumbled back and looked like was going to stay on his feet—an impressive task—except he stumbled over the boulder he had been sitting on. He fell flat on his back with a thorough *thud!*, and then I ducked in—avoiding his flailing arms—and punched him hard, three times in the sternum, right near his heart.

Those four total punches made him gasp and flounder like a large dumb shark being pulled on board, but I still had respect for him, which is why I went in and out quick.

I also dug into his jean vest and retrieved my hundred-dollar bills. It was a short-term investment, and I was calling the note due.

"Thanks for your help, Eddie," I said. "I appreciate it ... and think of this last message as a bit of payback from high school. You know what they say about revenge, don't you? It's a dish best served ... ah, forget it, I don't think you care that much, do you."

I stepped back from his hands and his feet, and let the torn halves of the original hundred-dollar bill flutter down to his heaving chest. He at least deserved that.

"No hard feelings, okay?"

He grunted something that could have been agreement or disagreement, but I didn't hang around to find out.

I took some time driving around, resting up, noting how swollen my right hand had become. It ached some, but I had gone through worse. I thought about driving over to Bellows Falls, to track down the living quarters known as the Green Mountain something-or-another, but it was dark and I was hungry. I decided to go home for a while, so I drove back across the border into New Hampshire—avoiding the checkpoints and guard towers—and twenty miles later, was having a nice, alone dinner at a Longhorn Steakhouse, where I had a filling meal, no conversation, and plenty of time to think about what had happened. And more importantly, what was going to happen.

Back again to Vermont, to the delightful Tracy Zahn, and I parked in her condo lot and rang the bell at the front door. I rang it twice, and then I saw lights come on, saw movement here and there through a curtain-covered narrowed window out front, and then she opened the door.

She was sleepy and she had on the same red robe with the dragon on the back. Tracy yawned. "I told you, I left the back door open so you can sneak in."

I walked into the foyer, closed the door behind me. "What, you're embarrassed to see me now? What am I, some tradesman that can only come in the rear?"

She took me by the hand and led me to the stairway. "You're not a tradesman, but a tool man, and for God's sake, will you stop dragging your feet?"

There was some odd scent about her, something that tickled my memory, and by the time I figured it out, I was occupied with much more pleasant activities.

———

In the morning I made breakfast again—which went quicker because by now I knew where all the ingredients were located—and it was ready by the time Tracy bestirred herself. When breakfast was completed, we returned upstairs. Eventually Tracy stood in her bedroom before a vanity, wearing a tight pair of black slacks, dark stockings, and black shoes. Her black bra and dark gray blouse were on the unmade made behind her.

I started making the bed while she fussed with a pair of earrings, her breasts delightfully swaying back and forth. "Ask a favor?"

"Ask away," I said. "But you know the answer is going to be yes."

"Because I'm so loving and dear?"

I pulled up the sheet and blankets tight, tucking them under the mattress. "Because of your stage of undress. Go ahead."

"I need to drop off my car for an oil change and inspection. Can you give me a ride to work?"

"Of course."

She came around to me and lifted up my swollen right hand. "Does it hurt?"

"Only when I make laughing noises with my hand."

"So you ran into Eddie Century."

"I did."

She kissed my hand again. "How did it go?"

"We had a frank and open exchange of views."

Tracy laughed, dropped my hand. "I bet you did."

———

I followed her to her local Volvo dealership, and when she climbed in I said, "All right, now it's my turn for a favor."

"As long as it doesn't interrupt my work schedule."

"I hope it won't," I said, driving out of the parking lot. "You know an inn or hotel called the Green Mountain something, just outside of Bellows Falls?"

"Sure," she said, balancing her black leather purse on her lap. "The Green Mountain Resort and Inn. Relatively new place, built near the Connecticut River, has a golf course, riding stables. Pretty damn pricey resort for this part of the state, but so far, they're making a go of it."

"Can you tell me where it is?"

She smiled. "I can do better than that. I can show you on the way to work."

———

Well, it really wasn't on the way to work, but I guess Tracy was just trying to repay me back for whatever she thought she owed me. We took Route 5 south, running parallel to the Connecticut River, and then she pointed out a turn-off with the sign for the inn. I took a left and the road quickly improved, and on the left again, I saw an impressive looking four-story building with wings and porches and other houses, looking like one of those grand hotels from the nineteenth century that had somehow missed the wrecking ball or arsonist's torch. The road went past the inn then looped back upon itself in a cul-de-sac.

Tracy was talking about the weather and such, and about an upcoming real estate showing, when I made a U-turn in front of the driveway leading out, and up by the main entrance there was a white

Buick parked, and I saw the man I knew as George get into the passenger's side of the car, the door being held open by a younger, bulkier guy.

In a matter of a second or two, I had made a decision.

EIGHT

I SPED OUT TO the road, heading back to Route 5. I said, "Tracy, would you say you have a spirit of adventure?"

She chuckled. "You're asking me that, when I still don't even know your name after all this time?"

"Glad to hear it," I said. "Make sure your seatbelt is nice and tight."

"What for?"

"Do it," I said, and I focused.

I braked as I got to Route 5, saw the way clear on both ends. I got out on the road and backed up, so we were facing south, the driveway behind us. I drove up enough to give me room for what I was quickly planning. Across the road was a drainage ditch and a stand of pine trees. The same geography existed on our side of the road.

I waited.

Tracy kept quiet. I wasn't sure if she was mad at me, or just intrigued at what was going to happen next.

I said, "Do me a favor, open up the glove box, pull out a road-map, and open it up."

She gave me an odd look and then did as I was told. She unfolded the map and said, "What am I looking for?"

"Camouflage."

I kept my Pilot in reverse, revved the engine, stood on the brakes as the engine shuddered. I waited some more, and didn't have to wait long after that.

The white Buick came out, halted at the stop sign, and the driver glanced at me.

"Tracy, drop the map and brace."

From the corner of my eye I saw her move, and that's when I re-leased the brakes and stomped down on the accelerator. The Honda jumped back like it had a Saturn F-1 rocket engine up its ass, and Tracy said something as I plowed the reinforced rear end of the Honda right into the driver's side of the Buick.

The impact was something else, a jarring, shuddering jolt I felt right through my bones.

I had my hands and arms locked on the steering wheel of the Pilot, so I didn't move much, though Tracy yelped. I kept my foot on the accelerator until the Buick was pushed to the other side of the driveway and fell on its side into a drainage ditch.

"Hey!" Tracy yelped.

I slammed the Honda in park and got out, Sig-Sauer in hand, and I had to give the driver credit, he was one brave and dedicated son-of-a-gun. By the time I was out and on the pavement, he had his own pistol in hand, aiming it out the now open driver's side window.

I quickly started shooting, advancing under fire, pumping round after round into the front seat of the Buick, depending on shock and awe to overwhelm my opponent. Forget what you see in movies and television about the shooter using a two-handed approach, squatting down, looking like he's about to expel an enema. That makes you immobile, makes you wide, makes you a target.

I don't like being a target.

I had spun around so I was rapidly walking toward him with only my side exposed, my right arm extended, quickly emptying my magazine. Moving like that is designed to shake up and startle the other shooter. I didn't get him with the first round, but I sure as hell got him with my second, third and fourth.

That seemed enough. I went around to the front of the Buick, to get a better view of the passenger's side.

Empty.

Damn.

The driver was slumped over, not moving. I jumped down the short slope that went to the drainage ditch, sailed over the little stream of water. The right rear door was open. I gave a quick glance into the car.

Empty.

The woods were in front of me. I was exposed.

I stepped back, went around so the Buick was between George and I, wherever he was. I went quickly back to the Pilot, making sure my back was to the Honda, still looking back at the crash scene. I suppose I could have spent some long minutes flailing around in the woods, but having had the initiative, I'd now lost it. A number of things were now on George's side, from time for someone to show up and call the cops, to finding concealment there in the woods. At this moment he might have even thrashed back through the trees and was running for the relative safety of the Green Mountain Resort and Inn.

I got back into the Honda, put it in drive and made a U-turn back onto Route 5. Tracy sat there, in shock.

"Are you all right?" I asked.

She didn't answer.

"Tracy, are you all right? Are you hurt? Does anything ache? Did you bite your tongue?"

"No ... no, I'm okay ... "

"Good."

As we drove to her real estate office, I started mourning the loss of my Sig-Sauer and the Honda Pilot. Both were too dangerous now to own, so I would have to get rid of them. The Sig-Sauer would be easy—just a toss into a lake or river—but the Honda would take some work.

"The airbags," she said. "Why didn't they deploy?"

"I had a kill switch installed a while ago, so I can disable them."

"Why?"

"To allow for what just happened, using the Pilot as a weapon," I said. "I also don't like the idea of having a shotgun shell pointed at my face. I drive safe and always wear my seatbelt. I trust that instead of an airbag."

"But who ... why ... "

The low buildings of downtown Bellows Falls appeared, and it was going to be another few minutes of driving before we got to her office.

I said, "That was the man who killed my coworker. I wasn't going to let him get away."

"But why didn't you call the police?"

"No time," I said.

"But ... you still could have called the police."

I was happy the Pilot seemed to be driving just fine, but I couldn't stay out here in the open too long with one heavily dinged-in rear bumper and hatchback. Even the dullest cop imaginable could probably make an easy link between the wrecked and shot-up Buick and my crippled Pilot once investigators arrived at the scene.

"For what reason?" I asked.

"To … get him arrested. What else?"

"All right. Hey, remind me, do I take a left or right up here?"

She ran a hand across her forehead. "Uh, left … no, right. Take a right."

I did just that, as we entered the pretty village of Bellows Falls. Traffic was light and I was happy not to see any concerned citizens, pointing at what was left of three-quarters of a functioning Honda Pilot.

"Say I call the cops. By some miracle, they actually track down the Buick and arrest the shooter. That means I have to come out of the shadows to testify, which ends my career and opens me up to a lot of unwanted attention. Then there's court dates, hearings, motions, depositions, and a year or two later … a trial. And with a good lawyer … he gets off … and my original goal is missed. And, by the by, I'd probably be going to prison after my record is finally breached."

Up ahead on the left was a block of red-brick buildings, and a small parking lot that abutted her real estate office. I backed in the Pilot so the damage wouldn't be visible from the street, and like the good gentleman I often try to be, I went around and opened the door to help her out.

Her hand trembled some but it easily slipped into mine, and we started around to the front of the building, but then she tugged me into another direction.

"Here," she said. "This way."

At an unmarked door, she stopped, pulled out a key from her purse, and unlocked the door. It led into a storage area, and she said, "Back way in."

To the left was a small bathroom, and to the right was a small conference room. We went into the conference room and she closed and locked the door, and then sat up on the shiny table.

Tracy's legs were shaking.

She hiked up her skirt to her waist, shifting her weight from one side to the other.

"Hurry up," she whispered, grabbing my belt, pulling me forward. "I have a client meeting in fifteen minutes."

I kissed her and whispered, "Are you sure you're up for it?"

Her hand caressed me. "You certainly seem to be."

———

In the city of Keene, over the border from Vermont, I parked on a side street, made a phone call, and waited.

The street had a hair shop, a corner grocery, and old three-story wooden buildings subdivided into apartments. It was a nice, sunny day. Lunchtime would be coming soon.

A tow truck rumbled its way down the road, backed up, and the driver came out, a stout young woman with a black ponytail pulled back, wearing a dungaree jumpsuit, who quickly went to work. Her hands were stained with dirt and oil, but her fingernails were painted a light pink.

In a few minutes and with a whine of the winch, the damaged Pilot was lifted up and, based on prepurchased plans and arrangements, would probably be shredded into scrap heading for Taiwan within a week.

The driver went back to the truck, winked, and said, "Happy motoring."

"You, too, ma'am."

She left, towing the Pilot behind her.

A few more minutes passed, and then another SUV rolled down the road, a black Ford Expedition. It took the space where the Honda had been parked, and another young lady came out, dressed better than the tow truck operator—tight blue jeans and a red turtleneck top—but just as attractive. She tossed the keys to me and I caught them with one hand.

"Aren't you the skilled one," she said.

"Years of practice." She laughed. I said, "You need a ride?"

"My dad always told me not to get into cars with strangers."

"What's your name?"

"Tiffany."

I shook her hand. "Tiffany, nice to meet you. I guess we're not strangers anymore, are we."

Tiffany smiled. She had a dimple on one side. "Agreed. I guess we're not strangers anymore."

I drove her to a car dealership out on Route 111, waved goodbye to my new friend, and went back to Litchfield.

———

After checking home base, I traveled out to a library in the near town of Merrimack. After spending a couple of minutes using the Great God Google, I located the website of the Boston field office of the FBI. It had a spiffy homepage with lots of links about cybersecurity, FBI employment opportunities, FBI news, and a color photo of the current special agent in charge.

However, if you were looking for information about how this office was corrupted by the local Irish mob years back and helped put a number of innocent men into prison, you were out of luck.

Once I scribbled down the phone number, I went outside and made a phone call with one of my numerous burner phones. After being passed around from one office to another and finally leaving a message, I returned home.

Along the way I paused by the Merrimack River and tossed in my Sig-Sauer and the burner phone.

The next day I got a phone call on a reserved burner phone from Special Agent Carla Pope, and much to my surprise and gratification, she agreed to a late lunch at my home. I did some shopping and spent some time on an outdoor gas grill—I know the mystique and glamour of cooking on real charcoal, but please, I have a life—and when she arrived promptly at two p.m., I was ready with small salads, cooked brown rice, and two nice little steaks, cooked medium rare.

I guess she was being more conscientious today, for she turned down my offer of red wine and asked only for water, while I went wild and had both the water and a glass of red wine, a nice Cabernet from Australia.

She had on a two-piece black suit similar to her first visit, except this one's skirt was a bit shorter, and the white blouse looked like it was bought at a real fashion outlet, instead of being issued from FBI Fashion HQ.

"I contacted the Vermont State Police," she said. "You're right, a woman's body was found in a motel room, throat slit."

"Do you know who she is?"

"Not at the moment."

"Really? The skills of the FBI are disappointing."

She expertly sawed of a piece of steak. "It's all about the turf. Boston is Boston. Vermont is run by the Albany office, hence, New York. You think New York and Boston ever get along?"

"They should. How long until you get an ID from the body?"

"Not sure," she said.

"And the water glass with the fingerprints?"

"Being processed as we speak."

"We're not speaking, we're eating."

Her fork stopped in midair. "Picky, aren't you."

"That's what makes me memorable," I said. "Anything else you can offer up?"

"No," she said. "How about you?"

I sliced off a piece of steak that had a nice charred bit of fat on the end. I know fat like that is bad for you, that it has potential carcinogens and can do no good for you and your heart.

I ate it anyway. It tasted delicious. I took a nice swallow of Cabernet, hoping it would at least thin out the fat.

"Yesterday, I was in Vermont."

"Oh?"

"Yep," I said. "I found out who repaired the house in Chester after the shoot-out, had a delightful conversation with the contractor, and then learned George and an armed companion were staying at the Green Mountain Inn and Resort outside of Bellows Falls. I hied my butt over there, whereupon I met up with George and his bulky and well-armed companion."

Carla put the fork and knife down, folded her hands tight. "What happened next?"

"We sat in the resort's hot tub, had some frozen drinks, and after apologies all around and exchanging favorite cookie recipes, we left."

"You…"

"I ambushed them. I ran their car off the road, and came out shooting. I shot and killed the driver, but George escaped."

I slowly sipped some more wine as about six minutes' worth of obscenities, curses, and questions about my intelligence and demeanor were raised and not answered. When she finally caught her breath, I gestured to her with my nearly empty wineglass.

"Your steak is getting cold. Finish it up and we can talk some more."

She jammed her fork into the remaining piece of steak, picked it up, and then tossed it against the stove. It bounced off and fell to the floor, the fork rattling around.

"Gee honey, was it something I said?"

"You stupid… bastard. Ignorant, thick… you shot them? Why the hell did you do that?"

I poured some more Australian Cabernet. "Who's being stupid now, Special Agent Carla Pope? The last time you were here I was quite clear what was on my agenda. I intended to find this George and kill him. You made it clear that you wanted to find him and arrest him. There you go. Just because I was faster and better at what I wanted to do than you, don't blame me."

"I told you I didn't want you to do that!"

"That you did. And I ignored you."

"But you didn't call me!"

I said, "How could I? Did you give me your phone number? An email address? Some other way to contact you? No. I was in Vermont and I saw my opportunity, so I took it."

I thought she was going to throw something again—this time at my head—but she regained a bit of composure and said, "Don't you see what this means?"

115

"Sure," I said. "I scared the shit out of George. He knows I'm after him. He knows I'm not going to slink back home and brood about what he almost did to me in Chester. That means he's going to be looking over his shoulder, he's going to be nervous, he's not going to sleep well at night. That all makes me happy, that's he going to be unsettled right up to the moment I blow his brains out."

Carla blinked a few times, and said, "You're unbelievable."

"Part of my roguish charm," I said.

"And what do you plan to do next?"

"Whatever makes sense," I said. "I'll probably go back to Vermont, poke around, see what I can find out."

"No. I don't want you to do that."

"Why?"

She looked at me like I was a college student asking why the sky was blue. "Because it's against the law, for one. And because I'm a member of law enforcement, and because I've told you not to. You get that?"

"You used the word *because* three times in a sentence," I said. "I think it's too many."

"I don't care what you think."

"But you care what I do."

She picked up her empty plate, tossed it across the kitchen. It made one hell of a noise as it shattered. "Got your attention?"

"You got it the first time I saw you in my shower, and unless you're going to put me in chains and handcuffs, I'm still going to be on the job. And congratulations to who gets it done first."

"Then forget about me telling you anything once those fingerprints come back."

"Gosh," I said. "Me not knowing the identity of a dead woman who earlier was about to shoot me. What will I ever do."

116

"She could be a good lead."

"She was left behind, dead, in a motel room. If her killers thought she was going to be of any intelligence value to the police, she'd be floating in the Connecticut River now, about ready to arrive in Long Island Sound."

I believe the look she was giving me was something called the death look. You know, the expression that says *Why don't you hurry up and have a coronary right now so I don't have to put up with you anymore?*

Hoping to distract her, I said, "Intelligence. Tell me more about Clarence Briggs. You said he was being investigated for something connected to national security."

"True."

"What is it?"

"Can't say," she said, and her eyes softened some, such that I didn't feel threatened that my chest was going to explode under her piercing gaze.

"Of course you can," I said. "Just open your mouth and sound out the syllables. Write them down first if that will help."

"No."

"Sorry, that's a bullshit answer, and you know it," I said. "Clarence was a lot of things. Had street smarts, worked for some crews in Massachusetts and New York, never let his emotions get in the way of getting a job done. Funny, loyal, quick with a weapon when it was necessary, in love with his boys and still in love with his ex, even though she kicked him out of the house."

"Is that all you know about him?"

"Well, I have sympathy for the ex," I said. "She came home early from a weekend trip and found Clarence in bed, not alone."

"With another woman?"

"With women, plural," I said. "Kind of hard to overlook that sort of thing in a marriage, especially when she took a shot at him."

"With her fist?"

"With a .38 revolver," I said. "The marriage was never quite the same after that. I'm surprised you don't know those details."

"Those details don't matter."

"Then tell me what details do matter. What else can you add to what I just said?"

"He … mostly what you told me. He worked in a number of illegal jobs, got a criminal record including arrests that were never prosecuted due to lack of evidence. He then became a person of interest at the Boston field office. We started looking into him, then we found out he worked with you … and once we tried to track you down, we came up against a blank wall. And we dug further … and came up against more blank walls. So here we are."

"Here we are," I said.

I took a hefty swig of my very good Cabernet—and God bless the Aussies for also having the roughest troops and most beautiful women in the world—and I put the wineglass down.

"My turn to ask a question?" I said.

Carla frowned slightly. "Ask away, but I won't guarantee an answer."

"Well, I hope you answer this one," I said, "for it's going to determine how much further I intend to go on this little enforcement adventure with you."

"Sorry," she said. "I don't understand."

"Oh, my bad," I said. "When you live alone you tend to lose your art of conversation. I'll say it this way: who the hell are you, anyway?"

Her face was troubled. "You know who I am."

"Maybe, but you're not a special agent with the Federal Bureau of Investigation, are you? An ID was shown but I called the Boston field office and, surprise, you're not an FBI agent there, or anywhere else."

There was a three-second long pause that seemed to go on for an hour, and then she broke away from the small dining room table and tried to make a run for it.

I got her in my living room, pulling on her hair and tossing her to the floor. I straddled her slim, fine-looking and sweet-smelling body, and I put the point of my very sharp steak knife to her throat.

NINE

I PUSHED THE TIP of the steak knife into her neck and a bright bead of blood appeared. My knees pinned down her arms. "Not a word, not a sigh, not a cry, or your body will be out of here in less than an hour, and I'll have new carpeting installed tomorrow. Now you're going to blink once if you hear me and if you agree to answer my questions."

No blink. A rather tough young lady. I moved the knife and pushed it again, drawing yet another bright bead of blood.

"Stubborn," I said. "Well done. But I don't have much patience left, Carla Pope—if that's your real name. You broke into my home, drew a gun on me, threatened me, and handcuffed me into working with you in finding the killer of Clarence Briggs. You did this on the false authority of being an FBI agent, fooling me, and a man in my position can't let it be known among his future clients that he can easily be fooled."

I moved the knife once more, again drawing blood. "I want questions answered. I want them answered now. And if they're answered to my satisfaction, I'll let you go. Can I have a blink now, if you please?"

She still looked up at me with contempt, but her eyes slowly blinked. I pulled the knife away.

"Bad grammar," she said. "You used the word *answered* three times in a row."

"We all have faults," I said. "You broke a fine piece of China that I got as a thank you from a customer in Shanghai. So let's move on. Real name?"

"Carla Pope."

"See, we're getting somewhere. And where do you work?"

"The Federal Bureau of Investigation."

"Oh, please," I said. "You're bleeding in three spots already. You really want to stick to that story?"

"It's the truth, damn you."

A pause. I said, "Oh. I get it now. What do you do? Human relations? Administrative aide? Wastebasket safety coordinator?"

"Office Services Supervisor," she spat back.

"Why the interest in Clarence Briggs? Why go through all this nonsense? I mean … reasons of national security? Please."

Tears quickly formed up in her eyes, trickling down her cheeks, down to her fine ears. "Because … "

I waited.

"Because … "

"Carla."

She worked hard to force me off of her. "Because he was my older brother, asshole!"

———

I got up and went to the kitchen, tossed the knife in the sink. I opened a drawer, took out a clean cotton kitchen towel, and from the refrigerator, I retrieved a brown plastic bottle of hydrogen peroxide. I soaked the cloth and went back into the living room, where I passed it over to Carla, who was sitting on one of my couches.

She pressed it against her neck, pulled it away.

"You cut me," she said.

"Poked," I said. "Hard enough to bleed."

"You like to fuck around with words, don't you," she said. She pressed the cloth against her neck once more.

"Sorry for screwing around with words, sorry I made you bleed," I said. "But if I may, this could have all been avoided if you had been upfront with me from the start."

"Like you've been upfront about your background and your name?"

"Different issue," I said. "I've been very upfront about not being upfront."

"And if I had come to you right from the beginning, about who I was and what I wanted to do, what would have happened?"

"We'll never know, will we? Hold on, let me get some bandages."

I trotted upstairs to the medicine cabinet, took out some small adhesive bandages, and came back down. I went to her and she said, "No. I'll put them on."

"Sure," I said. "And you'll do a sloppy job. Put your pride, anger, and other emotions aside just for a moment, all right?"

I gently lifted up her chin and moved it so the three puncture wounds were exposed. They were beginning to clot but I still slipped on the bandages. When I was done I said, "You can probably take those off tomorrow."

"Fuck you very much."

"If you say so."

I pulled over a footstool and sat down near her. "Tell me about you and your brother. Is Pope your married name?"

"Ex-married name. After the divorce, I decided to keep it, especially when Clarence started getting ... more active in his illegal activities. It's also a pain in the ass to change all those official documents."

"You didn't want the family connection recognized by your employer?"

She glanced down at her hands. "Those in the FBI who know, they know. But why spread the word? Why make it easier for me to get shit from higher ups or the DoJ in D.C.? So yeah, that's why I kept my married name."

"How did you find me?"

"Because Clarence wanted to make sure somebody in his family besides his ex-wife knew what he was doing when he was working with you, in case ... just in case something happened."

"Mmm."

"Why the drawn out grunt?"

"Because I thought I had done a pretty good job of insulating myself from Clarence. Not that I didn't trust him ... it's just, I wanted to keep things separate, avoid complications."

Carla brushed her fingers against the three small bandages on her neck. "I guess you made sure to change vehicles, make sure there were no tracking devices, doubled back, that sort of thing."

"You got it."

She smirked. "Did you ever think of seeing who might be following you from the air? Someone in a rented Cessna or helicopter?"

Clarence, Clarence, Clarence, I thought. Never thought you had the interest or inclination.

"I guess I didn't."

"So I knew where you lived, and from Clarence, got a very good idea of what you did for work."

"Not bad for an Office Services Supervisor ... whatever the heck that is."

"I have my days."

I got up. "Glass of wine?"

"God, yes."

Back to the kitchen and I killed off one of Australia's better exports and then returned to the living room and passed the glass over. "Why come to me, then? Why not go to your fellow FBI folks in Boston?"

She took a healthy sip. "I tell them that my ne'er-do-well brother is missing, what will they do? They'll issue a bulletin or two, but even if it's personal, do you think they're going to expend many resources to track him down? With nothing to follow up on?"

"No. They'd do nothing."

"Which is why I came to you." And another swallow of wine. "And why I want to see this right to the very end."

———

When we were both done with our wine, I went back to the kitchen, put the glasses in the sink, and picked up the broken pieces of the plate, the fork, and the chunk of steak that had all gone airborne a while ago.

Back once more into my living room, Carla was stretched out on my couch. Her skirt had ridden up some, and she had cuddled herself up against a couple of puffy pillows.

I took the footstool once more and said, "Now that you're secret is no longer a secret, what now?"

"We keep on. And remember that I know a lot about you and your illegal activities. So don't forget that."

"I'll do my best. By the way, how did you get that FBI ID produced, and what about that drinking glass from the motel?"

"How else?" she replied. "I have friends. Favors were exchanged. If you put in a request for assistance from my office, you could get it in three days. Or three hours. Depending on how I felt about you."

"I would think a fake FBI ID would be pretty high up on the feeling level."

"No, not really. Not if you say you're doing it for a Halloween party and promise to return it when you're through."

"This is May. Halloween's not for another five months."

"It was for last Halloween."

"And you still have it?"

"The guy who produced it for me is on a long-term assignment in Kabul, doing his part to save the world from medieval warlords. Once he gets back, then I'll square it with him."

"And the drinking glass?"

"With a friend as well."

"Must be some friend."

"What, you think I'm trading sexual favors for information? I don't like your tone."

I said, "I'm sure what you don't like about me is a long list. What's your plan once you get the woman's fingerprints ID'd?"

"What do you think? We'll do something about it."

"Still avoiding your coworkers?"

Carla said, "You know it. I … I want to get this handled. Once I get the fingerprint report back, I'll let you know, and we'll go on from there."

"Go on from where?" I asked. "You still looking to put your brother's killer away in jail?"

She didn't say a word.

"I think you'd agree that my way is quicker, more permanent, and will draw less publicity. A winner all around."

Carla kept on looking at me. I kept on looking at her fine legs.

"Come along to the dark side, Carla," I said. "We have chocolate."

She swung her fine legs off my couch and said, "I'll be in touch."

"I'm sure. Oh, and by the way. You left out something."

"What's that?"

"An apology, to start. For deceiving me."

Her face was sharp, indeed. "I follow the rules of Henry Ford in that one."

"Blaming the Jews?"

"No, what his son said, the other Henry," she explained. "Never apologize, never explain."

Then she left.

———

After she departed, I did the dishes and carefully took her wineglass, knife and fork and kept them separate from everything else. Then I made sure everything was locked up nice and tight, and went to bed, whereupon I slept just fine.

———

The next day I had a light breakfast of tea and cinnamon toast, and then decided it was time to return to the Green Mountain State, with one detour along the way. I placed the wineglass, knife, and fork in a plain paper bag, and then took the interstate up to Manchester, departing at Exit 6, getting on Bridge Street heading into Manchester. At the top of a rise that looked down upon the city and the Merrimack River, I pulled over and took a brief stroll into Stevens Pond Park. It was a sunny day, just a slight breeze, and I found my usual park bench and sat down, stretching out my legs, looking like an ordinary, peace-loving citizen, enjoying the view.

I waited a while and when I was reasonably confident I wasn't catching anybody's attention—not hard to do since I had this park to myself—I put the paper bag under the park bench, went back to my new vehicle, and started driving. A few minutes later, using one of my burner phones, I made a quick call, and then destroyed and dumped the phone along my route.

I got to Vermont about ninety minutes later.

———

I retraced my steps—or, more accurately, my poor late lamented Honda Pilot's route—and stopped at the road off Route 5 that led to the Green Mountain Resort and Inn. I parked my Ford and walked over to the ambush site. The brush and saplings were crushed and there were skid marks on the asphalt and gouge marks in the nearby gravel. Other than that, not much of a sign that a gun battle had taken place here the other day.

I got back into my Ford with the pleasurable new-car smell and drove the short distance to the Green Mountain Resort and Inn. As previously noted, it looked like one of those grand hotels of the nineteenth century that had missed being flattened to make a state-of-the-art parking lot. It had a center building, three stories tall, and attached wings on both sides that were a story shorter. The roof was red tile, the shutters were black, and the clapboards were a dazzling white. A wide front porch with white wicker furniture was in front of the center building, and I quickly bounded up the steps like I belonged there.

The main lobby was quiet. Oriental carpeting, comfortable couches and chairs, and a large stone fireplace in one corner that looked like it was big enough to cook an ox. I went up to the front desk and after a few pleasant minutes of lying to an eager young man wearing black slacks, a white shirt, and tartan bowtie, I was directed to a nearby sofa next to a coffee table and picked up a copy of that day's *USA Today*. I was still puzzling over the incredibly ugly design of the front page when a bulky yet sleek man came over to me wearing loafers, gray slacks, blue blazer, white shirt, and red necktie. On the jacket's right breast was a nametag with the inn's logo and a name. OLIVER SIMMONS.

"Mr. Simmons," I said, getting up and extending a hand. "Thanks for seeing me on such short notice."

He was clean-shaven, with a thick pompadour of jet-black hair that looked like it belonged in Tupelo, Mississippi, circa 1955. His handshake was firm and to the point, and we both sat down at the same time.

"As I explained before," I continued, "I'm a freelance writer, researching a book idea."

"I see," he said, sitting there, legs crossed at the ankles, soft-looking hands pushed together in a triangle above his waist. "And how does your book idea involve my resort?"

"The book idea concerns a new trend in crime," I said, doing my very best to spin a story that could be believed, "involving sudden outbursts of violence that take place in rural areas."

"I still don't see your point."

My smile didn't waver, but I had to wonder what kind of manager Mr. Simmons really was. "Then I'll get to the point," I said. "There was a deadly shooting out on Route 5 yesterday. At least one man was killed, another was possibly wounded."

"I see." He nodded in a slight and delicate way that indicated he didn't see at all. "But that crime didn't take place on our property, now, did it. It occurred out on the intersection of Route 5."

"You're certainly correct," I said, allowing him that slight victory. "But the gentlemen involved were guests of this establishment."

"Says who?" he replied, with just a hint of Vermont frost in his voice.

"Says some sources I've been working with," I said. "My book idea is just in its initial stages, so I'm looking for some background information about these two men, what they were like, what kind of guests they were."

Simmons nodded once more. "You seem to be a thorough individual."

"I do my best."

He grunted and got up from the couch. "If you'll excuse me, I'll check with the front desk and see what I can do for you."

"Thank you very much," I said, thinking to myself that perhaps the cautious old bean was going to help me out after all.

I was still thinking that when a detective from the Bellows Falls Police Department showed up and took me into custody.

Custody, I suppose, because he didn't have an idea of what to arrest me for, and because I decided to be a cheerful and cooperative guy and respond affirmatively to his requests. Detective Mike Shaye was a young guy, with a dark gray suit that looked like it was purchased in New Hampshire at some Wal-Mart—since Wal-Mart is still banned from the precious lands of the Green Mountain State. He had short black hair, streaked with some gray, a pug nose, and hard blue eyes, and he made it quick as he came into the lobby and showed me his badge.

"Can I ask you why you're so interested in yesterday's shooting?"

He was standing and I remained sitting. I looked up at him and said, "Yes."

He frowned. "Yes, what?"

"Yes, you may ask me why I'm so interested in yesterday's shooting."

He seemed confused at that and said, "Can I see some ID please?"

"Sure."

I passed over a New Hampshire driver's license, and in the spirit of today's activities, I also passed over an official press pass issued by the NH State Police. He glanced at them both and gave them back to me.

"How about we talk at my office?"

I stood up, surprising him, and I said, "Sure. Why not? Can I follow you?"

He shook his head. "I'd rather you'd ride along with me."

Feeling gracious and in a reasonable mood, I said sure.

"Oh, and another thing," he said, looking steadily at my coat and a slight bulge near my armpit. "Are you currently armed?"

"I am," I said. "I also have a permit for the pistol I'm carrying."

"Do me a favor and surrender it to me when we get outside, all right? I'll make sure I'll return it to you when we're through. Guns make me nervous."

"Guns make me nervous, too," I said, without stating the obvious, which was that the phrase *when we're through* was pretty open-ended.

Still, I continued to be in a gracious mood and I passed over my Beretta once we exited the Green Mountain Inn and Resort building.

I was surprised and pleased when Detective Shaye allowed me to sit up front in the old dark blue Crown Victoria unmarked police cruiser, since it indicated a certain level of trust. Otherwise, I'd be sitting in the backseat, with the door handles disabled so I couldn't get out on my own.

It only took a few minutes to get to the police station, a brick building on Rockingham Street that shared its quarters with the fire department. Before leaving the inn, he slid my Beretta under the cruiser's front seat. Along the way we both kept quiet, as I resisted an urge to ask him if I could play with the lights and the siren. We pulled into a municipal lot and then walked into the small police station, and Detective Shaye asked me to join him for a little chat.

So far, so good. I was sitting in his office, and not in an interrogation room. I've had some experiences with interrogation rooms and they don't frighten me one bit, but I liked seeing we were getting off to a quiet start.

"Tell me again why you were asking questions of the inn's staff," he said, taking a chair. The office was small, with the metal desk, three chairs—two now occupied—and metal bookcases and filing cabinets. No windows. I wouldn't like to spend too much time here.

"I'm working on a book proposal that ties into what happened near the inn yesterday," I said. "Small rural town, little slice of paradise, and shooting and mayhem breaks out."

"I see," he said. Next to his desk was a computer terminal, and he turned in his chair and started working the keyboard. After a minute he turned to me and said, "According to Google and Amazon, you've written exactly one book, about a cold case murder in California. Called *Dead Sand, Dead Sandals.*"

"That's right," I said, which was quite wrong, because the author of that book was dead and through some money greased here and there, the small publishing house that originally published the book thought he was still breathing and walking. And my driver's license and press pass matched the dead author's name.

"That book was published seven years ago."

"I'm a slow writer."

"Still ... seven years ago?"

"I'm hoping this book will be my lucky break," I said. "In fact ... speaking of breaks, this is a lucky one for me."

"What do you mean?" he asked.

"Because it happened within easy driving distance from where I live," I said. "What can you tell me about the shooting?"

He grimaced. "Not a thing. The State Police and the Attorney General's office have taken the lead on that, so you should talk to them."

"Oh, all right. I guess I will do that." A pause, and I said, "If that's all you can tell me, do you mind taking me back to my vehicle?"

"Yes, I do mind. Let's chat for a while."

"Sure. What's on your mind, detective?"

The grimace disappeared. "It's like this. Even though the State Police and AG has taken the lead, it doesn't mean that I'm just going to sit on my muscular ass and do nothing."

"Man murdered, another man getting away, vehicle shot up, I can see why."

His eyes snap-focused onto mine. "Who told you there were two men in that car?"

"That's what I heard."

"From who?"

"Sources," I said. "They said that one man was found dead in the car, and that another had escaped being shot."

"Considering the first people on the scene, plus EMTs and other responders, none of them saw a second party involved, that's some interesting information you got there from your sources. Care to share?"

I smiled the best way I could. "Please, detective, you know how it goes. First Amendment and all that. Why spoil a perfectly good conversation by raising a ruckus right from the start?"

He said, "I see your point, unfortunately. But if I can continue ... even though I'm not the lead, I'm still working some information, and if I find anything useful, I'll pass it along to the State Police and AG's office. You see, I don't care about getting credit. All I care is getting a hold of the guy who decided to shoot it up in my town. That offends me. Deeply. I like the town, its people, and most of all, I love it quiet and safe."

"An admirable point of view," I said. "And again, how can I help you?"

"Besides revealing your sources?"

"That's right," I said.

"Let's try this," he said, sliding open the center drawer of his desk. He removed a color photo print and pushed it across the desk at me. I picked it up and remembered how to secure my poker face. The photo seemed to be a surveillance camera shot—complete with time and date stamp on the bottom—and showed a Honda Pilot driving on the road adjacent to the Green Mountain Inn and Resort. The camera shot was clear enough to depict two people in the front section of the Pilot, and was also clear enough to show the driver.

He sure looked familiar.

I put the photo down.

"I'm sorry," I said. "I don't understand."

He gave me a quick glare as if to say he thought I understood pretty well, and he tapped the photo with his hand. "Camera surveillance photo. Taken a few minutes before the shooting started. This is a Honda Pilot that was in the vicinity at that time. Unfortunately we couldn't get a good view of the license plate. But look at the driver's face."

I made a point of peering down.

"Handsome-looking gent," I said.

"Don't you think that looks like you?"

I put an aggrieved tone in my voice. "Lots of people look like me. And why would I be here yesterday? I came here today only because I heard about the shooting. And as you saw back at the inn, I don't drive a Pilot."

Detective Shaye looked down at the photo, and looked back up at me. I could sense the wheels and gears spinning around back there, and I quietly said, "There hasn't been much news about that shooting, including the name of the dead man. Who was he?"

He still kept looking back and forth to me and the photo, like he was about to see a prominent mole on the man's face and match it to mine, which was going to be a waste of time, since I don't have such a mole.

"Out of state guy."

"How far out of state?"

"Far enough," Detective Shaye said. "Ohio."

"That's pretty far. And his name?"

He shook his head. "Mike Dillman."

"Have you tracked down his background?"

"Not as of yet," he said. "Why piss off the State Police and the Attorney General's office so early in the investigation?"

"I see," I said. "And his passenger?"

"Still looking into that, as much as I can."

"Sounds pretty thorough on your part," I said. "But if you don't mind … how did you come to visit the inn and talk to me? What kind of instructions had you left with the inn's staff?"

Like he was accepting defeat, Detective Shayle drew the photo back and returned it into his desk drawer. "What makes you think I left anything with the inn's staff?"

I gestured with my open hands, hopefully reaffirming the mistaken notion that I had nothing to hide. "Because you came so quickly after I got there. I don't think you were just wandering around the neighborhood and came in by chance. I bet you asked the inn to contact you if somebody arrived and asked a lot of questions about the shooting. True?"

"Not bad," he said, and from his computer terminal came a little bleep. He tapped the keyboard, frowned, and pushed his chair back. "If you'll excuse me for a moment, there's a gentleman from the Department of Justice who's here, who wants to see me about this case. I guess he didn't get word about the State Police and the AG's office."

"No problem," I said. "Can I leave as well?"

He headed out the door. "Wait until I come back."

Detective Shaye walked out and left the door open. I heard voices. Something tickled at me.

I got up and peered around the door, saw Detective Shaye talking to a guy just outside of the dispatcher's office.

Well, well, well … whaddya know.

I doubted the man was a gentleman, and I wasn't sure if he was from the Department of Justice or not.

But I did know this:

The good detective was involved in a very animated discussion with an older man I knew as George.

TEN

DECISION TIME ONCE AGAIN, and a quick one.

I walked out the hallway and turned left, strolled quickly and with my head held high, like I belonged here and owned the joint. I went past two crowded offices and only one raised eyebrow—from a secretary typing frantically away on a computer keyboard—and when I turned a corner, next to a bulletin board listing State of Vermont work rules, some Wanted posters, and a sign-up sheet to play softball next weekend against a local VFW team, there was a door blessedly marked EXIT.

I went through the door, got dumped into the municipal parking lot. I gently and quietly let the door close behind me—I didn't want that curious secretary to investigate the noise of a slamming door—and then I resumed my careful, law-abiding stroll.

But I felt empty, out of place, and quickly figured out why.

Something was missing.

In the parking area where Detective Shaye had left his cruiser, I checked the driver's door. It was unlocked. I opened it and reached a hand in, quickly retrieved my Beretta, and then felt much better.

It was a beautiful day.

I kept on walking.

———

After a pleasant and unobtrusive stroll through Bellows Falls, I walked into the offices of O'Halloran & Son and asked if Tracy Zahn was in. A pleasant young man, blond with brown horn-rimmed glasses, looked at a large scheduling book and said, "She's out on a sales call right now, but I expect her back in about fifteen minutes. Would you like to wait?"

"I certainly would."

I took a comfortable padded chair in the small lobby area. There were large plate glass windows overlooking the downtown at my rear, and before me was said pleasant young man, his desk, and three other desks, all of which were empty. Maps of the area and posters of ski areas and lake resorts were up on the walls. If I were a blushing man—which I'm not—I might have reacted to the site of the conference room toward the rear, where Miss Zahn and I had had a pleasant encounter the day before.

To pass the time, I picked up a copy of the local newspaper, *The Brattleboro Reformer,* which had a front-page story about yesterday's shooting, complete with a photograph of the shot-up Buick, stuck in the drainage ditch where I had pushed it. As noted from my conversation with Detective Shaye—no doubt wondering where in hell I had gotten to—I didn't expect much from the story, and wasn't disappointed. Buick was a rental, rented from Burlington International

Airport, about two hours north, and the ID of the man or men who had rented it was being kept quiet.

I kept on reading the story. The Vermont State Attorney General's office, along with the State Police, were investigating the death of the vehicle's driver. No identification released, even though I knew the man's supposed name, for whatever good it might do me. The vehicle also looked like it had been involved in a hit-and-run accident. Witnesses who might have seen an accident yesterday were asked to come forward and do their civic duty, and I pondered what my civic duty exactly was when the door opened up and Tracy Zahn strolled in. She had on crisp black slacks, a short black jacket, and a white blouse with decorative lace around the collar. In one hand she held a soft leather briefcase, and her pretty eyebrows seemed to fly off her face when she saw me sitting there.

"Well," she said. "What a surprise."

I got up, dropping the newspaper behind me. "A pleasant one, I hope."

She smiled. "The day's still young. What can I do for you?"

"A private word, if I may?"

"Certainly," she said, gesturing to me. "Patrick, I'll be taking … my friend here to the rear conference room."

"You got it, Tracy," he said.

I followed her and she made a point of leaning over to get phone messages from Patrick, and when she leaned over, she really put some thought into it, protruding her shapely behind right in front of me, and I quickly determined she was wearing a thong.

Back in the conference room, she closed the door, laughed, and dropped her briefcase on the floor. After a brief yet energetic greeting, I said, "I hate to say this, but I'm in a bit of a hurry. Could you give me a ride?"

She reached behind her, slapped the top of the conference room table. "Right here? We'd have to keep quiet so we don't shock young Patrick."

"No, you naughty lady," I said, rubbing her back. "I need a ride back to my Ford. It's parked at the Green Mountain Inn and Resort."

"Ford? You drive a Pilot."

"I did drive a Pilot ... but I think you'll recall how it got dinged up a bit."

"Oh, yes I do," she said, smiling widely. "So how did you get into town, then?"

"I was offered a ride by a fine police detective."

"Mike Shaye?"

"That's the one."

"So why aren't you getting a ride back from him?"

I rubbed her back. "Excellent question. It seems I've escaped police custody."

Another laugh. "For real? Are you under arrest?"

"Not at the moment," I said. "But that might change very shortly. I managed to walk away from the police station ... without him noticing. Or approving. Or giving me permission to depart police custody."

She squeezed me in a very intimate place. "Such a wicked boy. Sure, I'll give you a ride. Let's duck out the rear, then."

Which we did.

She drove me quickly and efficiently back up to the Green Mountain Inn and Resort, and I said, "How was your showing today?"

"Dull. Boring. Some days you feel like sitting in a corner and yawning as a house-buying couple fight in the kitchen over granite or Corian counters."

"So why do you stick with it?"

She got us onto Route 5. "Because when I'm good, I'm very good, and it's a great feeling to match a property to a client."

"Nice."

"But I won't lie to you, it's been a rough start to this year. Not much is moving in the market."

"Sorry to hear that."

Tracy slowed down at a stop sign. "And besides escaping from the police, how's your day been?"

"Interesting," I said, "with a chance of cloudy coming my way soon."

A slight pause, and she said, "There was a story in the newspaper about the shooting yesterday."

"I saw it."

"It said a man was killed."

"It did."

She said, "How do you feel about that?"

I said, "He was a bad man, working for another bad man. I don't feel much about it. How about you?"

"I was happy to see you alive and breathing before the shooting, and very happy to see you breathing and alive afterward."

"That makes me happy."

"Still, it was a pretty thin story."

"It was," I agreed. "Did you have any temptation to call the newspaper or the police to fill out the story?"

"No."

"Glad to hear it."

Up ahead was the intersection where the inn was located. "You want to know why I didn't call?"

"I'd love to know why."

She turned, her hair looking sweet indeed around her lovely face. "Because if I did that, you might get arrested. And that would mean I would never see you again. And I didn't want that."

Not sure what to say to that, except "thanks," and she smiled back at me, turned on her directionals, and we made a right.

"Stop," I said. "Right here."

She pulled the Volvo over to the side of the road. "Why? What's wrong?"

"Nothing's wrong here," I said. "It's up at the inn that I'm concerned about. They have a surveillance system up there to keep track of customers and traffic on the adjacent roads."

"Oh, shit," she said. "Did they catch the two of us yesterday?"

"Fifty percent of us," I said. "Me. The photo's fuzzy enough so I couldn't be positively identified, but it was good enough to catch Detective Shaye's very professional attention."

"I see," she said. "Thanks for having me stop here. What's next?"

"I get out, walk up to the inn, grab my Ford, and get the hell out of here."

"Oh." She pouted. "No time for dinner? Or fun?"

"I'd love a chance for dinner and fun," I said. "But I think Detective Mike Shaye is going to be looking for me, and rather quickly. Tell you what, you have any showings taking place over in New Hampshire?"

"No," she said. "But I can make sure I'll have one there tomorrow."

"Thanks," I said. "I'll let you know … and, well, there's one more thing."

She leaned over, kissed me, and I kissed her back. It felt damn good. "Most times I don't like men taking advantage of my good nature, but this must be your day. What is it?"

"You've got friends or contacts at the police department?"

"A couple," she said. "Go on."

"There was a man there just a while ago, claiming to be from the Department of Justice. I'd love to know his name and where he's spending the night."

"Is that all?"

"Do you want me to ask you more?"

"No," she said, kissing me again. "That'll be fine. Now, get going before I grab you and toss you in the back, and have my way with you."

I put my hand on the door handle. "I might put up a fight."

Another laugh. "No, no you wouldn't."

I got out, knowing she was right.

———

I walked through the woods back up to the Green Mountain Inn and Resort, thinking this was probably the same route that mystery man George took after I gunned down his driver. Along the way I searched for clues, like a leather wallet or man bag that might have been dropped in a panicked run away from the shot-up car. Alas, the only clues I found were a Pabst beer can and a Budweiser beer bottle, existing near each other in relative peace.

When I emerged from the woods and onto the finely manicured lawn of the Green Mountain Inn and Resort, I strolled briskly across the grass and onto the parking lot. Keys in hand, I got into my brand-new Ford and drove out of the parking lot.

Just for the hell of it, I waved in the direction of whatever surveillance cameras were at work.

Back in Manchester, I returned to Stevens Pond Park and went back to the earlier park bench, and I got my wineglass and silverware back. When I returned to my Ford Excursion, I made a phone call from my rapidly depleting stock of burner phones.

It was answered on the first ring.

"Yes?" a man answered.

"Yes," I said.

"All right," he went on. "The basic. Subject came back as one Carla Briggs Pope, with date of birth and Social Security number of"—followed by a string of numbers—"and currently resides at 14 Healy Drive, Quincy, Massachusetts. She's a GS 9 Office Services Supervisor with the FBI field office in Boston. Currently unmarried. One sibling, Clarence Briggs. Any more information required?"

"Not at the moment," I said.

"Have a nice day," the male answered, and I signed off, now down one burner cellphone and five hundred dollars from one of my anonymous Cayman Island accounts.

Back home, I drove down my street in Litchfield and noted a black GMC van parked about two telephone poles away from my house. The windows were tinted black. How about that.

I turned around and stopped for a moment. I was severely tempted to drive back and rear-end the van, claiming that I had lost control of my Ford because the sun was in my eye, a fly was buzzing around my head, or my naughty bits were itchy and needed to be scratched.

But damn it, I just had gotten this Ford. It still had that new car smell that made me feel like I was accomplishing something in my life.

So I slowly drove by the van—noted its license plate—and pulled into my driveway, and this time, I didn't wave at my watchers. There's having fun and then there's tempting fate and being stupid, and I didn't want to mix up the two.

Inside my house, I checked my telltales one more time, and then washed my silverware and wineglass, which were stained with graphite fingerprint powder.

When I went back out to my living room, the van was still there.

I decided to shake things up.

With another phone activated, I made a phone call to the Litchfield Police Department with a slow, querulous voice, saying I had just been walking my Dachshund dog Fritzie along Palmer Road, where I had strolled by a parked black van—with the following license plate number—and despite my advanced age and loss of hearing, I was sure I had heard a girl screaming from inside.

Oh. And my name?

"Oh," I said. "I forget."

And then there was one less phone in the universe.

———

I made myself a cup of tea and went out to my living room. I sipped at it and didn't have to wait long. A blue and white Litchfield police cruiser came down my road, went up and swung around, and then came up behind the van. An officer stepped out, cautiously approached the van, and did a very good job of standing behind and

145

away from the driver's side door as he talked to the driver. The window lowered, but I didn't see the usual and customary sliding over of driver's license and registration. I saw a brief motion of a hand, and even at this distance, I could see the Litchfield cop relax.

The tea was hot and soothing. Why not be relaxed? The driver had just produced some sort of identification from whatever law enforcement agency was keeping close view on my house and its favorite occupant. The cop and the unseen driver—unseen to me because of my angle—had an apparently friendly conversation, and the cop went back to his cruiser with a friendly departing wave.

The cruiser rolled away.

The van remained.

I finished my tea.

———

Later I was on my couch, watching one of the finest thriller movies ever made—*Ronin*, directed by John Frankenheimer and which redeemed him of the sin of *The Island of Dr. Moreau*—and thinking about what to have for a meal when my doorbell rang. I went up and took a glance through a side window at the front door. I do have one of those peepholes in my door but after seeing someone I had once worked with get an icepick in his right eye after being surprised one evening, I've never trusted them.

Carla Pope was there, looking impatient. I looked beyond her. My snoopy van and its friends were still there as well.

I unlocked the door, opened it up, and Carla came in, and before she could say a word, I closed the door behind her, said "Darling!" and gave her a big ol' sweet kiss on her mouth.

That earned me a muffled grunt and a knee to my private parts, which I managed to dodge fast enough so that it struck my inside upper right thigh instead. I broke free and made it quite clear what was going on by pushing my first index finger up to my lips and shaking my head.

She stopped whatever she was doing, looked at me, raised an eyebrow.

I nodded, putting both hands to the side of my ears, then rolling my eyes to the direction of outside. She nodded in understanding—she's a quick study, I had to credit her that—and then reached into her leather carrying bag. Carla took out a pen and small notepad, and I gently put my hand over hers.

"Honey," I said, "would you mind if we took your vehicle to dinner? My Ford's been acting up some."

"Your Ford—" And I knew she was surprised because she knew I drove a Pilot, but she hardly skipped a beat and said, "I thought you were going to bring that back to the dealership."

"I was," I said, nodding in appreciation. "But the day just got away from me. Let me get my coat."

I grabbed my coat and we left my house, with me locking the door behind me, and I noted Carla was driving a black Mercury Impala. She had her keys in her hand and I snapped them out of her grasp, and said, "Thanks, love bug. You know how I like to drive."

She gave me a smile with about one degree of warmth. "How can I forget?"

I made sure I stayed between her and the inquiring eyes up the street, and bundled her into the front seat. I was also tickled to see

147

that her Impala was registered in Massachusetts. I got into the front seat, started the car, adjusted the rearview mirror.

Carla said, "Mind telling me what the hell is going on?"

"In just a minute or so," I said.

I put my seatbelt on, and so did she, and I took a moment to make sure the side mirrors were also in place, so I had a good view of what was behind me.

Which was just an empty street.

I shifted the Impala into reverse and slammed my foot down on the accelerator.

———

We flew back with the engine humming like the warp engines on the original *Star Trek*, and Carla was also smart enough not to disturb me as I was racing up my street in reverse. With the way still clear, I stepped off the accelerator for a moment, made a slight motion with the steering wheel—at this speed and direction, even the slightest touch will have a large response—and the Impala started skidding to the right, the front end flipping around. I shifted into neutral, kept my foot off the accelerator and the brake, and when we had spun a nice round 180 degrees, I shifted the Impala into drive and goosed it.

We got to the intersection of Route 3, where I made a legal and lawful stop, and spared a second to look in the rearview mirror.

Nothing. "All right," I said. "Being this is a car registered in Massachusetts, the only license plate is on the rear bumper. Good chance the folks in the van didn't spot that. And the way I walked out with you, I don't think they got a clear shot of your face."

"Christ, you really do think things through."

"It's what I do," I said.

She kept quiet.

"Still hungry?" I asked.

"Yes," Carla said.

I drove up Route 3, heading to Manchester.

Less than thirty minutes later we were in downtown Manchester, at the Hanover Street Chop House, a fine old steak restaurant that's pretty well known in this part of northern New England. I left the Impala in an out-of-the-way parking spot, which gave us a brisk ten-minute walk to our dining spot. The restaurant was in an isolated three-story building almost directly across the street from a grand old pillared building that had NEW HAMPSHIRE FIRE INSURANCE CO chiseled overhead, but now housed the Manchester campus of the Hellenic American University.

After we settled into a corner table, and after salads, sea scallops, and a nice Pinot Noir from Chile was ordered, we got back to the issue at hand.

"Who's watching and listening?" Carla asked.

"Beats me," I said, buttering a roll. "But I'm pretty sure it's coming from your side of the fence."

She flipped a white napkin onto her lap. "That parked van up the street?"

"Very observant, Agent ... er, Office Services Supervisor Pope."

"Thanks," she said dryly. "I try to get good marks on that through my annual performance review. How certain are you that watchers were in that van?"

"Extremely certain," I said. "I made a bogus call to the Litchfield police about a suspicious van in the neighborhood. When the cop showed up, I saw the driver flash something, and a few minutes later, they were yucking it up like police academy chums from way back."

"Interesting," she said. "But now they know you know."

I took a bite out of the roll. Warm and freshly made. "Yeah, we're a couple of knowledgeable folks. Which means they'll have to work harder to get whatever it is they're looking for."

"Which is what? Information about my brother? The stolen painting? Anything else nefarious you've been up to?"

The wine tasted great. "Very good, Carla, it's been a long time since I heard someone use the word *nefarious* in a conversation. Let's take out Bishop Occam's Razor and give it a go. All of my business dealings over the … past periods of time, has ended in a reasonably peaceful manner. Save for the last one. And it's getting more complicated every day."

"What do you have?"

So I told her about my visit back to Bellows Falls and my encounter with the earnest Detective Shaye, and she stopped me when I told her I saw the man known as George standing in the police station, saying he was from the Department of Justice.

"George? The one who killed my brother?"

"That's right."

"You … fool. Why didn't you go up to Detective Shaye and have him arrest George?"

We kept quiet as the salads came. When the waiter left, I leaned over our booth's table and said in a low voice, "Carla, I know you're under pressure. You've had a rotten week. Your brother is dead, and his body's still not been recovered. You have my sympathy."

Her eyes teared up. "Thank you."

"You're welcome," I said. "But if you call me a fool, or stupid, or any other insult from this moment forward, then I am getting up, walking out, and that will be that. And before you get your FBI-issued panties in a bunch and threaten me with arrest, water boarding, or anything else, I've dropped out before, and I can do it again. All it will take is me getting up from this table and walking down the sidewalk. And you'll never see me or hear from me again, and your brother's death will go unsolved, and those who did it won't be punished. Is that what you want?"

Her voice was quiet but hard as steel. "No."

"Good. Now. Figure out why I didn't go race up to Detective Shaye and start yelling, 'He's the one officer, he did it!' For one, at the time he thought I was a true-crime writer. That means telling him I had been lying to him for the past half hour. Second, our killer George was there as an official of the Justice Department. Who do you think Detective Shaye would really trust then?"

"George is a killer. He can't be from the DoJ. It has to be a front."

"With a fake ID, right? Since you're the expert?"

She blushed. "Maybe so. And it's a small Vermont town. They tend to get ... overly impressed by someone claiming to be from the FBI or the Department of Justice. Did the detective tell you about the man you shot? George's driver?"

"Just his name, Mike Dillman."

"Where was he from?"

"Ohio."

"And what about his background?"

"Detective Shaye didn't have that with him," I said. "The State Police and the Attorney General's office are playing it all close to their vest."

"Did you find anything out that can help us?"

"Not at the moment."

She frowned. "Seems like a wasted trip, then."

Our main courses were served and I said, "Let's talk about something else for a while."

"Why?"

"Because I hate to dine on a fine meal with a companion who seems to want to chew on something else," I said, picking up my knife and fork. "Like my shin bone."

———————

With dishes cleared away and check paid with cash, I said, "And you, madam? What did you find out about our mystery woman?"

"Pretty much still a mystery."

"Oh? Did the fingerprints come back with any identification?"

"Yes, but that's about it. Her name was Kate Salzi, and she was from Pennsylvania."

I nibbled on a roll crust. "Really? That's all?"

"That's all I could get."

"Don't get pissy at me," I said. "I find it hard to believe that you'd get a fingerprint report with such a thin result."

"Oh, well, I was expecting more but my source … he got called away."

I stopped eating. "Carla, tell me more."

"My source … he called and left me a message. ID'd her as Kate Salzi, and that he'd have more in ten minutes. But he never called me back."

"Did you call him?"

"Yes."

"And…?"

"One of his coworkers said he had been suddenly called away."

"Any reason why?"

She seemed disquieted. "No … "

"Any follow-up? Email? Texts? Phone calls?"

"No," she said.

I got up from the booth. "Let's get going."

"Where?"

"Anywhere but here," I said, leading her out. "Tell me, your source, a close friend? Someone you've had a long relationship with?"

"No, not really," she said, scrambling to keep up with me. "Why are you asking me that?"

"Because I'm pretty sure he or she is dead," I said. "Or has been sent to the Boise field office. Whatever might be worse."

"You can't believe that. I'm sure it's just a coincidence."

"If you'd like to believe that, go right ahead. I can't afford it. Let's roll."

————

Outside on Hanover Street, I turned to Carla and said, "Your phone. Personal or government-issued?"

"Personal. What difference does that make?"

Too late.

Two men were on opposite ends of the sidewalk, quickly and confidently centering in on us. We were in the most urban city in this small state, which wasn't that urban. Nobody else was on the sidewalk save for us.

"I need two answers and need them quick," I said. "Number one, are you in this for real? To find your brother's killer, no matter what?"

"Yes."

"Number two, are you armed?"

"No, I'm not."

"Damn," I said. "Wish you had gone all-in on your FBI agent disguise."

With that, I pulled out my Beretta and opened fire.

ELEVEN

ON THE SLIGHT CHANCE that I was mistaken, I didn't shoot to wound or to kill. I'd hate to have the blood of two innocent Mormon missionaries on my already-crowded conscience. I fired twice at the near man, turned and fired twice at the far man, and then I grabbed Carla's upper arm and started running. Both men had professionally ducked and rolled when I started shooting, so I was pretty confident they weren't on a mission from God.

I ran just enough to get out of their immediate view, and quickly slowed down, now walking on Manchester's Main Street, which had more pedestrian traffic, and my hand was loosely grasping Carla's upper arm, while my Beretta was back in its shoulder holster. Carla's voice was shaky when she said, "Shouldn't we be getting the hell out of here?"

"Yes," I said, "but we need to be getting out of here in a smart way. Four gunshots were fired a few minutes ago a few blocks away. Two people running away would get a lot of interest. Right now, we're blending in, slowly strolling around on this nice day, and I'm happy."

We walked another block. Main Street was four lanes, two north-bound and two southbound. Traffic was steady. "About that cell-phone of yours, do you have it handy?"

"Right here."

"Pass it over."

She unzipped her leather bag, dug in, and passed it over to me. Based on so much experience that I forgot when I exactly had started it, I had removed the back, the SIM card—which I broke—and then came across a sewer grate. I paused, reached down like I was picking up a loose dollar bill, and I dropped what was once Carla's phone into the sewer.

"I was being tracked."

"Yep."

"By the same people who are tracking you?"

"Makes sense, doesn't it."

Carla said, "About George, and what you said about he being from the DoJ … "

"Yes?"

"I'm getting scared that you might be right. Maybe George is one of us."

"One of *you*," I said. "Not *us*."

We stopped at the intersection of Main Street and Concord Street. "What now?" she asked.

I took her upper arm again while we walked across. "You got anything in that Impala that's valuable?"

"No."

"Registered in your name?"

"Sort of," she said. "It's a rental."

"Well, it's probably burned, just like your phone. It's time for us to go dark, take a breath, and decide what to do next."

"Will the 'do next' part including getting to George and whoever killed my brother?"

I stopped in front of a coffee and pastry shop. "That's my plan. You can either come along for the ride or go back to Boston."

"Fuck Boston," she said.

I gently propelled her into the coffee shop. "What, are you a Yankees fan or something?"

———

We both had cups of strong coffee, and I added to my calorie fest with a vanilla Neapolitan pastry. We sat at a round table near the rear, just by the EXIT sign, and I kept a sharp eye as we let the time pass us by.

She said, "You're fast."

"I try."

"No, I don't mean you're driving or anything like that. I meant . . . back at the restaurant. You made a decision, and we got out of there. Out on the sidewalk. You saw a threat. You reacted. You're . . . fast."

"You ever hear of Edna St. Vincent Millay?"

"Sure. Pulitzer Prize–winning poet, 1920s, something like that."

"There's a short poem of hers that I've always used as a template for my life:

My candle burns at both ends;
It will not last the night;
But ah, my foes, and oh, my friends—
It gives a lovely light.

"Do you understand? That's how I move. No time to waste one's life or talents."

I tried to gauge what was going on behind those eyes of her and failed. I went on. "I take that as a compliment. Sitting still … you're a target. Moving … you shake things up, you disrupt other people's plans. That's what's gotten me this far in reasonable good health."

"Why do you do it, then?" she asked. "What's your background?"

I said, "Not enough money or pressure in the world to tell you where I come from, or what I've done before. But I learned a long time ago that the nine-to-five, cubicle office work with a fat 401k down the road with a wife and ungrateful kids wasn't going to work for me."

"It's safe."

"It's dull."

"Are you an adrenaline junkie?"

I shook my head. "Like those guys who do rock climbing with no ropes? Or climb the top of a thousand-foot TV antenna and do a parachute jump? Nope, not for me. I take risks, I go into dark places, but it's all calculated."

"And what's there at the end of the day? Besides a fat bank account?"

"Many fat bank accounts … with the knowledge that when I start to slow down, when my reflexes aren't what they should be, then I'll silently fade away and find something else to do, with the fine sense of accomplishment that I've done exactly what I wanted in the previous years, no compromises, no illusions."

The slightest of smiles. "Perhaps you'll end up in a cubicle anyways."

"Only if I get a good dental plan."

Carla picked up her coffee mug, stared out at the bustling Main Street, and put the mug down without drinking from it. "Whatever my brother was involved in … and you … and now me, it's gotten big. Out of hand."

"That's right."

"What's going on, then?"

"Pretty easy," I said. "Either some criminal element or a group from the government. Or maybe both."

"I don't believe it."

"We know my main man George ID'd himself to the Bellows Falls cops as somebody from the Department of Justice."

"Like I said, that might be a lie. Or a cover story."

"Or maybe the truth. If he's illegal, he's going into the belly of the beast: law enforcement. He'll be looked at, videotaped, and maybe a discreet phone call or two to check up on him. That's pretty edgy. Which means I think George is either with the DoJ or working with them."

Carla shook her head. "I can't believe that… no matter what I said earlier, about being scared, you might be right."

"Oh, honey, honey, honey …"

She looked like she'd like to pop out my eyeballs, one after another, using a grapefruit spoon. "Don't call me honey."

"Then don't say stupid things," I said. "You think the FBI, the Department of Justice, the federal government is all run by Boy Scouts or Girl Scouts. Damn, you work from the FBI field office in Boston. Do I really have to remind you of Whitey Bulger and his Irish gangsters, how they were protected by corrupt FBI agents? How they concealed their crimes, hid evidence so innocent men were sent to prison? Or do you and your coworkers all suffer from collective amnesia?"

Her voice was flat, with no emotion. "That's past. History. We don't dwell on it."

"Well, you should dwell on it," I said. "Your friend who ran the fingerprints for you … that triggered something for somebody. Which means he's either dead or has been disappeared."

"Or something innocent."

"Innocent? Well, look at this … you were next up on their hit parade, until we managed to scramble away. But they're still out there, either from your Boston office, or someplace else in the Northeast, or anywhere else. Corrupt feds, or somebody working with the corrupt feds."

"Over what? The Rembrandt painting? That's how this all started. What's the deal, then?"

"Who knows?" I said. "It's a murky world. Maybe somebody knows where the Isabelle Stewart Gardner paintings are located, and wants to make a side deal with the FBI, for money or glory or something like that. And before he proceeds, he wants to make sure the paintings are the real deal. Clarence and I go to Vermont, I verify the Rembrandt is the Rembrandt, and when that was achieved, it was time for George and Kathy Salzi to eliminate us both."

She played around the edge of her coffee mug, pushing it slightly with a thumb against the handle, until it revolved a complete 360 degrees. "What's your thought process now?"

"Now? Short-term, we enjoy our beverages. Long term … this is how I see it. We can do one of two things. Sit around and scurry and wait for them to come at us again. Or we can go on the offensive."

"I don't like sitting around," Carla said.

"Neither do I."

She gulped down the last of her coffee. "I'm done enjoying my beverage. Let's roll."

———

Unlike most metropolitan cities, getting a cab in Manchester takes more effort than standing on a corner, waving madly. That's not how it works here. After talking to the young lady who had seated us, she made a phone call and told us our ride would be coming by in ten or so minutes. I slipped her a couple of dollar bills and walked outside back on Main Street, with Carla at my side.

Sirens sounded in the distance. Carla winced and I said, "Take my hand, we're a young couple out for a stroll, nothing to get worked up about."

She didn't pull away. "You're not that young."

"Oh, such a charmer," I said. "I can't see why your husband left you."

"I left him," she said, squeezing my hand hard.

We walked two blocks and at the intersection of Palmer Street and Main Street, we waited, until a dented white Ford Taurus with stick-on letters saying QUEEN CITY LIVERY pulled up. I opened the rear door, she slid in, and I joined her. The driver was a heavy-set woman with white-streaked black hair wearing a dungaree jacket and a Manchester Monarchs baseball cap. "Where you going, folks?"

I told her, and off we went.

———————

About fifteen minutes later, in a run-down industrial section of Manchester, I stepped out of a fence-enclosed parking lot that contained scores of metal buildings, holding storage units. I got back into the Ford Taurus, holding a black nylon duffel bag with web handles. Carla eyed me as I got in, the bag on my lap.

"What's that?" she asked.

"Stuff. You know, bird watching gear, books, that sort of thing."

"And you store it here?"

I patted the top of the bag. "You never know when you need bird watching gear in a hurry."

———————

An hour later, I was by myself, slightly chilled, but feeling pretty good. I had changed out my clothes and was wearing a camo wrap designed to be used by trackers and snipers, both professions I have a serious and high regard for. I was now back at my home, in the stretch of woods behind my house, on my belly, keeping eye on the neighborhood. With 7 x 50 Zeiss binoculars in hand, my birdwatching and other gear at my side, I could see everything that was moving, everything that was going on, like the two Smith girls playing in their back yard.

And also including something that wasn't moving.

My friendly surveillance van from earlier in the day.

Hadn't moved a bit.

"Well, guys," I whispered. "Even by doing nothing, you're telling me a lot."

Which was this: at least two, maybe three guys in that van. They were still sitting here, which meant another two guys had been out there, near the Hanover Street Chop House. That means five. Plus a Mister Big or Doctor Evil either hiring George or being George, along with a minion or two (without the goggles and gobbly-gook dialogue) to help him out.

Lots of serious men and—including Kate Salzi—at least one serious woman.

I gently put the binoculars down on the leaves and pine needles at my side, picked up a Remington .22 semiautomatic rifle, with a nice 10x optical sight attached to the receiver. A long time ago a very helpful gunsmith made some adjustments to the rifle so it could be broken down and carried in a duffel bag like the one nearby. It's a very popular weapon, not particularly high-powered or dangerous, but as I learned a long time ago, there's no such thing as a dangerous weapon, only a dangerous man.

Or, thinking of Kate and her H&K MP 5 pointed in my direction, a very dangerous woman.

That gunsmith also made me a fair number of highly effective and highly illegal sound suppressors, one of which was attached to the end of my rifle's barrel. I lowered my head, sighted through the scope. I probably could have made the shot using the open iron sights that came with the Remington, but like most things in life, I didn't want to leave anything to chance.

I kept steady, narrowed my aim, and fired.

A harsh *chuff* and the *clink* of the bolt ejecting the tiny spent .22 round.

Three more shots, and I was finished.

I quickly broke everything down, took off my camouflage wrap, and walked across my back yard like the responsible and tax-paying citizen I was. I gave a slight and silly wave to the folks in the surveillance van—now resting on four shot-out tires—and I got into my Ford with the new car smell, started it up, and drove off.

I still felt good, though I admit I was a bit concerned about starting up the Ford, thinking maybe things had gotten so far that an explosive device had been attached, but nothing happened, which went a ways to renewing my faith in whatever humanity rested in my pursuers.

I stopped and took a right onto Route 3.

Check that, I thought. *Our* pursuers. For better or worse, I now had a representative of the FBI working with me.

I almost doubled over in laughter at that thought.

TWELVE

IT WAS A RELATIVELY short drive to where I picked up Carla Pope, at Manchester's famed Airport Diner, about five minutes' drive to the silly over-named airport that served this city and its neighbors: the Manchester-Boston Regional Airport. Yeah, right.

She got in and said, "Any more coffee and I won't sleep for a week."

"Worse things could happen."

"How did it go?"

"Went fine."

"Seemed to take a while."

"Oh, I had to make a quick stop on the way over, at that Irving gas station back there."

"To gas up?"

"Among other things," he said. "I found two tracing devices on the undercarriage of the Ford. They're now under a Chrysler mini-van with Connecticut plates. I'm hoping the mini-van brings our tracers right to the Nutmeg State."

"How do you know there were only two?"

"Are you doubting my abilities?"

"Every minute I'm with you I have doubts," she said.

Carla started yawning and I knew what was going on: even with the caffeine, she was coming down with the Winston Churchill effect—the relief and let-down that comes from being shot at with no injury.

"Let's take a break," I said, pointing out the windshield at the nearby Holiday Inn Express. "Spend the night here, sleep in late, head out to Vermont tomorrow."

"I want to go now."

"We go now, it'll be late by the time we get to Vermont. We'll be even more tired, more fuzzy, and we'll make mistakes. We'll shoot ourselves in the feet. Maybe literally."

"But—"

"That Holiday Inn is used by a lot of flight crews. Fairly anonymous. We walk over, I pay in cash, and we're gone in the morning."

"Separate rooms?"

"Of course."

"Room service?"

"Sure."

"Any limits?"

"Use your best judgment," I said. "If you have any left."

———

I like hotel rooms, I like their sameness, the quiet, knowing I'm not responsible for cleaning or dining or anything else.

So a number of quiet hours passed.

In the morning we walked back to the diner, had a quick and late breakfast, and then got back into my Ford and started driving.

I got us onto Route 101 east, planning to take Interstate 93 north a while to Concord, the state capitol. "National technical means of verification," I said.

"What?"

"Don't you remember your history?"

"Some history, but I don't even know what you're talking about."

"Yesterday. The tracking devices. The espionage. Spycraft."

We sped east, past the Mall of Manchester and a whole slew of big box stores. I had the quick feeling that I hoped Robert Frost wasn't looking down, shaking his spectral head in dismay at what happened to his home state. Stopping in the woods on a snowy evening my ass.

"Back in the days of nuclear weapons talks, both sides agreed that the telemetry for some of their missile launches would be broadcast in the clear, making it easy for the other side to track the performance and ensure there was no cheating going on. But in addition, it was always understood that spying and spy-tools—also known as national technical means of verification—would be used."

We were now approaching the tollbooths in Hooksett. From there, we would eventually find a state highway that would take us west to Vermont.

"Yesterday I checked the undercarriage of the Ford with my eyeballs. Didn't find a thing. But among my bag of tricks was a surveillance tracking device that located the first one, no doubt descended from something that was used to track Soviet missile tests. But I didn't stop there and I kept looking ... and I found the second one.

And this one was tricky, using some sort of new battery technology I couldn't initially recognize, and which wasn't picked up by my detection device."

"Serious players."

"Very serious. But I hope they have a sense of humor when they ended up in Stamford or Hartford."

"They'll probably find out sooner rather than later."

"Still, it gave us time to get to Vermont."

"Besides the obvious," she said, "what else is in Vermont?"

"My *personal* technical means of verification."

————

We were eventually on Route 113, a state highway that led us through some wooded and pasture lands on our way west, and I felt better about the status of Robert Frost's spectral viewing from up above somewhere or somewhen. There were small towns, grassy commons, and the occasional statue of a Civil War soldier standing forever at guard. Think state highway and you might think of a four-lane ribbon of concrete and asphalt; in New Hampshire, you'd be thinking wrong. Here, a state highway can be just two lanes of a better-than-average paved road, which we were currently on and driving steadily along.

I had the radio set low to some classic rock station, but still, the dead air inside the Ford was making me quite uncomfortable, with Carla just staring out the windshield, occasionally squeezing her hands together. So I decided to break the ice, or at least scrape it around some.

"Tell me more about your brother," I said.

"Why?"

"To pass the time, to learn more about him, that sort of civilized thing."

"You worked with him for a couple of years."

"Not long enough to know him," I said. "We had the ultimate professional relationship. He worked well with me, I paid him handsomely in return, and when the job was done, we had a nice meal at a restaurant and then went back to our own respective corners."

"You start," she said. "Then I'll fill in the blanks."

"All right," I said, driving by a beautiful white Colonial farmhouse, with neat barns and pastureland. Perfect for tourists and landscapers. Disneyworld New Hampshire.

"Rough and tough, with a fine sense of humor," I said. "Grew up in Boston, worked off and on for a number of not-so-wiseguys. Freelance at what he did. Divorced with twin sons. Adores his kids and still has fond thoughts about Wanda, his ex-wife, though they've been apart for a while."

Carla laughed. I had to turn my head to make sure I was hearing what I thought I was hearing. She had a merry smile on her face. "Not bad, save for one thing. He didn't grow up in Boston. None of us did. We grew up in Providence."

"Ah, home to the quiet ones."

"H. P. Lovecraft?"

"No, organized crime. The Providence mob ... they're content to let their Boston cousins to the north get all the notoriety, headlines, best-selling books, and Oscar-winning movies while they quietly did their business. How did your brother get hooked up with them?"

"High school bored him. What else can I say?"

Up ahead was an intersection with a blinking red light dangling overhead. I took a left. We hadn't seen a real traffic light in nearly an hour.

"What did he do for the boys from Federal Hill?"

"A lot of traveling, I guess. All up and down the East Coast, running errands, meeting people, doing … whatever he was told to do."

"Were you the typical younger sister, trying to get big brother back home where he belonged? Tried to keep him on the straight and narrow? Is that it?"

She turned her head to look at the peaceful landscape sliding by. "No."

Carla said not another word, even when we drove over the Connecticut River and were back in the Green Mountain State.

A couple of phone calls later, I met up with Tracy Zahn, my own private intelligence agency, who was taking the day off and had on faded blue jeans and a thick black turtleneck sweater. Even with the bulky clothes, she looked pretty damn fine. We met at a Little League baseball field outside of Bellows Falls, which was empty of fans and players. I parked near a squat green concrete building that looked like it served as a concession stand and dugout for the home team.

Tracy had parked under a maple tree and I walked over to meet her, sitting next to her on the hood of her light green Volvo station wagon.

"Well, hello there," she said.

"Hello there," I said.

She looked over my shoulder. "You cheating on me already?"

"Not hardly," I said. "She's … assisting me on this search, from another angle. Two minds being better than one, that sort of thing."

Tracy kept looking over my shoulder. "Lean-looking wench, isn't she."

"Haven't noticed."

She returned her look to the baseball park. "Bring back any fond memories?"

"No."

"What, no Little League, peewee football, semipro soccer?"

"I don't like team sports," I said.

"Says you."

She laughed, a sound I decided I still liked. From the rear pocket of her jeans, she removed a folded over piece of white paper. I took it in hand, opened it up. It was still warm from being tight up against her butt.

George Windsor was written out in neat handwriting. *The Putney Homestead Bed and Breakfast.*

"That's your man's name," she said. "And as of this morning, he was staying at the Putney Homestead."

"Where's that?"

"Just south of here in Brattleboro. Nice little inn. I'm surprised he's there, after having stayed at the Green Mountain. The Green Mountain is a much better facility."

"I don't think he has fond memories of the place," I said. "What else can you tell me?"

She bit her lower lip. "Not as much as I wanted, my friend. All I know is that he's somebody important, from D.C., and that the cops here are lining up to kiss his bony ass."

"Do you know why?"

"Only if you answer a question."

"Go ahead," I said.

She gestured to the ballpark. "Why are we meeting here? Why not in town? Or at my office?"

I refolded the piece of paper, slipped it into my coat. I said, "Things ... might get pretty interesting over the next day or two. I don't want you to be involved."

"I'm already involved."

"I like you," I said. "Any more involvement ... bad things might happen."

"How bad?"

"Very bad."

She nodded. "All right, thanks for the warning. And here's a warning right back to you, friend. George Windsor is up here on some sort of federal investigation, looking for a very bad man, and once he finds that man, he intends to, quote, nail his balls to the barn door, unquote."

"Ouch," I said.

"Be careful," she said with a sly smile. "I've developed an affection for your balls, and the body attached to it."

————

Back in the Ford, Carla Pope of the FBI said, "Local talent?"

"Local real estate agent," I said. "She's got connections, knows the news and the gossip. She's helping me out."

"I'm sure she is," she said.

I glanced down at her folded hands. "Gee, look at those claws pop out. You're something else, Miss Pope."

"It's Mrs. Pope, and you can still keep on calling me Carla."

————

From Bellows Falls to Brattleboro is about thirty minutes on Route 5, bypassing Interstate 91, to enjoy the view and to avoid snoopy State Police troopers and overhead aircraft or drones.

"What did you find out from the hot real estate agent back there?"

"A full name," I said. "George Windsor. And where he's currently residing, the Putney Homestead Bed and Breakfast, outside of Brattleboro. He certainly doesn't enjoy staying at a chain hotel."

"George Windsor," she said. "True name?"

"True as it gets, if it gets him into a police station and feels confident he's not going to get rousted."

"True name, true job?"

"Department of Justice? I ... I don't know. It just doesn't seem right."

"What does?"

I stopped at an Irving Service Station, made a quick inquiry of a cheerful teen boy working inside, and then went back out to the Ford. I kept on driving. On Main Street in Brattleboro I pulled in, just by the Old Brooks Library, a hundred-plus-year-old Victorian-style building.

"What's here?" Carla asked.

"A bit of anonymous surfing," I said as I got out.

"Then why here? We must have passed about a half dozen libraries from the time we left Manchester."

"This library's small, but not too small. We go into a small town library, then we're remembered. I don't want to be remembered."

She looked up at the old edifice. "You really need me in there?"

I smiled. "I've grown accustomed to your chilly face."

———

Inside the library had the hushed silence, smell of old books, and the low hum of knowledge being stored that still gave me a brief frisson of joy, years after I had gotten my first adult library card some years and miles ago. A helpful male librarian with a black Van Dyke beard and a pierced eyebrow directed Carla and I to the banks of the computers, and as we sat down, Carla said, "What a waste of space."

"Say again?"

"All these old books, all these crowded shelves." She started tapping on the keyboard. "Everything out there can be scanned and stored."

I pulled a hard plastic chair next to Carla. "Then what? An EMP pulse, a screw-up in some computer file, or a zombie apocalypse later, these books will still be patiently waiting on shelves, waiting to be read. What do you think of when I say the word *archipelago*?"

The keyboard tapping went on. "You haven't said that word."

"I just did."

"All right, I suppose Indonesia. Or the Philippines. Or maybe the old Soviet prison system."

"Extra points for the Gulag reference, Carla. When I think of archipelago, I think of all these hundreds of libraries, spread across the country, all of them a little island of knowledge. Each existing by themselves, each connected to each other."

She cocked an eye at me. "You certainly had the interesting upbringing ... whoever you are."

"You have no idea," I said.

The thought of sharing Google and Bing searches with someone else gave me a queasy feeling, like sharing my toothbrush with a roommate who was coughing and hacking up his lungs. But Carla was quite good at making Google and Bing dance to our tunes, and we went hither and yon looking for the elusive and currently dead Kate Salzi. We did the usual Facebook, home address, and general searches, and Carla was able to dip in and out of some semi-secret federal databases.

Within an hour, we were finished, in more ways than one.

Kate Salzi didn't exist.

And neither did George Windsor.

THIRTEEN

On the sidewalk in front of the library, Carla and I leaned against the still-warm front fender of my Ford.

"She doesn't exist," she said. "And neither does he."

"On the contrary, they both do exist."

"But there's nothing out there ... nothing."

"Wrong," I said. "There's two things out there. One is my intimate connection to the deceased Kate Salzi, just a few days back, along with the fingerprint hit from that water glass. And the other is my equally intimate connection with George. They're both real. As real as me."

Carla said, "Interesting point. As real as whoever the hell you are. Her fingerprint came back, but not the source. Which means she entered the criminal justice system at one time, or was interviewed for a job requiring fingerprints."

"Then her records were scrubbed."

"As well as George Windsor's."

"By whom?"

"I know you don't like me bringing this up, Mrs. Pope, but all signs point back to the Department of Justice. Or maybe some other none-such-agency using the DoJ as a cover."

"If that's true, then there should have been info on George Windsor being a member of the DoJ."

"He was scrubbed as well for the purpose of this op."

"And what's the purpose of this op? To capture or kill you? Or have that Rembrandt painting verified? The Department could have done it much simpler by setting up a trap to arrest you, and having that painting examined by its own experts."

"I'm pretty hard to catch," I said.

She gently kicked my foot with hers. "I seem to recall trapping you in your bathroom."

"And I seem to recall wiggling free and getting you wet."

"Don't get cocky."

"Wouldn't dream of it."

We got back into the Ford and drove slowly through downtown Brattleboro, which was lovingly rebuilt and restored, with lots of trendy shops and boutiques. At the outskirts of downtown, we both spotted the Putney Homestead Bed and Breakfast, a two-story bright yellow building with wraparound porch, lots of bay windows and decorative scrollwork.

"Nice," she said.

"Only the best for our hardworking…chasers."

I took a parking spot across the street, near a barbershop and a bakery cum sandwich place called St. Anthony's. The barbershop and the bakery were both popular and busy. We were maybe seventy-five or so feet away from the inn's front porch, a quick walk from where we were parked.

"Well," I said.

"What now? Go inside and find George, guns ablazing?"

"It's an idea."

"Not very bright," she said. "You don't know if he's there, or if he's there, where he might be. He might be in his room with a couple of rough and tough bodyguards, or might be having a late brunch with innocents sitting around him."

"It was an idea," I repeated. "I didn't say it was a good one."

She swiveled in her seat. "Here's another idea. I'm starving. Would you mind going into that place and grabbing something to eat?"

"Takeout?"

"Sure. We could sit here, eat quickly, and keep an eye on the place."

"You paying?"

"No."

I undid my seatbelt. "Do I need to remind you of that rescue effort back in Manchester?"

"I didn't need rescuing, and I can still remember it."

I opened the door. "What would you like?"

"Turkey club and an iced tea."

"You want sweetened or diet?"

Carla pursed her lips. "Does it look like I need a diet anything?"

I got out and proceeded to the bakery.

———

Inside it was warm and steamy with conversation and cooking. There were small round tables with wrought-iron chairs, nearly all of the tables occupied. I shouldered my way up to the counter, ordered two turkey clubs and two iced teas, and I was told it would be ready in twenty minutes by a tall, strikingly attractive woman in a black tanktop and whose entire right arm was tattooed with orchids and skeletons.

Any other time, a twenty-minute wait would have been irritating. I was seeing it as a gift today.

———

I went back to the entrance, pretended to scan a bulletin board, which had adorable postings about a local ham and bean supper, a knitting collective, a string quartet playing to benefit Tibetan refugees, and a student production of Shakespeare's *Julius Caesar*.

While I was pretending, I was also watching what was going on outside. Carla was still in the passenger seat of my new Ford, but she had something held up to her head. It seemed like she was talking into her hand, but I didn't think that was logical. The fact she had a hidden cellphone with her—okay, that was logical.

Then the door opened and she stepped out onto the sidewalk. She gave the bakery a quick glance. From the angle of the door and where I was standing, I was pretty confident she didn't see me.

Carla turned again and ran across the street, right up the front lawn, and then to the porch of the Putney Homestead Bed and Breakfast.

The front door of the Putney Homestead swung open, and there was movement. Two men stepped out, the younger one dressed in a dark suit with no tie, white shirt with open collar, and the look of a hungry hunter around his full and curious face.

The other man was considerably older, wearing khaki pants, a gray cardigan sweater, and an Irish tweed cap, and that was the man known in some circles as George Windsor.

"How about that," I said.

———

The conversation was brief but animated. Carla was waving her arms around a bit, and George gave it back as good as he got, also with plenty of arm movement. The other man stepped back, as if to allow his two betters to do their business while he did his job, which was to keep his boss safe, if not happy.

Temptation.

I could walk out of this bakery, go across the street by those lilac bushes, and then scoot across the lawn, and in a manner of seconds, start shooting and Get Things Done.

But George wasn't alone. That hard man was moving his head, looking back and forth, scanning and evaluating. Even if I were to stroll up the flagstone pathway like I was getting ready to check in or review the brunch menu, George's buddy would immediately zone on the approaching threat and drop me without hesitation.

I could go in a sudden blitz, but if that guy was good—which he definitely looked like he was—he could push George behind him and start ripping off rounds at me. In the subsequent exchange, I might get him, and then George, but only by being very, very lucky would I be able to avoid getting hit myself.

Plus, in the ensuing crossfire, Carla Pope might get hit as well.

She started walking briskly back to our Ford. George and his bulky buddy went off the porch, to the rear, and then a few seconds later, a black Chrysler Escalade exited the rear parking lot of the building and went out onto Main Street.

Carla got back into my Ford.

"Hey, number nineteen," called out the tall woman with the deadly tattoo. "Your order's up!"

Carla being shot in the crossfire.

I was surprised the thought didn't bother me at all.

———————

Back into the Ford I went, grasping two bottles of Lipton iced tea in one hand, and a white wax paper package with our respective and identical lunches.

"Anything happen?" I asked, passing over her lunch.

"Like what?"

"Like George emerging from that house and begging forgiveness?"

"Nope." She opened her bag. "Where's the chips?"

"You didn't ask for chips."

"That's part of the agreement when it comes to a sandwich," Carla said. "It comes with chips."

"It also comes with napkins, but I didn't have to ask for napkins. You want chips? You know where to find them."

We ate quietly after that, the noise of the wax paper and napkins being rustled around. As she ate, Carla Pope had no idea how lucky she was. If she had encountered the younger and angrier me, I would be considering taking her out to another rural Vermont road, not in search of any more leads in this matter, but a place where I could easily dump her body.

But my age was her good fortune. Plus a curiosity in wanting to know what was going on, although at my own pace and speed. I could force the issue now with Carla, but now it seemed like George had left the scene. Perhaps she and he would meet again, at a time when I hadn't been sent away on a food run. In the meantime, well, perhaps I could figure out what this FBI bureaucrat was really doing. And I'm sure she would be stunned at what I was currently thinking, but I was wondering how much she'd really liked her older brother, and maybe she had something else going on that didn't involve avenging Clarence.

Maybe something else … like recovering that stolen Rembrandt on her own and giving her major props among her FBI crew.

Maybe.

I ate and looked out at the B&B, running through thoughts, options, and ideas. Nothing settled, just randomly tossing things up in the air and seeing where they land and how they fit together.

"Good sandwich," Carla announced.

I grunted in reply. I was thinking of other meals past, before I had hired this woman's older brother. Once I had been on Rue Elgin, in the old town section of Quebec City, a part of the city that looked like it had been transported from a medieval section of France and plopped down on the banks of the St. Lawrence River. The waitstaff was older men and women who took pride in their profession, and the five-course meal was a gourmet's delight, from start to finish, with three different kinds of wine being served.

Another time soon after that, I was halfway up a remote mountain valley in Afghanistan, eating cold mutton and bread, with cold weak tea, a flickering fire before a circle of men that barely warmed our faces, shivering under a scratchy and smelly wool cape.

I took another bite of the sandwich. Funny thing was, I had fond memories of the cold mutton rather than the medium-rare sirloin steak with sautéed mushrooms and a Merlot reduction on the side. You see, in Quebec City, I was involved in a complicated negotiation between a Montreal motorcycle gang, and another motorcycle gang based in California. The object of their desire was an intricately designed, constructed, and painted memorial Harley-Davidson motorcycle that had enormous sentimental value for each gang.

The dinner was held at this supposedly neutral spot, and the gang members had arrived without their colors, dressed in what I guess passed for their best clothes, yet none of the dressing up could hide the dirt under their fingernails and the contempt behind their eyes. One gang was in one private dining room, and the other was in another. Between courses I shuttled back and forth, and when dessert and café au lait was offered, I skipped out and left, not bothering to even go back to my hotel room to fetch my stuff.

The next day, before I left the city, I picked up a copy of the city's daily newspaper, *Le Soleil,* where the lead story was a bloody shootout that had erupted the night before, near Rue Elgin, with one dead, three wounded, and enough bullet holes in nearby windows and masonry to outfit a Michael Bay movie.

But the cold mutton, though, that was a more pleasant story. It involved a negotiation between a Pashtun warlord who had a bit of pressed and hammered copper jewelry that may—emphasis on the word *may*—have belonged to Alexander the Great when he had been traipsing through these very mountains back during 330 BC or thereabouts. The other party was a very tired and frightened woman from the New York Metropolitan Museum of Art, who was covered in a full burqa, and whose voice shook every time she said something to our hired translator. The warlord wasn't quite sure of the valuable nature of his possession, but he eventually passed it over to us in exchange for two small gold bars, a large herd of goats, and eight cases of 7.62mm ammunition.

The warlord had been a joy to be with, for he went on and on with stories about these mountains and the fights that had gone on for centuries, and I had been so entranced with his talk that I spurned my usual fee and only asked to hold that piece of jewelry in my hand before we successfully returned to Pakistan.

That food was a pleasant memory, as pleasant as the Quebecois dinner was unpleasant.

I crumpled up my sandwich wrapper. The next few hours would determine where this sandwich would go into my memory banks.

"Tell me more about Clarence. Was he popular? Lots of buds? Lots of girlfriends?"

"I told you before and—"

"And I'm not satisfied. C'mon. Give it up. I've been extremely clear why revenge is on my menu. But you? Threatening your career, maybe even your life, for a criminal brother?"

She slumped lower in her seat. "He was more than just a criminal ... he was ... loving. He stood up for me at school, whenever the mean girls tried to make my life miserable, and I paid him back by trying to help with schoolwork. He was also protective. And innocent, almost like a gentle giant."

I had a series of memories quickly flash by, all of them concerning Clarence and me on a job, from one extreme to the other, from jobs that wrapped up quick and clean, all the way up to jobs that ended with Clarence dragging me out by my collar from a blown meeting place, using his other hand to put down suppressing fire.

"Please don't be offended, Carla, but innocent isn't exactly the first thought that comes to mind when you mention your brother Clarence. Not even the fifth thought. Or tenth."

She sighed. "Clarence was good at what he did. He could be scary. Threatening. Deadly. But he never … he never came up with a scheme or a plan of his own. He was always just the follower, never a leader. He was a loaded weapon, and he was content to be used like that … aimed and forgotten after he got paid. And paid from whomever he was hired out to, no matter the job."

"How much of an embarrassment was it to you, working for the feds and having a crooked brother in the background?"

"Not embarrassing at all," she said, "since it's been three years since I last spoke to him."

So there you go. And I left my follow-up question unasked: then why are you here?

———

That took care of the conversation for a bit, and I idly tapped on the steering wheel, thinking of what Carla had just said, and also thinking of what she had done earlier, going out on her own to talk to George Windsor, for whatever reason. I wanted to be suspicious of her background, but I recalled my own fingerprint research on her. She was who she said she was, unless the FBI was very good at hiding folks like Carla in plain sight, making everyone think she was just a lowly bureaucrat.

No offense to the boys and girls at the J. Edgar Hoover building, but I didn't think the FBI had that particular skill set.

I then stopped tapping on the steering wheel. "Okay, that's it. We've been sitting on our collective butts for too long."

"You thinking of going away?"

I started up the Ford. "No. In fact, hell no. We're going to drive over to the Putney Homestead and see if our man George is staying there. I'm tired of doing surveillance, waiting for him to make a move. Time for us to make a move."

"He might be in there, waiting for us."

Considering what I had seen of the Cadillac Escalade, I doubted that, but I wasn't going to let that on.

"Then he'll be in for a big frickin' surprise, won't he."

She paused. Why? Because I was screwing up whatever plans she and George might be working on?

Finally Carla said, "I don't like it."

"I don't really care," I said. "Besides, I'm not as sprightly as I used to be. The days of me being on a day-long stakeout and using an empty Pringles can for relief are long over. I need to hit the head."

"Stakeouts," she said. "What kind?"

"Mostly the boring kind."

I parked at the rear of the bed-and-breakfast, where there was one open space available in the tiny paved lot, which wasn't surprising considering who I had seen earlier drive off. If God was working miracles in this neck of the woods today, it would have been fine if George were to drive up, so we could once meet again, face to face, and get everything settled.

But God must have been busy elsewhere, so Carla and I walked around to the front of the Putney Homestead, unmolested and unbothered. Yet I walked with my hand within easy reach of my holstered Beretta, more to keep Carla thinking that I was being cautious, even though I knew George wasn't around.

We went up a porch, enclosed by screens, and went through the front door. The charming interior nearly knocked me back. There were two settees on the right, a covering of roses and flowers on a round coffee table, and a small dining room to the left. Before us was a staircase going up, and an ornate wooden desk. A young woman—late twenties, early thirties—got up and extended the both of us a smile. She had shoulder-length brown hair parted to one side, bright brown eyes, and a small nose. From what I saw she had on a gray skirt and scoop-necked yellow sweater, and after exchanging greetings, I said, "Tell me, I've missed George, right? He and his friend? He told me he wouldn't wait for me, the son-of-a-gun."

Our gracious host hesitated just for a moment, and I laughed. "Oh, that's my George. He's so secretive and mysterious, especially when he's hooking up with his friend." I added air quotes to the word *friend*. "You know who I mean, nice older man, about my height, several pounds heavier, looks like a slimmed down Santa Claus that had to shave off his beard."

The hostess—named Natalie—blushed. "Yes, he left a few hours ago."

"Checked out?"

Natalie glanced down at an open appointment book on the desk. "I'm afraid so."

"Dear me," I said, turning to Carla. "Sorry, honey. I guess we should have left the zoo earlier." Carla wasn't sure how to respond, so I went on. "Tell me, the kitchen smells great. Any chance of dinner later on?"

Natalie sat back down behind her desk. "I don't see why not."

"Hey, thanks," I said. "And … okay, I'm pushing it, I know, but do you have any available rooms?"

Natalie ran a cute finger across the book. "Well … since your friend and his friend left, we do have their rooms available. They're among the older rooms we have, each a single with a connecting bathroom."

I turned again to Carla. "Gosh, honey, think you can survive a night without snuggling up against me?"

Carla said, "I'll manage."

———

After checking in and bringing up our respective coats and belongings, we settled in our new lodgings. I opened both doors leading into the small bathroom and examined our new home for the night. The rooms were twins of each other, with small beds, a comfortable chair, bureau, armoire, and nightstand with lamp, phone, and digital clock.

Carla said, "What are we doing here?"

"We're going to be eating, and then we're going to be sleeping," I said. "We're also going to talk to the other guests at dinner, see if anybody can remember George and what he might be up to."

"That's a stretch."

"No, that's a hell of a stretch, unless you can come up with a better idea."

She frowned. "No, I can't."

Liar, I thought, but I let it slide.

———

While Carla was in the shower, her side of the bathroom door locked, I took off my shoes and padded around to her door, where a minute or two of lock-picking expertise got me into her room. Using a tension wrench I held the lock cylinder firm, and with a skinny metal lockpick, I quickly moved back five lock pins. Then I rotated the tension wrench and undid the lock with a satisfying *click*. Door open, I headed straight into her room and to her large black purse, lying on the edge of the bed.

Bingo, I thought as I dug into it. A TracPhone disposable cellphone. I turned it on and saw that I needed a four-digit password to get access.

Suspicious young lady, I thought, and switched the phone off, put it back into her purse. Something else was in the bottom of her purse, and it was bingo squared.

A .32-caliber Smith & Wesson semiautomatic pistol.

"Very suspicious young lady," I whispered, and then that went back into the purse and I got the hell out.

———

Dinner was a surf and turf for me—lobster tail and filet mignon—and some sort of salmon dish for her. I ordered a split of a French Bordeaux, and we shared it throughout the meal. The room was small, pleasant, and twice I got up to use the restroom. Both times I struck up idle conversation with three other couples—of various ages and conditions—who were staying at the Putney Homestead. Alas, nobody could tell me anything of interest about George and his muscle man. I passed the time by pretending to be a friend of George's who had arrived late, but due to the lack of responses to my questioning, George must have holed up in his room, playing cribbage or hearts with his companion.

As Carla examined the dessert menu, she said, "You expect to get anything out of that stupid chit-chat?"

"You never know unless you try."

"How original."

"No, it's not original, but sometimes the old sayings, they still work."

For a slim-looking woman, Carla had one heck of an appetite, and put away a hot fudge sundae, which sounded so good I had one as well. But she turned down the coffee, and I went with two strong cups.

That caused an eyebrow to rise. "You're going to be staying up late tonight."

"Might just be my plan."

"What kind of plan?"

"To finally finish reading *War and Peace*. How about that?"

"I'll believe it when I see it," she said.

"You looking for a book report?"

She scraped her spoon across the bottom of her dessert dish. "Maybe an oral report."

That caused me to smile and to sit back.

Maybe I had misjudged her once again.

Time to confront her?

No.

———

After dinner we sat out in the reception area in front of a roaring fireplace and we both looked through old picture books of Vermont, me having another cup of coffee, Carla having a glass of ice water. We sat, watching the couples either going outside or walking up the stairway. When the room was empty I said, "How about we retire for the night?"

She closed the book she had been reviewing. "I suppose that was going to happen, but what's next in our chase?"

I checked to make sure we were alone, and I said, "Later tonight, after all the good people and bad people have gone to sleep, I'm going to come back down here and root around the Putney Homestead's computer system, maybe check the receipts. There should be something there to tell us more about George."

"That's it?"

"You got a better idea?"

She stretched her back. "At the moment, no."

Again, I thought, another lie.

———

She retired to her room and I retired to mine, and I listened to her wash up and then flush the toilet, and then I knocked on the bathroom door, and not receiving a reply, entered to do my business. I washed up and brushed my teeth and did what had to be done, and then went back to my room.

I had a slight buzz from the Bordeaux and the coffee as I prepared myself for bed. I checked the lock on the door leading to the hallway, which was perfectly adequate for a nice bed-and-breakfast that wasn't prepared for crime, but which wasn't perfect for me. I had hoped for a straight-back chair to jam underneath the doorknob, but that wasn't going to happen tonight.

Darn.

The lock on the door leading into the bathroom was a simple deadbolt, which I secured. I opened up the bureau and the armoire, found spare blankets and a light blue down comforter. It would do very nicely. On the window side of the bed, I spread out the bedding on the floor, and then stretched out on my homemade and quite unofficial bed. I kept my clothes and footwear on, in case I had to move quick.

Not bad. I've certainly slept on worse. From a nearby carry-on bag, I slipped out a Petzl headlamp, which I put over my head. I switched it on, reached up, and tugged down a pillow, and then switched off the lamp on the table.

I settled in, pulled out a John Lukacs history of World War II, and read for a bit, my Beretta within easy reach. When my eyes got heavy, I turned off the headlamp. The room wasn't completely dark, with illumination coming from outside and the nearby streetlamp.

Looking good.

I was reasonably comfortable, well-armed, and I was set for the night. With a dark room like this, if anybody broke in and started blazing away, they'd aim for the bed, and they'd miss me. And in my position, I'd be in a good place to return fire without being hit.

Not a bad plan.

As I fell asleep, I should have recalled that other folks have plans as well.

———

The ringing phone sat me right up, and I knew instantly it wasn't one of my burner phones, and that it belonged to the Putney Homestead, and it was three a.m.

I kept my profile low, just in case the call was designed to stir me up and silhouette me against the window.

I grabbed the phone and said, "Yes?"

"Ah," a man said. "Did I wake you up?"

"No, I was detailing my toes when you called. Who's this?"

A short laugh. "My, the great negotiator, he draws blank on a moment like this? I'm quite surprised."

Then it came together.

"Hello, George."

"And a cheery early good morning to you as well."

FOURTEEN

I SAT UP AGAINST the bed, phone in my left hand, right hand grasping my Beretta.

"Hey, George, a cheery good morning right back to you as well. How goes it?"

"It goes. Hey, are you as good a negotiator as people say?"

"Pretty much."

"You open for a negotiation?"

"I can't imagine where this is going, but in my business, I've learned to never say no from the start. What do you have in mind, George?"

"You have something I want. Your friend had it, now you have it. I want it back."

"Nice opening statement," I said. "Brisk and right to the point. You've told me what you want. Now, let's move on to the second part. What do I get in return?"

"Your life."

"Ah, George," I said. "Now we've reached our first road block, because you're being unreasonable. You're trying to close a deal with something not in your control and your possession—i.e., my life."

George laughed. "Don't be stupid."

"Don't be insulting."

"I almost killed you once."

"And I almost did the same to you," I said. "You caught me by surprise. Won't happen again."

"Pretty self-confident."

"Pretty self-evident. And by the way, speaking of deals, you still owe me for my work on the Rembrandt painting."

Another confident laugh. It was starting to get on my nerves. "Let's leave that be for a while, get back to the subject at hand. You have something I want."

"Which is what?"

"You shitting me?"

I paused, then said, "You don't appear to be on the floor underneath me, so no, I'm not shitting you."

"Hah. Let me repeat: you, and only you, have something I want. And I want it now, in exchange for leaving you alone."

"Sorry, George, this is becoming very unproductive. And at such a late hour. You're not being very considerate as a negotiation partner."

"All right, if you're not that excited about negotiating with your life on the line, let's try somebody else's."

"Excuse me?"

A slight *click* and *clack* of the phone being handed over, and then another voice, female and frightened.

"This … this is Carla … who's this? Please?"

———

If I had been awake earlier, now I was flying high and wired, every sense of mine tingling with anticipation and danger. "Carla, you know who this is. What's going on?"

"I … I've been abducted … and Christ, I'm so fucking scared … "

"When did they do it?"

"An hour … two hours ago … I'm not sure … they came into my room and grabbed me … tied me up, put a hood over my head … Christ, can you help me? Please? Can you help me?"

"Give the phone back to George."

A sob. "Thanks … okay … thanks … "

The phone went back to George. "Well?"

"George?"

"Yes?"

"Can you hear me clearly and distinctly?"

"Of course I can," he said. "What's this about?"

"Just wanting to make sure there's no confusion over what I'm about to say."

"Which is what?"

I took a breath. "No."

"Hunh?"

"No, *non, nyet*."

And I hung up the phone.

And just for good measure, I disconnected the phone from the room.

Then I went to work.

———

Another quiet entry into the hallway, and another quick work with my locksmith tools. In a few seconds I was in Carla's room. I carefully closed the door and just waited.

Odd, I know, but sometimes I like to stand quiet in a room, just to get a sense of the place. After years on my uncertain career path, I've learned to note things just out of earshot, just out of eyeshot. Like furniture moved around, a television set on to a blank channel, water dripping from a faucet, a phone buzzing because the receiver is off the hook.

Nothing seemed to speak to me.

I switched on the Petzl headlamp but kept it cupped in my right hand and not around my skull. The bed was before me, and the bedding was tangled at the end of the bed. I moved around to the other side, and then flashed the light around the rest of the room.

Empty.

The bathroom door was open, and I ducked in there as well.

Empty.

I went around the room, flashing the light on the floor.

No clothes or shoes on the floor.

No luggage left behind.

No beauty supplies left in the bathroom as well.

Maybe Carla had just packed everything up, preparing for an early start in the morning, and her alleged kidnappers had grabbed it all on their way out.

Perhaps.

I switched off the Petzl lamp, and then went back out to the hallway. Noises from downstairs. Probably the morning chef getting ready to start the preps for breakfast. A rough way of life.

Back in my room, I locked the door behind me and plugged the phone back in and checked the phone console. There was a cardboard square that marked the phone number for this room, and I saw that any outside caller could dial directly into the room, bypassing the Putney Homestead's main switchboard.

There was a digital readout above the keypad, and I was tickled to see that it allowed me to view the last number dialed in. I pushed the keypad for that function, and it quickly came up BLOCKED CALL.

Thanks, George, I thought. Working smart.

But not smart enough.

I unplugged the phone again, because I didn't want to be disturbed.

I stretched out on my homemade bed on the floor and relaxed my muscles, took a series of deep breaths, and eventually fell back asleep.

————

I woke up two hours later, showered and shaved with the doors locked and closed, and with the shower curtain open. When I was presentable, I got dressed, reconnected the telephone, packed and went downstairs, bag in hand and coat over my arm. It was six a.m. and breakfast was being served, but I didn't have time. I checked out with Natalie at the front desk, and after sliding over a twenty-dollar tip, I made a request.

"I just got a new cellphone and number, and I want to make sure George can reach me if he calls here," I explained. "I know it's a long-shot, but if George calls here, would you pass on my cellphone number?"

"Absolutely," Natalie replied, her eyes bright and face smiling. I wondered how she and her husband managed to juggle all the responsibilities of running a B&B—dealing with demanding guests, keeping the rooms clean and orderly, and serving good meals day and night—and still keep an attractive smile on one's face at such an ungodly hour.

"Will you be staying for breakfast?" she added.

"No, I'm sorry I've got to get going," I said.

She smiled wider, revealing a dimple on one side. "Well, if you ever get back in the area … "

"I'll make sure to stop by, thanks," I said.

"We look forward to it."

I gathered up my belongings and strolled out onto the porch, down the walkway, trying to plan my day, and I started to the rear of the inn, where my Ford was parked.

Then my planning was put on hold, because someone else had gotten there first.

A sour-looking man in an ill-fitting dark gray suit was blocking the walkway.

Detective Mike Shaye of the Bellows Fall Police Department.

———

I paused, and he stared at me. His black hair was a bit disheveled, and his pug nose was reddened, like he was coming down with a cold.

"Hey," he said.

"Good morning."

"Here's the deal, final and not open to any discussion. Got it? I see your hands, which are great. But if they start moving, then I'll blow a hole in your fucking stomach and drop you right there."

"That seems pretty direct."

"It sure is," he said. "Designed to be. Well?"

"Got the message, Detective," I said. "I'll do my best not to move."

"All right," he said, and there was a hint of disappointment there, like he was looking for an excuse to shoot me and get vengeance for what I had done at his police station the other day.

And no surprise, that's exactly the subject he started with.

"Who the hell told you that you could leave my custody two days ago?"

"Nobody."

"But you still did it?"

"I wasn't under arrest and I wasn't in a locked room. So I decided to leave. That suddenly against the law here in Vermont?"

His eyes narrowed and darkened. "You also trespassed and took your pistol back."

"I apologize for the trespass, as brief as it was," I said. "And the pistol … it's my property. I wanted to retrieve my property with a minimum of fuss or paperwork. No apologies, I'm sorry to say."

He continued to glare at me. "Your background … pretty sketchy."

"Is what it is."

"Almost as sketchy as the Department of Justice fellow that came in the day you walked out, who was also looking for you. He said you were a writer, but that you were also a person of interest in a financial matter involving international terrorism."

"Dear me."

"Tell you what," he said. "Let's go back into the Homestead, you buy me breakfast, and we'll sort out some things."

"Detective, you're a charming fellow, and I appreciate the offer for a breakfast companion, but I'm really pressed for time."

"Book research and all that?"

"Absolutely."

"That's truly fascinating, but you're going to have to delay your research. Either we have breakfast and talk things through, or you'll be in the back of my cruiser, under arrest."

"This isn't your town, your jurisdiction."

"My ex-brother in law is the police chief here," he gently explained. "Need I say more?"

I said, "Well, I am hungry. So let's go in."

He nodded crisply. "After you."

If Natalie was surprised to see me back so quickly, she kept it under wraps. She took my belongings and stored them in a rear closet, and Detective Shaye and I had a corner table on an insulated porch that offered a nice view of empty farmland and rows of trees that would be cut down in several months for Christmas.

After coffee was poured and breakfast was ordered, Detective Shaye said, "Not to sound rude or anything, but do you think I'm a fucking idiot or something?"

I briefly thought of the correct answer and let it loose: "No."

"Funny, I think otherwise," he said. "First of all, you disrespect me, and then you disrespect my department. I bring you in as a gentleman, I secure your weapon, I bring you into my place of work, and what do you do? Do you respect me in return? No. You leave my place of work, retrieve your weapon, and leave, impeding my investigation. Does that sound accurate?"

"Pretty accurate."

"Glad we seem to be making progress," he said.

"Me, too."

"Do you have any idea who I am or where I've been?"

"No," I said, "but I'd love to hear more if you'd care to share it."

He cocked his head a bit. "That bullshit or are you for real?"

"Quite for real," I said. "I apologize for the disrespect, and I appreciate you not arresting me."

"See?" he said, as our breakfasts were served. "I love it when two reasonable men can talk together."

I had French toast with sausage on the side, and he had waffles with strawberries and homemade whipped cream on top. As we started eating, Detective Shaye said, "Me first. Grew up here in Vermont, up in the Northwest Kingdom, probably one of the most rural, poor, and isolated spots in New England. After getting out of high school, not much seemed open, so I joined the Marines. And please don't say thank you for your service. I went in on my own, eyes wide open, and did a good job."

"What was your MOS?"

"Very good," he said. "My MOS was zero-one-thirty-seven. You recognize it?"

I did, but I didn't want to let on that I knew his background. I briefly shook my head and Shaye said, "Scout sniper. Where I grew up, hunting in and out of season was sometimes the only thing that supplemented the food banks. So I had the aptitude. Trained at Camp Lejeune and then shipped out."

"Iraq or Afghanistan?"

"Both," he said. "Fallujah and Mosul in Iraq. In Afghanistan, outside of Kandahar and some mountain villages."

"Tough places."

"You know it," he said. "Did three tours, opted out, and decided to come back home and get into law enforcement. And just so we're clear, I saw a lot of shit and did a lot of shit, but I'm one of the lucky ones who did his job and got home with a clear mind and clear conscience. Not many can say that."

"How do you think you escaped that?"

A shrug as he sawed through a sausage link. "Luck, I suppose. I got clean targets and clean kills. No women, no kids carrying a soccer ball in one hand and a hand grenade in the other. But when I did come home, I made a vow—I was going to protect my own, and protect my town. No matter what."

I didn't know what to say to that, so I kept my mouth shut, thinking the steady ex-Marine would continue if he was interested.

And he was.

"See, in my line of work, you expect and prepared for a certain amount of crime, certain amount of lawlessness. You try to adapt when new things come up, like all this cheap heroin flooding the markets. And I also have that sniper sense, of something not right, something wrong ... just about the time you showed up."

I gave him a good look. "Your town and your people have nothing to fear from me."

"So says you," he replied. "But this is what happens over a few days, so bear with me. First things first, down Chester way, some neighbors on a rural road hear a series of gunshots, and one hears a vehicle drive away at a high rate of speed. One of my cop buddies checks things out in the neighborhood ... finds nothing, but interestingly enough, the next day, some repair work gets done on a house, performed by one of our less reliable citizens, Eddie Century."

I kept eating, still keeping an interested yet slightly bored expression on my face.

"I go see Eddie," Shaye said, "but he's not talking. Seems like somebody had tuned him up pretty good. And my buddy down at the Chester PD, he goes back and finds a recently spent 9mm shell in among some juniper bushes at this particular house."

"Fascinating," I said.

"I'm sure," he said. "As with many things, it does get better. A motel in Chester also reveals a dead woman contained within, with her throat slit. A day later, we get a call for a shooting outside the Green Mountain Inn and Resort. A white GMC sedan was found in a ditch, filled with bullet holes and one dead driver. The State Police and the FBI swooped in and took over the case, leaving me behind. Okay, I'm a big boy, I can handle that."

I kept eating like I was in a cone of silence or something.

He said, "I ask the Green Mountain staff to call me if anyone suspicious rolls in, and voila, there you are. We chat here and there, and then you depart . . . just as a man appears at the police station, saying he's interested in looking at all aspects of this shooting, including you, in one amazing development."

"Hell of a coincidence. Who was he?"

"He said he was from the Department of Justice, which got me tingling even more, and after he departs, I do some checking and learn my mysterious visitor is, in fact, not a member of Department of Justice, despite his earlier impressive set of credentials and references. And now I find you here, still in the vicinity, doing God knows what. What does that tell you?"

"Tells me that this is a much more interesting part of Vermont than one could be led to believe."

It seemed he took a moment or two to decide on how much I was being a smart-ass, and then he decided to give up and go on. "Back in Iraq, only one thing really got me pissed, and that's when the Bigs intervened. You ever hear of the Bigs?"

"No, I haven't," I said, and this time I was telling the truth.

"The Bigs … the Big Boys, the Big Cheese, the Big Kahuna … those guys who decide it's their job to come in and fuck around with things. One example … my sniper unit was chasing down this mullah who was a real piece of work, who had a sniper's target permanently tattooed across the back of his head. He was responsible for stirring up the tribes, getting them to hate us … he interfered in our civilian work, like building clinics and schools. And he was a conduit for the Iranians shipping over the shaped-charged IED's that were sophisticated killing machines for our guys in their armored vehicles."

"This mullah was public enemy number one, then."

"Yeah, we couldn't get much higher. But we were closing in. And the day I got that goat fucker in my sights, we got word to stand down. Our target was no longer a target. It seems some Big Guy somewhere—or a host of fucking Bigs—decided it was more importantly diplomatically or politically to keep him alive for some future possible negotiations. And there I was, seeing him emerge from a Mercedes-Benz with tinted black windows, easiest goddamn target in the world. And I didn't take the shot. Even though I knew this asshole was responsible for a number of American deaths—including buds of mine—I let him live. That really pissed me off."

"And that's why you don't like the Bigs."

"That's right. And after all the blood, toil, tears, and sweat to clear out Fallujah and Mosul, the current Bigs in D.C. decided to give it all away a couple of years ago. Now they're doing the same in Afghanistan. You can tell they're not on my Christmas list, ever."

"I got that."

"And right now, I don't know who they are, or what they're doing in my neighborhood, but I can sense the Bigs are among us. And I don't like it, not one particular bit of it. So here's the question of the day: Are you a Big, or are you working for one?"

"No to both," I said.

"Then what are you?"

I was going to answer in my usual rote manner and decided that wasn't the smart thing to do. "I'm an independent contractor, working out an employment issue."

That caused him to smile. "What, you mean you really aren't a true crime writer?"

"No."

"So that surveillance photo of you in that Honda Pilot?"

"That was me."

"And do you have ... *knowledge* of the car accident that happened later, and the shooting death of the driver?"

A bunch of things were bouncing through my mind right then, like that game show trick where they put you in a bubble full of dollar bills and run a whirlwind, challenging you to catch the hundred-dollar bills scattered within the singles, seeing just how lucky you were.

But the detective was opening a door for me. He wasn't asking if I was involved, or if I was the shooter, or anything else to put me on the spot at this particular moment. Yet he was also leaving himself room if he decided not to trust me and go back on the hunt.

"Yes, I have knowledge of the shooting."

He just nodded and his expression changed, like he was starting to show some sympathy for me, which I found heartening. "Appreciate that. I haven't heard word one from the State Police about that dead driver. Which means he is or was under some Big's protection."

"A good guess," I said.

"Mind telling me your real name?"

"That, I do mind."

A pause. "All right. Then what the hell are you doing out in my neighborhood?"

That gave me hesitation—a law enforcement official asking me such a direct question—but I decided to go with the flow. "A coworker of mine was murdered. The man who came to your station, the one who said he was from the Department of Justice, he's the one who pulled the trigger. I've been looking for him."

"For what purpose?"

"I'll leave that to your imagination."

"You think he's a Big?"

"The biggest. He's involved in something wide-ranging, something cruel, something bad."

"How bad?"

"Bad enough to kill my coworker, bad enough to slit a woman's throat when she could no longer work for him."

"Yeah, that's pretty bad," he said. "The woman at the Chester Motel?"

"Yes."

"Sounds like a Big all right."

We ate in our own separate worlds for a bit, and he said, "I'm looking for some guarantees."

"I'm open to hearing you."

He wiped his hands on a white cloth napkin. "I could arrest you now, bring you in. Charge you with a variety of offenses. Maybe disrupt your day or two. But in the end … what would be served?"

"So far, so good."

"Shut up," he exclaimed. "Like I said, what would be served? You'd lawyer up, clam up, and in a day or two, you'd be on your way. And the Bigs out there, the ones tromping up and down in my towns and neighborhoods, they get away with whatever they're doing. I don't like that."

The waitress dropped off the check in a black leather holder. I picked it up and carefully laid out enough cash to cover the bill and a nice tip.

Detective Shaye said, "This is what I want. I want you to keep a low profile, do what you have to do, and get the Bigs the fuck out of my life and world. But whatever you do, make sure it doesn't hurt innocents, doesn't make a mess for me or law enforcement, or otherwise piss me off. How does that sound?"

"I like it," I said. "Can I ask for a favor?"

"Seems like I'm doing you a lot of favors already," he said.

"You are," I said. "And I appreciate that. But the Big I'm looking for … he called my room here at about four a.m. this morning. My room phone said the incoming call was blocked. If you could find a way to unblock that incoming call and give me the source phone number, it would help me a lot." I gave him the room phone number.

A nod. "Call me later today. I'll see what I can do."

"Thanks."

I looked around our breakfast nook, at the nice quiet innocents having a nice quiet breakfast. "Am I excused?"

"You are."

"Glad to hear it," I said, pushing my chair back.

"And what's on your schedule for today?"

I stood up. "What else? To do good."

"Where? Around here?"

"No," I said. "Farther south."

For the first time the detective laughed. "Good luck with that."

FIFTEEN

LATER THAT DAY I took a long and roundabout trip, going someplace I should have gone to earlier, but because of my busy schedule and cowardice—which I freely admit—I had avoided making this journey.

But it was time.

I had driven from Vermont down to Massachusetts, and eventually got on the dreaded concrete and asphalt highway called the Massachusetts Turnpike, aka the Mass Pike, and got to the urban sinkhole in and around Boston. I went north to Saugus, a city known for its strip clubs, a former steak restaurant that featured plastic cows out in the front, historic ironworks, and for being the birthplace of a famous author who writes about werewolves. I got off the highway and drove around some suburban streets until I found the place I was looking for: a quiet two-story home with white siding and black shutters on Tremont Court. The lots here were small, most of them fenced so that any encroaching neighbors couldn't steal a shrubbery, or some grass, or a handful of dirt.

I parked the Ford and got out. The hum from the nearby Interstate 95 was a constant noise. This was only the second time I had ever come here, and the first was only after a vehicle breakdown eight months ago that had forced me to give somebody a ride here for some assistance.

I took a breath, went past the sidewalk, opened up the gate to the waist-high chain link fence, and strolled up the path, past a Virgin Mary statue standing in a circle of white stones. I rang the doorbell and waited.

Movement from the inside.

The door opened. A woman in her mid-forties stood there, wearing blue jeans and a white sweater. Her face was made up and her hair was thick and black. "Yes?"

"Wanda Briggs?"

"Yes? Who are you?"

I just stood there. "I was Clarence's boss."

She bit her lower lip, and her body shuddered, like she had just taken a punch to the gut. "Come in, then."

"Thanks."

———

She led me to the living room, which was tidy but which also had some kids' toys scattered around the carpeted floor. I took a settee and Wanda sat down on an opposite chair, crossed her legs. A couch, coffee table, two comfortable chairs, and flat-screen television filled out the room. There were numerous photos of Wanda and her twin sons hanging from the wall, and on the shelving containing some books and knick-knacks.

There were no photos of her ex-husband, Clarence.

"Well?"

"I'm sorry to say that Clarence is dead."

She folded her arms. "I know that."

"Who told you?"

"Carla, his younger sister."

"When?"

"A few days ago. Clarence didn't show up for the boys' Little League awards ceremony. And he didn't call, or text, or show up the next day to apologize. That's when I knew, deep in my gut, that he was dead. Carla just confirmed it. He adored Sean and Dennis. We would have never hurt them like that. Oh, I was hoping that maybe he was in some sort of accident, a coma or amnesia, but really, what are the chances of that?"

"Pretty slim."

As she talked, her voice went up and down in octaves, like it was deciding to find one level to work on, and her eyes wandered as well. Then she snap-focused on me and said, "So how do you know he's dead?"

"I was there when he was shot."

She closed her eyes. "Did … did he suffer?"

"No," I said. "It was instant."

She opened her eyes. "When?"

"A week ago."

"Where?"

"Chester, Vermont."

"Never heard of it. What happened?"

In this quiet little suburban oasis of supposed domestic bliss, it seemed obscene to haul out the memory of what happened a week ago, but I did it anyway.

"Clarence and I were at a job. I was asked to evaluate a stolen painting, and then assist in the negotiation of its sale. As we were working, the man I was dealing with opened fire and shot Clarence, killing him instantly."

She closed her eyes for a moment, opened them up. They were steady and unflinching. "How did you get out?"

"Out a second-floor window."

"Was it open?"

"After I tossed a chair through it."

"And Clarence's ... body?"

"Gone."

"His SUV?"

"Gone as well. I don't think we're going to locate his body. The gunmen were ... thorough."

"I see. Ask you a question?"

"Absolutely?"

"What the fuck took you so long to come here?"

"Three things," I said, feeling my face flush. "I was trying to save my own life, I was trying to track down the man who killed him, and I was too chicken to come here right away."

"But you're here now. Why?"

"Because I was tired of being a chickenshit, and because I wanted to see how you were doing."

Her gaze was steady and unyielding. "Is that all?"

"No. The guy who killed your husband—"

"Ex-husband," she corrected.

"—who killed Clarence," I went on, "said later that I had something valuable that belonged to Clarence."

"And do you?"

"No, I don't."

I now noticed that the hum of the interstate was felt and heard throughout the house. I couldn't spend a night here, never mind live here.

"Who's the guy who shot Clarence?"

"A man named George. Initially he said he was just an old-time art collector from small-town Vermont. Later he presented himself as a representative from the Department of Justice. I don't know his real name or background."

She crossed and recrossed her legs. "Now what?"

"I'm curious ... did Clarence ever say that he had something valuable in his possession?"

"You looking to steal it?" she said, voice sharp.

"No, I'm looking to know what it is, so it'll end up in your hands."

She looked away, squirmed in her chair, and I think I knew what was going on: Wanda was trying to decide whether or not she could trust me. I suppose I could have pled my case, but I decided to sit still and keep my mouth shut.

Wanda turned back to me, eyes watery. "Clarence ... said you were the best boss he's ever had. Smart, reasonable, well-paying ... you were the best."

"So was he."

"Hunh," she said. "He was a man of the streets ... not those thugs who break into houses or run drugs or steal cars. No, he just was big, hard, and wasn't afraid of violence. And he moved in rough circles. The ones that make shady deals, that don't pay taxes, don't live in what they call the civilian life. And when you came along, he couldn't believe how fortunate he was."

I started to say something, and Wanda kept on talking. "The thing is, that wasn't enough. I wanted him to do something legit, something he could talk about with his sons. He said he would do that … one of these days, but Clarence also said the job with you was his last one, so he could keep on supporting me and the boys. Did you know that?"

"No."

"I talked to him, over and over again, about what it meant to have him out there, and he always said, 'No worries, hon, I got it covered. I ever end up dead, you wouldn't believe what I've got set up for you.'"

"Like what?"

"Like he didn't say." She quickly brushed at her eyes with her right hand. "So now he's dead. No insurance policy. Nothing. Not even a body to bury. That means I gotta wait before the will gets sent to probate. And what am I going to do now? Get a job at McDonald's or an Irving gas station?"

"You'll be taken care of."

"How?" she demanded.

"Because I'm going to make it right."

———

A few moments passed as she wiped at her eyes a couple of more times, and said, "How?"

"Not sure," I said. "But it's going to happen. Clarence … before he worked for me, did he exclusively stay in Rhode Island and Massachusetts?"

"No … he'd travel a lot. Wouldn't say where, but I figured it was in the Northeast. He was never gone that long, and he didn't pack like he was going on an airline. Just driving distance."

"Anything stick out from those trips?"

"Well … sometimes he'd come home late, most of the time laughing, and buzzed that he had gotten some job done. Then he'd want to wake me up and tell me stories, have me make him breakfast … and then … you know, crawl back into bed and get reacquainted."

She paused in her telling, and I gently pressed her. "But was there one day that was different?"

She slowly nodded. "Yes … three years ago, just before we split up. He came home late … practically snuck in. He had dried blood on his shirt and coat. Not his, thank God … but he didn't make the kind of fuss that he usually did. Just quiet. Stripped off his clothes, took a shower, went to bed … slept nearly a full day. And later, he said, no more traveling for a while. Said it had been dangerous, he had … what was it? Oh, yeah. He had gone off the reservation. He had seen his opportunity and took it."

Wanda clasped her hands together. "He stayed home for about a month. I mean, stay in the house, not even go out for a drink or to buy me dinner. Nearly drove me and the boys crazy, and then he did a little pick-up work, and then started working for you. And then … well, we split up."

"But he never said what he had done that night."

"No."

Horns were blaring outside from something going on at the Interstate.

"Since … he didn't come home, have you gotten any strange phone calls? Somebody in the neighborhood? Maybe an attempted break-in?"

"No, nothing like that. But that's not surprising."

"Why?"

"Because Clarence insisted I take back my maiden name ... like he wanted me to cut whatever legal ties I had with him. So I'd fade in the background."

Interesting. And time for a quick change of topic. "His sister, Carla. What's she like?"

A quick burst of laughter. "That ice queen? A bitch on wheels, that's what she is."

"But you do know where she works, right?"

She waved a hand. "Oh yes, the high and mighty Eff Bee Eye. Hunh. You think she pissed Mountain Dew and shit Skittles, the way she carries herself. She's just a glorified secretary, an admin person, but she always held herself like she reported to J. Edgar Hoover himself."

"J. Edgar Hoover is dead."

"Then whoever's running the show, whatever. But she ... she'd see Clarence every now and then, for family get-togethers, birthdays, Easter ... and it always ended the same way. They'd get into a fight and—no, that's not right. No, she'd always pick a fight with Clarence, show how better she was. Always tried to tell him in so many words to leave the life, if not for her, then at least the family."

"I've spoken to her some," I said. "She says she hadn't seen Clarence in three years. Is that right?"

"Yeah, right after we split up, and he moved out."

I thought about the last time I talked to Carla, and said, "Do you know where she is? Have you talked to her lately?"

"No and no." Wanda paused. "Do you know where she is?"

"Yeah, she's in some trouble."

"Gee, too bad." But there was a smile on Wanda's face.

I looked again at the family photos, my eyes drawn to the twin boys, photos from infants to them now as burly eleven-year-olds in Little League uniforms.

"Your split up … I'm sorry, what caused it? I mean, I know Clarence, well, I know he had a wandering eye."

Another short laugh. "Hah. You mean a wandering dick, that's more like it. No, that's not what split us up. It was his choice."

That surprised me. "Excuse me? That's not what I heard."

"Really? Then whoever told you that was lying. Sorry. Look, I could overlook a few things. His job, for one. And how hard it was to get blood stains out of his clothing. But that's the life he chose, and I chose to be with him. It meant good money, trips to Aruba and Disneyworld—both Florida and California—and Catholic schools for the twins. So if he picked up a little strange on his trips, all right … I made it clear that he needed to be protected so he didn't bring anything home, and that whatever he did, it happened while he was away. Not home, not in this part of the state."

That really caught my attention. "I'm sorry, Wanda, I heard that there was an argument, a fight, that you fired a shot at him after coming home early one day and finding him bed with two women."

"Didn't happen that way."

"You mean there wasn't a fight, and there wasn't a gunshot?"

"Christ, yes, there was a fight—we always fought, we were like water and oil, the two of us—but I can't remember what it was over. I can tell you one thing, it didn't involve him being in our marriage bed with two bimbos."

I kept a steady look at her. She said, "Okay, there was also a gunshot, but it didn't mean I was trying to kill him. It was an accident."

"How?"

Her face reddened. "It was a hot August night. We came back late from some party. We have these A/C units that cool down the whole house. One here in the living room, one in the boys' room, and one in our bedroom. Clarence was supposed to turn on the one in our bedroom before we left, but he forgot."

"I see."

"So we come back home and because the windows were closed, the bedroom was a fucking oven. I started bitching at him about being dumb, about being stupid, about having to sleep in a hot bedroom, and he said, 'Christ, just shut the fuck up and take the A/C remote out of the drawer, turn it on.' That went like that for ... thirty minutes or so. I won't get into any more of the details."

"All right, that's fair. What then?"

Her face reddened even more. "After a while he said he was tired of all this bullshit, that he was going to go to the drawer and get the A/C running, 'cause we were wasting all this time fighting, and by now, the place would be cool if the A/C had been turned on when we first got in. And I told him, don't you fucking dare, I can't trust you to do anything around the house, so he started moving around the bed, coming to the nightstand, and I beat him to it, opened the drawer, pulled out the remote, and pressed the switch."

I got it now. "You didn't have the remote."

"No. It was a pistol."

"Wasn't the safety on?"

"It was a Glock. No safety. And it was loaded, with a round in the chamber. And I was drunk, and I didn't see what I had in my hand, I just pushed and pulled with my fingers, and the damn thing went off. Nearly took off his head, went into the ceiling and up into the attic. Broke the bottom half of a plastic Santa Claus."

"Wake up the boys?"

Her face was grateful. "Christ, no, thank God. They were on a sleepover. After the gunshot ... Clarence and I cried some, hugged, and he said he was moving out the next day. And he did."

"Did he say why?"

"Because … he said he was a dangerous man, a wanted man. The gunshot reminded him of that. And he wanted to protect us."

By God, so he had, I thought.

We took a break while she got a glass of water, and she didn't offer me anything—whether from forgetfulness or anger at who I was, I really didn't care—and when she came back, I said, "Where's his home?"

"Dumpy little Cape over in Lynn."

"Do you have a key?"

She sipped from her water tumbler. "No, but there's a brick patio in the rear. Loose brick at the right corner, facing the woods. What, you going to look inside his house?"

"That's right," I said. "George—the man who shot Clarence—he thinks Clarence had something valuable. Something I supposedly have. And I want to see if it might be at his house. Did many people know he lived there?"

"No … he tried to keep it pretty quiet."

I looked at her and felt something odd burrow inside me, the thought of the love of a woman who would stick with you, stay by your side, and always look out for you and defend you, year after year, no matter the overdue bills, the flat tires, the oil heaters that break down, the laundry that needs to be done, the groceries that need to be bought.

What would that be like? I thought. What would that be like.

And it came to me, that it was a sort of loyalty, similar to what I was doing on Clarence's behalf ever since he was killed, the loyalty of a man to his partner.

"Anything more?" Wanda asked.

"No ... just directions to Clarence's place in Lynn."

"Sure. I'll write it down for you."

She put the water tumbler down on a coaster with Mickey Mouse's head on it, and she started to get up, and then she sat down.

"I see it now," she said, her voice almost a whisper.

"See what?" I asked, although I saw some sort of light of recognition in her eyes, and I knew she had arrived at the same place I had gotten to, about five minutes ago.

"Clarence ... he came back from that last job, three years ago. His sister Carla, she tries one last time to get him to leave what he does, and when she's not satisfied, she never speaks to him again. That was three years ago. Just when he split up with me and the kids."

I said, "That's what I think, too, Wanda. He had done something ... notable. He had a sense he was always going to be in some sort of danger from that day forward. And he left you and moved away, to protect you the best way he could."

"Then this George ... "

"Either he's the wounded party, or he's working for the wounded party. They want back what Clarence stole. But they moved too quick and too fast, and killed him."

"What could it be?"

"I don't know, but I will find out."

She reached over to the coffee table, slid open a drawer. Took out a pad of paper and a pen, scribbled some notes.

"There. The address to his house in Lynn. Be careful, all right?"

"I will."

I got up and she saw me to the door, and she said, "You've asked a lot of questions. Mind if I give it a go?"

"Go right ahead."

"Clarence said you were funny ... a guy with lots of secrets. You had a few ... made-up names, what you call 'em. Pseudonyms. He didn't even know your real name, am I right?"

"That's right."

She opened the door, leaned against it. "What's your real name? Will you tell me?"

I did. Blame my weakness, or the moment, but I did.

"A good, strong name." She came over and kissed me full on the lips, then touched my cheek.

"Go kill that fucker."

"On it," I said, and I went out to the fresh Saugus air, now knowing what had really happened—that the trap in Chester baited with Rembrandt had not been set for me, but for Clarence.

I had been so very wrong.

I didn't plan on being wrong again.

SIXTEEN

From Saugus to Lynn took about twenty minutes, with traffic a breeze, and I followed Wanda's directions, which were clear and to the point. Lynn is what is called a North Shore community—meaning it was north of Boston—and it was mainly known for three things. One is its famed history of political corruption, which led to the second thing, a schoolyard jingle that goes, "Lynn, Lynn, the city of sin, you never come out, the way you went in."

A number of convicted state representatives, state senators, and the odd congressman would no doubt agree.

The third thing is its quiet feud with its northern neighbor, Salem, home of the famed witch trials and also home to a nearly year-long festival and Halloween circus invoking its witch history, and bringing in hundreds of thousands of tourists each year to spend their cash.

Fortunate for Salem, and unfortunate for Lynn, the real history is that back in the day, Salem was a much larger community, and most of the witch-related activities—including the bulk of the hangings—took place within the current Lynn boundaries. But the tourists don't know that, Salem doesn't mention it, and most everybody ignores poor old Lynn when they try to bring it up.

Clarence's house was in a sorry-looking cul-de-sac just a couple of minutes from a highway exit leading to Route 1, nearly running parallel to I-95. I got out and checked out his house, again hearing the hum of nearby traffic. The house was a Cape, similar to its neighbors, and its white paint was peeling in places. It had an attached garage, and the grass was about ankle-high. Some kids were playing around two houses down, tossing a football back and forth, two older teenagers and two younger guys, all dressed in blue jeans, hoodies, and backward baseball caps.

I went across the lawn, thinking with melancholy that in a while, this lawn will probably be boasting a FOR SALE sign, and then swung around to the rear. As noted, there was a brick patio back there, right up against some brush and saplings. Two unfolded lawn chairs with rust and an equally rusting outdoor grill were back there. I went to where Wanda had directed me, and yep, there was a loose brick at the very edge.

Underneath the brick was a single key, with a plastic tab attached. I grabbed the key and instead of going back to the front of the house, I went to the rear entrance, and the door opened up right away, into the kitchen.

And into chaos.

Everything in the shelves had been tossed to the floor, from dishware to frying pans to silverware. I slowly walked through the kitchen, and then to the big living room, and the two bedrooms upstairs, taking my time, my hand on the butt of my pistol. The place had been viciously, violently, and professionally searched. Even with the damage and destroyed furniture and broken glassware and framed photos, there was a method and plan to this destruction: to look for something of value. Things weren't just dumped, they were evaluated and carefully piled up, so there was no confusion of what had been examined as the search progressed.

Examined for what?

Damned if I know.

After some minutes in the house, I stood alone in the living room and tried to piece together what I was seeing. Mentally putting everything back in its place, I saw a bachelor pad—not a swinging bachelor pad, mind you—but a place where a single dad came home to relax. And what were his vices? Being a Red Sox and Patriots fan, watching TV, reading books—paperback novels about military adventures—and not much else.

Yet there was something here, something desired.

I toed a broken photo frame that contained a photo of his twin boys in their Little League uniforms.

Had the mysterious item been located already?

Probably not. It was hard to tell but everything in the house seemed like the damage had been done some time ago, before Carla had ended up in George's company.

Which meant Wanda and her boys would be in danger until I settled accounts with George and whoever his boss might be.

I reached down, picked up the color photo of the twins, brushed off the glass, and gently placed it on the side of an overturned couch, where the stuffing and insides had been torn out.

———

I went back out the rear kitchen door, made sure it was locked, and then I returned the key to the brick.

Back around the side of the house, the four guys were still tossing the football around, and one yelled out, "Hey, bud, here it comes!"

So it did.

The football arced high up in the air and I stood next to my Ford, waiting to catch it, when two of the older boys ran as if to intercept it, and instead, hammered me right into the ground.

———

I fell back and felt foolish, being surprised and knocked down like this. It may have been foolish, but it was also effective. I fell on my back, the kids doing their best to hold me down, and there was a hesitation on my part—I mean, they were still high school age—that gave them an advantage. I started resisting and they were all over me, and then one of the older boys showed up, swore, knelt down, and took out a hand-held Taser, which he pushed into my side.

———

I grunted and howled, and rolled, and managed to slap at the older boy's hand, and then I started shaking, trembling, spit flying.

"Good … good … the fucker's down … now, where the hell is Mel?"

A loud engine came to my attention as I writhed on the lawn. Two of the boys started working on my hands, pulling them together, fastening them tight with plastic zipties.

"Hurry! Hurry, damn it!"

My shins were the next attention of the eager boys. I moaned, kicked, and rolled back and forth, spit dribbling down my chin. A white van rolled to a stop behind my Ford, the driver jumping out and opening a sliding door. I was grabbed, dragged, and dumped into the van. The rear seats had been removed, and there was a dirty carpet I was now lying on. The driver—Mel?—went around the van, the two older boys got in—one in the front, the other joining me in the rear—and the door slid closed and we were off.

The shock of the Taser still reverberated through me, like the waves of water from a tossed stone in a puddle, bouncing back and forth. When I had been dumped into the van, I managed to roll and duck so that my legs were facing the front, where Mel and the other boy sat in individual bucket seats. The interior smelled of grease and old doughnuts, like this had once been a delivery van. With all the doors closed, the van sped away from the cul-de-sac, skidded to a halt at a stop sign, and then got on the road, regaining its speed.

Inside there was a jumble of shouts, commands, and curses. Mel focused on his driving, yelling, "Shut up, okay, I'm trying to fucking drive! Shut the fuck up!"

His companion up front turned, looking back at me, eyes wide, holding a revolver in my direction. The third was kneeling over me, and I thrashed my head, spit flying, groaning, and he yelled, "Shit, what's wrong with him? I think he's fucking dying!"

"How the fuck should I know?" the boy with the gun yelled.

"You fucking tased him!"

"I tased my younger brother once," he shot back. "He sure as fuck didn't act like this!"

"If he dies, what the fuck are we gonna do? We sure as hell won't get fucking paid!"

Mel the driver yelled back, "I'm trying to fucking drive! Shut up!"

The other one said, "He's got a gun on him! Find it."

His shaking hand went underneath my coat, tugged the Beretta free. "I got it," he said, voice wavering. "What do I do with it?"

Mel said, "Christ, shove it up your ass for all I care."

I let out a really loud groan, and my companion in the van's rear said, "Fuck! I think he's dying!"

The guy with the gun started to answer his friend, but I got so busy I didn't quite hear what he said, not that it made any difference. The boy in the rear was kneeling down, looking down at me with concern, poor fellow, since I repaid him by abruptly leaning up and pounding my forehead right into his nose, shattering it.

————

He screamed and fell back, both hands up to his nose, and things really got interesting. The thing with Tasers is that if you can knock the electrodes away from you in a rapid motion—like I had done back at Clarence's front lawn—then you can drastically cut down on the impact of the thousands of volts slamming through your body.

Which allowed me now to propel myself forward on my muscular butt, raise up both legs, and slam my bound feet into the side of Mel's head. He yelped and fell over, the steering wheel falling out of his grasp. "Fuck!" came from his buddy up front, and he got off a shot—damn loud in the closed interior of the van—that seemed to go into the vehicle's roof.

I rolled myself in a ball as best as I could as the van shuddered, screeched, and roared off the road, falling over into a drainage ditch or something. I had no idea what was going to happen next, only certain that when you've been snatched like this, time is your enemy. If you're going to make a break for it, do at it at the very beginning, before your captors get comfortable and are no longer operating on fear and excitement.

I bounced around in the van like an old soccer ball, someone's foot hitting my head, and the van rolled, crashed, and both rear doors flew open.

More shouts.

The van stopped.

I forced myself out, rolling and pushing, until I stood up. I was riding high from the endorphins racing through my system, and I knew I was hurt, but I didn't know the extent of my injuries. That would come later. I raised up my arms, aiming at a piece of the rear bumper, and brought them down briskly.

The plastic zipties burst. My hands were free. Zipties look secure but they can be easily broken if you've practiced … and my, how I've practiced. If you don't believe me, spend a couple of minutes on YouTube.

I ducked back into the van. The boy with the broken nose was in a corner, crying, holding his hands up to his face. I found my pistol. Grabbed it, and then seized a tire iron that had flown free from a stored spare tire on the side.

One quick motion later, my legs were free.

Next time, I'd make sure I was carrying my Ka-Bar.

Yeah. Next time.

I went around to the front of the van.

Mel was dead, although I hadn't killed him.

"Seatbelts," I murmured to the bloody head pushed through the shattered windshield. "How could you forget seatbelts?"

I went around the front of the van, broken, bowed in, fluids leaking out. The passenger door flew open, and the third young lad emerged, blood trickling down his forehead. His baseball cap was missing, revealing a very elaborate haircut with zig-zags and designs razored in. His mouth was bloody, and one eye was closed, but despite his injuries, he started to bring up his revolver.

"Drop it," I said.

He kept on moving, and I gave him that one and only chance, and then I shot him in the chest.

"Sorry," I said.

———————

I went back to the rear of the van, where the third boy remained, still sobbing. I got in on my hands and knees, holding my pistol, and I tapped it on his right foot.

"You."

He lowered his hands, shaking. Blood was smeared over his hands and his face. "I … I … "

"Shut up," I said. "I don't have much time." I tapped his foot again. "Who was in charge?"

"Gill."

"Who's Gill?"

"You … I think you … he's been shot."

"All right. What was the job?"

"We … we had to watch that house … somebody looking like you showed up … we had to snatch you … "

"How long have you been watching the place?"

"Three ... days. Three days ... "

"Who wanted to snatch me?"

"I don't know." I raised up my pistol and he screamed. "I swear to God, I don't know! Gill ... he was in charge. Asked me and Mel ... asked us if we wanted to make a couple of hundred bucks, easy ... "

"After the snatch, where were you going?"

"Uh ... the North Shore Mall ... in Peabody. We was supposed to meet a guy there after Gill called him ... "

"Who?"

"I don't know, Christ, please, don't shoot me! I don't know! Gill ... he set up the meet ... he was in charge ... oh shit, oh shit, I wish I had never known him ... oh shit ... "

I kept my pistol pointed right at him. He brought his hands back up to his face, sobbed some more. He looked to be fifteen or sixteen, if that.

"You."

"What?" He refused to look at me, and I knew why. He didn't want to see me or the pistol that was about to shoot him.

"Is there anything you can tell me to help me find out who ordered the snatch?"

"Mister ... please ... I wish I could ... I'd lie if I could ... but if I knew, I'd tell you ... oh God, please don't shoot me ... please don't shoot me ... " The sobbing resumed, louder than before. A wet spot started widening in his crotch.

I tapped his foot again. And again.

"What? Please ... what?"

"I'm leaving. You're going to tell the cops whatever you want, but you're going to leave me out of it, including the snatch part. Tell them you were carjacked, tell them some random terrorists shot you up, tell them you got in a fight over some girlfriend, I don't care …"

I hammered his foot with my pistol. "But I know a lot. I have a lot of friends and contacts in this part of the world. And if I find out you mentioned a syllable about me and what I look like, then you'll wish at the end of the day I had put a bullet through your forehead."

Then I left.

———

I casually walked across the street—no running!—and then cut through somebody's side yard. In a very few minutes, this neighborhood would be packed tightly with police cruisers, fire trucks, and an ambulance or two. And if it was a slow news day, maybe a TV crew from one of the cut-throat competitive television new stations from Boston.

But I had to be quiet, inconspicuous, and I had to smoothly get out of here.

The side yard led to a narrow stretch of woods. I pushed through, breathing hard, my pistol now back in its shoulder holster. I didn't even remember putting it back there.

I emerged through the woods. A housing development, with better homes than those in Clarence's neighborhood. Somewhere a dog barked. I cut through the yard and resumed my slow stroll. Clarence's place … it had to be over there, to the northwest. I wiped at my eyes, kept on walking.

Sirens were beginning to sound.

I kept on walking.

———

I tripped three times getting to Clarence's house, including stumbling through a muddy stream or ditch, depending on your point of view. As I bumbled my way across this rural section of Lynn, I kept on thinking and rethinking what I was doing. When I had started this little adventure, it had been pretty straightforward: find George and whoever helped him kill Clarence and nearly kill me, and then put them all in body bags.

At some point I may have thought of going to ground, because George and his partners were numerous, tough, and nearly everywhere—from my home in Litchfield, to ambushing me and Carla in Manchester, to being over in Vermont at the Putney Homestead. That was a lot of firepower to go up against, especially since Carla may well be working with George on her own agenda.

Not many options there. It would be smart to go cold dish on their asses, i.e., revenge being a dish best served cold, and wait a month or a year or five years.

Yeah, that would be smart.

I emerged in a back yard with a swimming pool, swing set, and the lawn littered with abandoned toys. Such a beautiful, peaceful oasis. Hard to believe that in a few minutes' walking distance, there was a semi-destroyed van with two dead young men and another man who would probably have nightmares for the rest of his life.

A young girl stepped out from a rear door of the fine-looking house. She looked at me, I looked at her. She seemed about six or seven. I gave her a cheerful wave, and then briskly walked along the side, across the street, and then into another tidy suburban yard.

Smart. Yeah, who was being smart? I should step back now, but today, that choice had been taken away from me, once I met Clarence's ex-wife and saw photos of his twin boys, both at the carefully decorated home and the smashed residence that belonged to Clarence.

They were now mine. I couldn't help it, couldn't resist. If I were to go to ground and stay quiet, George and his hunters would keep at it, and eventually, they would go to Wanda's home and her two boys, and go to work on them.

That wasn't going to happen.

But, damn it, what did I have to negotiate with if I approached George? To allow him to keep his life if he stayed away from Wanda? I doubt he would take that deal. That wasn't how he operated. Wasn't how I would operate if I were in his place, as depressing as that sounded.

No, he wanted what Clarence had stolen, something I supposedly had. That would be the focus of a negotiation, nothing else.

I came out on a familiar road, feet wet, hands raw, and various aches and pains beginning to make themselves known as the endorphins began wearing off. Before me was Clarence's house, and the other quiet homes as well. I walked across to my Ford, reached into my coat pocket, and retrieved my keys. How lucky could a guy get, that through all of this nonsense, I hadn't managed to lose my keys.

Lucky, indeed.

Luck.

I'll be damned.

I gave the neighborhood one more look before I left, and I spotted something on Clarence's lawn. I went over and with some difficulty, bent down, and picked up the football that the boys had been tossing around earlier, and which they had used to trick me.

I juggled the football in my hand, went back to my vehicle, and shoved the football underneath the front left tire. I unlocked the Ford's driver's side door, and got in, and started up the Expedition.

I drove forward, destroying the football in one satisfying *bang!*, and then left what had once been a kill zone.

SEVENTEEN

NOT MUCH FOR OPTIONS, not many choices in where I could go. My home in Litchfield had been blown, I wasn't going back to Wanda's, and Carla was among the missing, and deservedly so.

So where now?

Back to the home of Ethan Allen, of course, and I don't mean the furniture stores.

———

The drive had been a grueling one before I made it back to Bellows Falls, Vermont, a community that I was getting very familiar with. I had to stop twice on the way over to the Connecticut River and beyond, once to gas up the Ford, and the other to gently pull over, go into the woods, and throw up from coming down from the high I had felt when the van had started rolling around.

With each mile that passed, my pain and discomfort increased. My head ached, my right shoulder made an obscene crunching noise every time I lifted up my arm, and there was a wet spot at the base of my skull. I had pushed a couple of paper napkins up there and they had come back sodden with blood. It also hurt to breathe.

Other than that, things were going great.

Nearly three hours after leaving Lynn, Lynn, the city of sin—and I was definitely not going out the way I came in—I crossed over the Connecticut River, and I thought I'd feel better.

But I was wrong.

I parked in a condo parking lot and waited and waited. My mind bounced around, thinking things through, running through perceptions, options, and chances of success.

I took my last paper napkin out of my glove compartment, used it to sop up the blood at the rear of my head. I took the napkin away. Not as much as before. Maybe things were healing back there.

It was getting late, later than I wanted, but I didn't think I had many options, and besides, I was hurting.

A familiar-looking light green Volvo station wagon rolled in and parked in its numbered spot. Tracy Zahn stepped out and with leather carrying case in hand, strolled confidently to her unit. I got out and walked as fast as I could across the lot and caught up with Tracy just as she was getting ready to shut the door.

"Hey," I said. "Feeling lonely tonight?"

She turned and for the briefest of moments, there was fear on her face. Then there was pleased surprise, and then concern.

"My God, what happened to you?"

"That bad?"

"Worse." She stepped in and said, "C'mon, let's see what we can do."

————————

She sat me down on a straight-back chair in the living room and went upstairs, and then came back down carrying various bandages, creams, and ointments. She had on dark khaki slacks and a buttoned blue-striped blouse. "Get that jacket and shirt off before you get them even dirtier."

I got my jacket off with a minimum of fuss, but the shirt … damn, did that hurt. First off was the Bianchi holster with my Beretta nestled inside, and I lowered that to the floor. Tracy made to pick it up and I said, "No, leave it be."

I unbuttoned my shirt and winced, and Tracy helped me take it off. "What happened to you?"

"Car accident."

"Damn. Where?"

"In Massachusetts."

"Massachusetts … You didn't go to a hospital? You drove all the way here?"

"Since I'm here, that's pretty apparent," I said.

"No hospital?"

"I thought I'd get a better level of treatment here."

"Ha."

She worked on me for a few minutes, and I drank some ice cold water as she did. She mopped up the remaining blood at the base of my skull and then put on two butterfly bandages, and a larger gauze strip. "How did the accident happen? Was there more than one car?"

"No," I said. "I was in a van that ran off the road, rolled over a couple of times."

"You were driving?"

"Nope," I said, as she took a warm washcloth and started wiping down my torso. She seemed to enjoy her work, and I was glad. "I was just a passenger."

"And the other people? What happened to them?"

"You really want to know?"

She wrung out the washcloth, went to the kitchen, re-wet it again, and came back. "Sure."

"There were three of them. Something went wrong. I was … seized."

"Kidnapped?"

"No, I don't like that word. It implies I was taken in exchange for some sort of ransom. No, I was taken to go on that proverbial one-way trip."

"Oh. Then what happened?" Tracy resumed her washing.

"I didn't want to be seized. I fought back. The van crashed. I managed to get out."

"God," she said, working on my back this time. "What happened to the men in the van?"

"Boys," I said. "Teen boys. The three of them were hired to grab me and take me someplace. Only one walked away."

Her hand stopped. "The other two?"

"One died from the crash. The other one threatened me with a gun. He wouldn't drop it."

"Did you kill him?"

"Yes."

She kissed the top of my head. "Good."

———

Tracy assisted me in taking off the rest of my clothes, and I limped upstairs, carrying my Beretta and nothing else. I left the Beretta on a vanity in her bathroom, and I locked the bathroom door and showered with the curtain open. I winced a few more times and managed to at least get refreshed.

When I was done and dried myself off, Tracy knocked on the door and said, "Are you decent?"

"Not even close," I said as I unlocked the door and let her in, all the while keeping my Beretta in my hand. She gave me a good steady look and then handed over a light blue cotton robe.

"Something to wear while I do some laundry." I took the robe from her and she said, "You must be hurting."

"I am."

"I've some old Percocet that my OB-GYN gave me last winter, when my periods were really ripping me apart."

I put the robe on. "No," I said. "That's got Oxycodone in it. That'll slow me down, and I can't afford to slow down."

"Really? You've got enough bruises and scrapes to outfit an NFL team, and you plan to be moving fast anytime soon?"

"As soon as I can," I said. "How about some Ibuprofen? And a big glass of water?"

"On its way. See you back downstairs."

I fastened the robe and with Beretta in hand, I walked back downstairs, keeping my eyes open. Tracy was in her kitchen and passed over the glass of water and a generic brand of Ibuprofin. I opened the bottle, shook out three tablets, and chased them down with three big swallows. I put the glass down and said, "How was your day, dear?"

She smiled, eyes twinkling. "Dull, boring. One possible sale fell through, and another appointment never showed up. Going to be a bad month."

"Sorry."

Tracy removed the glass, put it in the sink. "The life I chose. When I was young, I was really young and dumb. Drank, smoked dope, and couldn't wait to get out of high school. Wanted to get out and see the world, married a guy who wanted to see the world as well ... so long as we never left Vermont, as it turned out."

"Sorry again," I said. "Didn't end well, did it."

"Nope." And there was a lot of weight in that voice. "He wanted to support me. I was lazy. Sounded like fun. Pop out a baby or two ... stay home, have fun. But no babies arrived, he blamed me, words and fists flew, and then I left him. And what was there for a single woman who barely made it through high school?" A shrug. "Not much. Which is how I ended up in real estate."

"Good for you."

"Yeah, good for me, not so good for my bank account."

I stretched my arms and rotated them, tried to see what range of motion I had. Answer: not as much as I wanted.

"I'd like to use your real estate knowledge, if you're amiable."

Tracy leaned over the kitchen counter. "Not sure if I can spell *amiable*, but sure, I can help. What are you looking for? A hide-out? A fortress of solitude? A bunker?"

"A place to make a sensitive exchange," I said.

"Sensitive? Like a prostate exam?"

"No," I said. "Sensitive, like if it doesn't go well, there'll be blood on the ground and gunpowder in the air."

"What are you looking for?"

"Someplace open, remote, with easy access in and out."

"If you're making an exchange, why not make it a public one? Like downtown Bellows Falls or Springfield?"

"Too much chance of something going wrong, either by cops or curious civilians coming by. Besides, remote gives one opportunities."

"I see," Tracy said. "What's being exchanged?"

I made a point of raising an eyebrow. "Valuables, and that's all you need to know."

If she felt like I had insulted her, she didn't seem to make a fuss about it. "So you're looking for an open space, like a field, rural, then?"

"Yes."

"I think I know the place."

"Nearby?"

"Less than two miles. It's where a charter school had been set up in an old nursery school building. Lasted a couple of years before it went out of business. Still for sale, and its grounds are being maintained. There's a large field behind the building. It's adjacent to Yukon Road."

"Yukon's in Canada."

"The selectmen who named the roads that year were a funny lot. But it's easy to get to."

"What's the name of the school?"

"The Cornerstone School for Exceptional Children."

"Sounds like a school where you learned a lot about weaving ponchos and the mating habits of Galapagos Island terns."

"Maybe so. What do you need now?"

I moved around a bit, didn't feel like crying out. Improvement, perhaps?

"Please don't be offended," I said, "but I need to make a couple of phone calls."

"Privacy?"

"The same."

She got up, brushed her hands together. "I'll get some laundry going, check in with you a bit later. And I'm not offended, honest."

"I'm glad to hear that."

Tracy came around the kitchen counter and gave me a very thorough and lengthy kiss. "I get the feeling you want privacy to protect me."

"That's right," I said. "I want to give you plausible deniability if anything goes bad."

"You expect things to go bad?"

"Absolutely," I said. "But I plan to be the one making them go bad."

———

I gave her a few minutes and listened to the water being run upstairs for her washer. Bad design. It's convenient to have your washer next to the second-floor bedroom, but if a water pump or hose were to fail...ouch. A mini waterfall would be tearing through the house in no time, and if you're away for a couple of days, disaster would be eagerly waiting for you when you get back.

I took out my latest cellphone and made a phone call to the Bellows Falls Police Department, and when I got ahold of Detective Shaye, he said, "No," and hung up.

I hung up as well.

I waited and listened to Tracy move around upstairs. I had a brief temptation to go up there and ask her if she needed her unmentionables sorted, but I bravely resisted, and was glad I did.

My cellphone rang and I picked it up.

"You there?" Detective Shaye asked.

"I am."

"Good," he said. "I wanted to get out of the building so I could talk without any fuss."

"I understand," I said. "Any success?"

"Sure," he said. "But not much depth. This is the phone number that called you this morning"—and he rattled off twelve digits for me, which I scrambled to write down on the back of a Hannaford's supermarket flyer—"but I tried to dig deep, find out who the phone belonged to, its billing and travel history, and no joy. That's one black phone, and I don't mean that in a racist manner."

"I see," I said. "Using your experience and excellent deduction skills, what does this tell you?"

"This guy's a Big, and I'd be careful about pissing him off."

"I'm not a particularly careful guy sometimes," I said. "And I think the pissing off train has already left the station and this time zone."

"I get that feeling from you, for sure. Plus ... there's one more thing."

"The location?"

"Yeah," he said. "Usually we can do a trace and do a cellphone triangulation, locate your caller down to a few meters. But not this one. All I can tell is that it's within a ten-mile area, here and over in New Hampshire."

"The man's got heft."

The detective agreed. "Lots of heft. Which tells me he's law enforcement, a member of the so-called intelligence community, or someone connected with both deep pockets and lots of drive."

"A Big, indeed. Thanks, Detective."

He didn't hang up, and I didn't push him. He cleared his throat. "You know how I feel about Bigs."

"I do."

"Just, well, just wanted to let you know."

I said, "I think you've just opened the favor bank."

"If I have, it's for a very limited time only."

"I appreciate that," I said. "Are you familiar with Rudyard Kipling?"

A brief snort. "I served in Iraq and Afghanistan, and on down time, I read a lot of fucking books. So yeah, I know Kipling."

"Do me a favor," I said. "Reread his poem, 'The Ballad of East and West,' and maybe we'll talk."

Then I hung up on him, but I hoped I did it in a cheerful and polite manner.

———

The washing machine upstairs was rumbling along, and I looked down at the supermarket flyer. The twelve digits stared right up at me, as if they were mocking me. *Well*, they seemed to be asking, *are you going to call? Or are you going to wimp out?*

"No wimps here," I announced to the empty kitchen, and I picked up the phone and quickly dialed a number.

It was answered on the first ring. "Yeah?"

"Good evening," I said. "Is George there?"

A grunt. "There's no George here, bud."

"All right," I said. "Maybe George isn't his real name, or maybe you're under orders to screen his calls. Let's try this. I'm looking for an older guy, pleasant-looking fellow, white hair, looks like a Santa Claus who enjoys fondling little girls and boys when they sit on his lap. That strike a bell?"

"Fuck you," he said.

"No thanks, I'm good," I said. "One more time. I'm looking for the guy who's seeking something in the control of Clarence Briggs. Get him on the phone right now, or I'm hanging up and then booking a trip to Aruba."

"Hold on."

A few seconds passed and there was a familiar voice. "Yes?"

"Hey, George, how's it hanging?" I said. "You still on the hunt over there?"

"You stupid fuck, nobody hangs up on me."

"Well, that's a statement that fails its logic test right from the start, because I hung up on you the last time we talked. You want me to do that again, so there's no confusion?"

"You do that and I'll cut off a finger from that Carla bitch."

"Maybe you will, George, but you're operating on a fact that hasn't been put into evidence."

"What?"

"You're assuming Carla Pope's safety is of interest to me. It's not. So let's get that out of the way."

I was sure I could hear his breathing increase, but maybe it was my overactive imagination. "All right, that's put away. For now."

"You believe I have something that was under the control of Clarence Briggs."

"That's what I said the first time, you fool. And then you denied it."

"My apologies," I said. "As a negotiator, I should have been open to additional information, no matter how off-the-wall it sounded. If you're amiable, I'm up to negotiating a deal."

"Okay, here's the deal," he said. "You turn it over, and I'll let you live. And if I'm in a good mood, I'll let the FBI bitch live as well."

"Not much wiggle room there, George, is there."

"Not my problem."

I sighed loudly, hoping he could hear it on the other side of the phone. "George, you've presented your case, and you've been quite clear. Still, I'd love to meet you face-to-face, so we can conclude these negotiations."

"I'd love a face-to-face," he said, and I could sense his wolfish smile out there, wherever he was sitting. "But I'll tell you this, if anything goes wrong, someone's gonna get hurt."

"I can take care of myself."

"That's not what I'm talking about. Here, talk."

A brief sound of noise, and then Carla was on the phone. Her voice was low, shaking. "Is this . . . is this . . . "

"If you're looking for your white knight to come save you, forget it," I said.

"Please . . . "

"Not happening," I said.

She sobbed. "You . . . you saw me then . . . right? Me meeting George at the inn . . . "

"Very observant, Carla. It looked like the two of you were pals. So what are you running?"

Another sob. "Nothing . . . except showing you how stupid I am . . . "

"No argument here."

"Please ... help me ... they've already hurt me ... "

"Your friends? Really? They seemed so chummy when they took you out of your room this morning. Nothing overturned, disturbed ... I didn't even hear a thing."

"I ... I was stupid ... I wanted to do this on my own ... I wanted to see if George ... who he was working for ... so I could ... so I could ... "

Laughter in the background, and George's voice, faint: "How did that work out for you, bitch?"

"He ... he was my brother ... and if ... and if ... there was going to be revenge, it was going to be mine ... not yours."

"What were you saying to George?"

Carla coughed. "I ... I was using the same FBI agent scam ... telling him if he'd cooperate ... give up the rest of the crew ... I'd protect him ... "

I didn't believe her, yet her words rang ... true? Something close to the truth? Reasonable, perhaps.

But I still didn't want to believe her. It complicated an already very complicated situation.

"If ... if you don't help me ... they'll kill me ... honest ... please help me ... please ... "

The phone was taken back. "Well?"

"George, who the hell are you?"

A chuckle. "What, you want my driver's license? My Social Security number? My waist size? Not coming your way."

"I know that, but what are you? What do you do?"

"Oh, that ... I guess I can tell you that much. You're the negotiator, eh? Well, I'm the securer. The one who gets things. For a price, I'll get you what you want, or desire, or need. No matter what."

"All for a percentage."

"Nothing ever happens for free."

"And what you want, need, or desire is what I have, what once belonged to Clarence."

"Now you get it. Congratulations. So are we on? What you have in exchange for this federal employee?"

I closed my eyes. It seemed like the laundry upstairs was still going on. "Yes," I said. "We're on."

"Good, this is what we're going to do."

"Nope," I said. "I've already made the arrangements."

"Fuck you, pal, this is—"

"No," I replied. "This is how it's going to happen. Or you can keep Carla. Sell her into white slavery, harvest her body for organs, it doesn't matter to me. But I know you've done a lot, and paid a lot, to get to this point. Hiring men, chasing me around, setting up the initial sting, losing Kate Salzi, Mike Dillman … I get the feeling you're running out of time, maybe running up the bill."

"Fuck you."

"See? I know I'm right, because you're starting to repeat yourself, George. So this is the arrangement. Eleven a.m. tomorrow, off the Yukon Road, there's an abandoned school. The Cornerstone School for Exceptional Children. There's a playing field out back, two roads leading in. I'll take the south road, you take the north, we walk and meet out in the field."

No answer.

"We'll make it quick and simple. Carla for what I've got. Then you've secured what's needed for your boss, and we each leave by the way we came in."

There was the briefest of pauses that seemed to go on for an hour.

"Okay," George said. "We do this—and do it right—and we'll all end the day happy. No guns, though. I know you carry a shoulder holster. You get to that playing field, before you start walking, you show me that you're not carrying. Or the deal's off."

"Can I expect the same from you?"

"Sure," he said. "But pal, don't fuck with me. Or I'll take what I want, and I'll make sure I leave the two of you behind, dead."

"That sounds wonderful."

"Yeah, well, we'll see you tomorrow."

"Fine."

EIGHTEEN

TRACY CAME DOWNSTAIRS TO find me stretched out on her couch, her robe wrapped loosely around me, my pistol on my chest. She gently kissed me and pulled up a footstool, upon which she sat.

"Laundry's almost done," she said.

"Thanks."

"Getting blood stains out ... always a challenge."

"Thanks again," I said. "I've never had anyone extend me this courtesy."

"You have lots of experience getting blood stains out?"

"Some experience, but then again, I usually try harder."

"Why?"

"I always try harder when it's somebody else's blood," I explained "I don't want a reminder kicking around."

She wrinkled her nose at me. "That sounds disgusting ... and perfectly reasonable. How's your pain doing?"

"The pain seems fine," I said. "It's the rest of me that's not doing well."

"You feel like dinner?"

"Absolutely," I said. "Can I help?"

One more kiss, and she got up from the footstool. "Yes," she said. "By staying out here and out of the way."

Tracy bustled around in the kitchen and I worked very hard to stay awake, mostly by running through options and scenarios of what was going to happen tomorrow. I worked very hard at imagining what was going through George's mind, how he might be evaluating my talents, and what his options might be. It was a long list, it was a long exercise, and that's what kept me going, kept me conscious.

Eventually Tracy came out to retrieve me, and I went into the dining room. It was a simple meal—homemade macaroni and cheese, a salad, and fresh heated rolls. She offered me wine and to her surprise, I declined.

"You're really hurting, aren't you," she said.

"You should see the van," I said. "Looks much worse."

"I doubt it."

I offered to help her clean up and she kissed my forehead and said, "You stay there and just heal."

"I'll do my best."

She cleaned up the kitchen and then left to get my laundry, which she folded and placed on the couch in the living room.

Dessert was coffee made from one of those funky Kuerig coffee makers that I always resolve to get one of these days, and a slice of cheesecake with frozen strawberries dribbled over the top. It was so damn homey and domestic that it almost made me forget about the Beretta I had placed on the spare chair next to me.

She said, "Are you ready for tomorrow?"

"Yep."

"And the man called George … who killed your coworker … he's going to be there, too?"

"Yep."

She made to say something and I raised a fork that had a nice healthy chunk of cheesecake dangling from it. I said, "M'dear, there's a chance that things won't go well tomorrow, and in tracing my movements, the Vermont state police might be able to track me back here. If that happens, and if you're interrogated, I want you to be able to say in good faith and conscience that I kept you in the dark."

"Sometimes I don't like being in the dark."

"Gee, that's a surprise."

Tracy licked her fork and said, "Want to go upstairs?"

"Would love to, but as you say, I'm healing."

"I promise not to hurt you. Much."

"Fair enough."

———

As we later rested in bed, Tracy whispered, "You scared?"

"Of you?"

"Ha. No, are you scared about tomorrow?"

"Not right now."

She said, "I did what you asked me to do."

"What's that?"

"I saw *The Maltese Falcon* movie, the one you talked about." She started making long, looping scratches on my chest with her painted fingernails. "After his partner gets killed, Sam Spade says something about having to do something about having his partner killed.

Didn't matter what you thought of him, you had to do something about it, or else the killer would get away. Which would be a bad thing for everyone … everyone in the business."

"Good memory."

"That's what you're doing, right? Taking care of it because otherwise, it's bad for you and your business."

I thought about a widow and her two sons, living alone and scared in a small home in Saugus, with the drone of the highway hammering at you, hour after hour, day after day.

"Among other things."

She kissed my chest. "Be careful … and will you come back to me? To tell me what it was like?"

"I'll come back to you."

"That's not what I asked."

"That's how I answered."

———

She murmured some more, kissed me more, and then fell asleep on my chest. I kept still for long minutes, her weight upon me both comforting yet oppressive. I kept still, waited during the night, as she murmured, shifted. At some point, she made to roll to the side and I slipped away, so we were at last separated.

I waited some more. I wanted Tracy to be in a deep REM sleep and so I kept still. I stayed awake from the choices running through my mind, and the pain starting to reassert itself as the Ibuprofen wore off.

A deep rattling snore from Tracy next to me, and it was time.

I slipped out of the bed on my bare feet, waited again. Nothing from Tracy. From the nightstand I picked up my pistol and holster, and then paused. I nearly shook from the dark thoughts that suddenly coursed through me.

No loose ends, came the whisper. No loose ends. Loose ends can be tugged and tugged and then made into a rope that will bind and eventually capture you.

Those words … whispered to me by old vets above me. Maybe they were top car salesmen in my region in Southern California. Or grizzled lawyers on Wall Street. Or master sergeants in the Army. Whatever, they were whispered, again and again.

No loose ends.

It would be so easy to climb back on the bed, put a pillow over Tracy's head, push the muzzle end of my 9mm Beretta, and with two pulls of the trigger, remove her from the complicated equations I was dealing with.

So easy.

Pistol in hand, I quietly walked around the other side of the bed, to where she was sleeping. In the ambient light from the clocks, telephone and cable box, it was so easy to make out her sleeping form, the pillow she was resting on.

I bent down. Brushed my lips across her forehead. Stood back up.

"Damn," I whispered to myself, "what's wrong with you?"

I got out of her bedroom.

Downstairs I got dressed and then left her condo, walking as fast as I could across the parking lot. At my Ford, I got in and didn't slam the door … I just gently closed it and then started up the SUV, and then slid out of the parking lot without turning on my headlights.

When I got on the main road, I opened and slammed the door, switched on the headlights, and drove out into the darkness.

———————

Maybe it was karma, or my sick sense of humor, or God's even sicker sense of humor, but I needed a place to rest up for a few hours, and the only place that came to mind was the Chester Motel. So that's where I went. I went to the office and rang a doorbell, then an older man, yawning, came out from a doorway and unlocked the door.

"Hey," he said, scratching at his chin. He had gray-white stubble on his worn face.

"Hey," I replied.

I went in and we made it quick, as he yawned some more. From his demeanor and the way he moved around, I guessed that he was the owner. He had on blue sweatpants, a long-sleeved T-shirt, and a baseball cap that said VIETNAM VETERAN up front, complete with a couple of badges, one depicting a rectangular blue bar representing the awarding of a Purple Heart and the other showing the wreathed musket for a Combat Infantry Badge, indicating the older man before me had been in some rice paddies decades ago, getting fired upon.

I signed some paperwork and he passed over a plastic room key that had the numeral 9 imprinted on it ... thankfully, not Room 14. I'm not particularly superstitious, but why tempt whatever fates are out there?

I paid for one night and he said, "All set?"

"I am," I said. I slid over an extra twenty-dollar bill. His eyes widened some.

"For waking you up."

"Hey, my job."

"Still, I woke you up."

He grinned, pocketed the cash. "I guess the hell you did."

———

After I settled into Room 9, I locked the door and its deadbolt and then dragged a chair over and shoved it under the doorknob. I also drew the curtains and then went into the bathroom to check my wounds. Scrapes, bruises, and contusions, but I was still secure, still serviceable.

I went to the small writing desk next to the bed and spent some time scribbling around on a sheet of paper, drawing arrows and crosses, thinking things through.

Then I stretched out on the bed and let my mind relax and decompress. Jitters. Pre-op, pre-job, pre-sale jitters. They can always happen, but I find that if I've done enough research and planning, I'm able to sleep.

Which I did.

———

I woke up when the sun started beating through the drawn shades, and I checked the time. 6:06 a.m. I got up, dressed, and after packing up my belongings, departed the tender care of the Chester Motel, a recommended waypoint for murder victims and avenging … well, *knights, angels, and the forces of good* really didn't describe me, so I left it at avenging fill-in-the-blank.

Assisted by the directions provided by Tracy Zahn—who was probably waking up puzzled about my quiet departure—I found Yukon Road and carefully drove down its length. It had a mix of farmhouses, doublewide trailers, and two nice old renovated Colonials. At the left was a faded blue and white sign, stating CORNERSTONE SCHOOL FOR EXCEPTIONAL CHILDREN, and painted on the sign as well were old-fashioned building blocks and two teddy bears. There were bullet holes in the forehead of each teddy bear. I hoped that wasn't a sign.

I drove past without stopping, took a left onto MacKenzie Road, and pulled over and stopped. Time check: 6:21 a.m.

Plenty of time.

I got out and then really went to work.

———

I carefully walked through some heavy woods on my way to the grounds of the Cornerstone School. It was quiet and I took my time, going from tree to tree—mostly pine—and then slowed down as I saw the woods ahead thin out. I went to the edge of the tree line, scanned the field. For some reason it was still being mowed, so the grass was short. There were faded lines on the field, marking a baseball diamond and a soccer pitch. I took out the notes I made back at the motel room, sat against a birch tree trunk, did some more sketching.

From where I sat, the one-story school building was to the left. The windows were covered from the inside by sheets of brown paper. From the building the ground gradually sloped to the playing field, about a hundred yards wide. Two single-lane roads were on either side of the school building, leading to a rear parking lot.

I waited. The morning sun felt good on my face. I relaxed, my eyes flickering around the field before me, again running everything through. Something caught my eye and I saw a red-tailed fox scurry along the opposite wood line. So peaceful, so safe. My stomach grumbled and I had an urge to leave, get a cup of coffee and some sort of breakfast sandwich, and just return here and watch the sun slide its way across the morning. Just have breakfast and ignore a man escorting a woman across the field in a few hours, wait and ignore some more, and then get on with life.

It certainly sounded attractive. Just to get up and walk away and ignore it all, for in my absence, somehow, things would be concluded, without my knowledge or activity. Just leave.

The fox disappeared from view.

But I wouldn't—or, more accurately, I couldn't.

Two lines of poetry echoed in my mind, from the famed British-Canadian poet Robert Service:

> *There's a race of men, that don't fit in*
> *A race that can't stay still*

I got up from my viewing point. "Ain't that the truth, Bob." I slowly made my way back through the woods. I got into my Ford, started her up, and with my stomach grumbling even louder, I went to make one more stop before the day's activities were to begin.

———

The time passed quickly. Later I went back to the school, made a left, and drove down the short lane, stopping before it moved right into the rear parking lot. I got out, left my keys in the ignition—having a brief pang of memory of Clarence doing that in Chester so many days ago—and then I removed my Beretta, slid it under the front seat. I walked away, keys jingling in my coat pocket. Earlier I had decided against wearing a Kevlar vest. The vest offered protection, of course, but also advertised to my opponent that perhaps concluding a satisfactory deal for the two of us wasn't forefront in my mind.

I left the woods and walked across the field, thinking of the scores of children who had played here before the school had shut down. All those children, playing and having fun, running around, screaming and yelling, and now there was just silence, and for the moment, just me.

I went out about a third of the way and stopped. I opened my jacket, turned in a circle. With my jacket up, I also pulled up my shirt and moved the same way again, making sure anybody out there could see there was nothing hidden in my waistband. My clothes went back down. I lifted up each pants leg, showing that I wasn't wearing an ankle holster.

I checked my watch. It was exactly 11:00 a.m. A gunman out there could very easily cut me down with no fuss and no witnesses, but that would leave open the possibility that I didn't have in my possession the very valuable thing that Clarence had stolen from George's employer. So if I was killed now, George and his paymaster would risk not getting anything today.

I checked my watch again. 11:09. George was late, and that wasn't a surprise. He was no doubt pissed at me for having tried to kill him the other day, along with my lack of respect in my dealings with him. George was just going to play the delay game, to prove he was the man in charge, that he could show up any old time he wanted to.

Fine. I would allow him that satisfaction.

Another watch check. I didn't really care at the moment what time it was, but I knew I was under observation, and I wanted my watcher out there—either George or someone in his employ—to see my continuous glances and assume I was getting worried or anxious about the passing of time.

Fine. I would also allow him, or them, those thoughts.

I guess one would say that I was feeling in a pretty generous mood.

Movement then.

It seemed like I was holding my breath. I resumed my breathing and three figures emerged from the other wood line.

Three. How about that?

There was George, then the muscley friend I had noted on the front porch of the Putney Homestead, and Carla Pope. They walked in a ragged line, George walking by himself, and Muscular Friend walking with one long and beefy arm around Carla's waist, and his other arm held up at an angle. That arm ended in an equally beefy hand, which was holding a revolver, which was right against Carla's right temple.

Things were getting downright interesting.

When they had reached about the same distance I was, I resumed walking as well, until I got to the middle of the field. A faded white chalk line extended before me, and the trio approaching me stopped about five yards away.

I nodded. "There's three of you. I don't remember agreeing to more than just you and Carla."

George smiled, his face ruddy and looking to be freshly washed and shaved. "Then I guess you should have mentioned something, moron. Some negotiator you turned out to be."

He had on a blue L.L.Bean jacket, zippered open, and a black turtleneck shirt along with black dungarees. Muscular Friend had on a dark green commando-type ribbed sweater, with patches on the elbows and shoulders, and black dungarees as well. His eyes were small and focused right on me.

Carla … she had on black slacks and a brown leather jacket, and her face was puffy, red eyes swollen from tears.

"I guess I should have," I said. "Carla, how are you?"

Her voice was faint. "I've had better life moments."

"I'm sure. Hey, George, what's the name of your big friend in the middle?"

"Him? Oh, he's called Mister None-Of-Your-Fucking-Business."

"Has a nice ring to it." I caught the man's attention. "Hey, Mister None, has George told you about the challenges of working for him?"

He didn't say a word. I added, "Did George tell you that the last guy who was his best buddy and hired gun ended up dead in a ditch?"

George's face reddened even more. "Shut the fuck up."

"I guess he didn't," I said. "So I don't know how much he's paying you, if you've got dental insurance or a pension plan, but being in his employ is the true definition of a dead-end job."

Muscular Friend didn't waver, hesitate, or even blink. It made me think that perhaps he didn't even speak English, that perhaps he was from away and could only communicate via Serbo-Croation.

"Shut the fuck up, will you?" George said.

"If I did that, how will we ever conclude a successful negotiation?"

In another time and place, perhaps MF and Carla would have laughed or smiled, but no, their expressions didn't change. And neither did George's. He just said, "Let's get on with it."

"All right," I said, "but I need to clear up a couple of things first. You know the successful outcome of negotiations relies on frank and open communications. So tell me this, George, you're offering Carla to me in exchange for the property in Clarence's possession. But I have a suspicion that you and Carla are working together. What do you have to say about that?"

"Fuck you, Charlie," he said. "This stupid bitch phoned me up at Putney, telling the innkeeper that she was from the FBI and wanted to talk to a guy with white hair. I met her on the porch, she threatened to do all sorts of nasty things to me unless I gave up my employer …" He burst out with a laugh. "Like fuck that was going to happen. So I pretended to be scared and later that night, we scooped her up."

"Her room looked very tidy, indeed," I said. "No sign of a struggle."

George smirked. "You see my buddy there? He can be very persuasive in convincing folks to leave quietly and smoothly."

That was a thought. Carla said, "Please … "

"Got that?" George said. "Is that convincing enough?"

"Please … " she murmured. "Just so you know, Henry Ford … he was an asshole. Just so you know."

Henry Ford. Not the Jew-hating one. His son.

Got it.

"Question answered," I said. "Time to show the goods. I'm right-handed. So I'm going to slowly lower my left hand to my coat pocket, and come out with what you're looking for. And you don't have to say a word, I know in advance that if my hand moves too quickly, or comes out with a weapon, you'll shoot me dead. Followed by Carla."

George nodded. Carla's eyes were open. But the third member of the party across from me, he stood as still and lifeless as the former governor of California.

I lowered my left hand, feeling awkward in doing so, into my coat pocket, felt metal there, and slowly lifted it up. It came out of my pocket, out into the open, where the warm Vermont sun warmed it up.

A set of keys attached to a Red Sox plastic logo.

———

Something that might have been a smile slithered across George's face, and with the fingers of my left hand, I worked around the keys until I located the one I was looking for.

"Safety deposit box key, am I right?" I asked. "Clarence probably set this up when he was on some freelance job. Maybe he found a case full of hundred-dollar bills, or jewelry, or bars of platinum, and decided to make his move. So he stole the goods, went back home to Massachusetts, placed it in safekeeping, and then tried to cover up his trail."

George said, "Give me the key."

"It had to be somebody connected to the mob, maybe in the Philly area. The FBI has said the Isabelle Stewart Gardner museum paintings ended up with the mob in Philly. I bet you sought professional courtesy and asked if you could borrow one of the paintings, for bait, to get me and Clarence in one place. And I bet you knew that Clarence never, ever left this key out of his possession."

"The key," George said.

I dangled the keys so they jingle-jangled. "But you screwed up, George. Didn't you. You thought you'd kill Clarence, then me, and then scoop up the keys." I made a *buzz* noise, like getting a question wrong on a television game show. "Sorry, wrong answer. I got out and kept the keys. So here we are."

George's face looked like it was sliding from scarlet to heart-attack red. "Give me the key, or that bitch's head is going to be splattered all over this grass, and you'll be next."

"I moved pretty fast last time, George. You think you can beat me again?"

"I don't have to. There's two of us, and one of you. And my friend here ... he's fast, deadly, and as you can tell by his standing there, he's never been beat. The keys. Now."

Just then, my damn stomach decided to remind me that it hadn't been fed in a while. I learned a while ago that filling up with food

264

before a questionable task was not a good idea, leaving open the threat of infection if bullets go a tumblin' through your stomach and intestine while they're busy digesting a breakfast burrito.

And what do you know, George smirked. "What, your belly growling? You feeling nervous?"

"Not nervous at all," I said. "You made an offer. Here's my counteroffer. You left Clarence a widow with two young boys. How about you agree to take the key, let Carla go, and also give her ten percent of whatever's in the box as a sign of good will. What do you think?"

He laughed. "Do I fucking look like I'm overflowing with good will?"

"Well, I gave it a shot. Can't blame me for that."

"I'll tell you what I will blame you for, though, is if that key isn't here with me in the next five seconds, I'm going to kill this FBI bitch."

"You want to have the whole FBI chasing your butt when this is done?"

"She's some sort of office clerk, not an agent. They'll get over it. Last time, now, the key."

From the slight way MF was moving, I knew he was prepping for a shot, and I said, "All right, George, thanks for your patience. Here they come."

And I tossed the bunch of keys right at his head.

———

Damn.

George had been right.

MF was quick, whipping Carla to the side to open himself for a clear shot at me, and that took less than a second. George was quick, too, for a man of his age, batting away the keys and going into a crouch, pulling out a small semiautomatic pistol from his waist that was also pointed at me.

My chest grew cold, instinctively knowing that bullets were moments away from tearing through and ripping it to shreds.

I dared not move, nor breathe.

George got up from his crouch, lowered his weapon. MF took that as a sign, and resumed his position, hugging Carla with one arm, holding his revolver back up against her right temple.

"That was stupid," George said.

"My hand slipped. Sorry."

George picked up the key chain, the Red Sox plastic piece still dangling. He examined the keys and spotted the one for the safety deposit box.

"Satisfied?"

"Pretty much," George said.

"Then let Carla come over here, and we'll all go away happy."

George put the keys into his pocket. "No, I think I'll keep her for a while."

"Not part of the negotiation, not part of the deal."

"True, but how do I know this key isn't a fake? I can let Carla go and by the end of the day, a friend of mine will be at a certain bank with a key that doesn't fit. Where does that leave me? I take Carla and if the key works, then, maybe, I'll let her go later."

"A successful negotiation depends on trust," I said. "George, please don't go against your word."

He laughed. "Or what? You gonna be mad at me for the rest of your life? What the hell are you going to do now, asshole? I got the key, I got the hostage, I got everything." George took a couple of steps back

266

away from MF, and I knew exactly what was going to happen next, for he didn't want to be splattered with my blood and tissue.

"George, you're right," I said. "I surrender."

I lifted both of my arms up.

NINETEEN

THERE CAME THE SOUND of a baseball bat striking a pumpkin, and Carla yelped. George looked on, stunned, as his bodyguard fell right on his back, like he was a special marionette whose invisible strings had abruptly and violently been severed.

"Carla, down!" I yelled, and I went right after George, lowering my body down, attacking him like an NFL tackle pissed that his divorcing wife had just seized his Aruba condo. George raised up his pistol, got off a shot that whizzed right past my left ear, and I barreled right into him, flattening him to the ground, his arm still coming back at me with the pistol, but I knocked his arm free, and when it came back, I twisted and broke his wrist.

George howled. I loved hearing it. I now had one forearm digging into his throat, and with my right hand, reached down to my right shin, lifted up the pants leg very high, and quickly retrieved my Ka-Bar knife from a scabbard I had taped to my upper shin. The knife came up and with my forearm against his throat, the blade pushing in, George calmed right down.

"George?"

"Yeah," he said, strangling out a whisper up at me.

"Forgive me, but I want to get your attention."

I then slit his cheek.

———————

He howled some more but then eventually calmed down, even with a broken wrist and bleeding cheek. "You fucker. You set us up. You fucker."

"Go complain to the Better Business Bureau," I said, pressing the now-bloody knife's edge to his throat. All of my senses were on high alert, like one of those old Air Force radar warning systems seeing a squadron of Soviet bombers coming over the North Pole. I could hear sobs from Carla, heavy breathing from George, and I could smell his scent of sweat and fear, mixed in the smell of spilt blood, drifting in the peaceful Vermont air.

"Besides," I continued, "you broke the rules first."

"Fucker," he strangled out once more.

I pushed in deeper with my forearm and the knife's edge. He gurgled. "Despite what's happened in the last minute, George, this is turning out to be a very, very lucky day for you. My original mission in this negotiation was to get you in a position to kill you for killing Clarence."

George was wheezing and his face was turning red, almost sliding into light blue. I had to talk quick or lift up my arm before he passed out underneath me.

"But goals change, George, don't they. And so did mine. Now you have this opportunity to live. Interested?"

I released the pressure on my forearm just a bit. He struggled to take in a breath. "Yeah … I'm interested."

"Here's the offer, no negotiations," I said. "Deal is, you leave Vermont, you leave New England, you never come back. I don't give a damn what your employers think or respond, but you tell them Clarence ate the key and you lost his body or something else like that. You agree to that, then you're free to go, with just an ER visit and a trip to the Laundromat to worry about."

"How … can I trust … you?"

"Sounds like a personal problem, George. Do we have a deal?"

"Why … I got to know … why … "

"I mentioned it earlier," I said. "A widow and two sons. They need to be supported, and they need never to be bothered."

"Deal," George said.

"Tell me what you understand, before I get up off of you. Sign of a good negotiator, you want to make sure the terms are very precise and clear. Got it?"

His cheek was bleeding like hell, and his throat was raspy from me having almost strangled him, but George came around.

"I … never come back to New England … I tell my guy, mission failed … and I don't bother the widow or sons …"

"And what about the guys in the surveillance van? Or the shooters in Manchester? Or the kids in Saugus?"

Spittle was drooling down his chin. "One … time … hires … local talent … that's all …."

"Outstanding," I said, starting to move, "it looks like we're going to—"

270

The sound of the gunshot was so loud and abrupt that I rolled off George's body, knife held up, looking for a threat, for an enemy, maybe George's bodyguard had come back to life, looking to see what the hell was going on.

Carla stood there, slightly weaving, George's pistol in both her hands. Blood was trickling down the right side of her face. George moaned, brought his hands down to his left side, where a blossom of blood was quickly growing.

"I wasn't part of the negotiations," she said.

She moved the pistol, shot again in the direction of George's head.

Missed.

"Carla..."

George yelped, but before he could say anything, Carla shot again. She didn't miss this time.

———

I got up, sheathed my knife in my shin scabbard, and grabbed Carla by her arm. She held up the pistol and said, "Do you want it? I think I'm done with it."

I managed to speak. "Sure. I'll take it off your hands."

Carla stood away from the two bodies, legs shaking. Before she turned away from me, she said, "They... hurt me. Both of them."

"I see. Wait just a sec, okay?"

I went over to the body of George's muscle, whose upper head was pretty much... well, I don't want to describe it. I took out my handkerchief, wiped the pistol down, put it in the muscle's hands, forced his trigger finger through, and fired off a shot. Carla didn't even flinch. I dropped the pistol and found Clarence's keychain, grabbed it, and put it in my pocket. I gently took Carla's upper arm, and we moved as quick as we could back across the field and to my Ford.

"Your head? Are you okay? What happened?"

She brought up her hand, touched the side of her head, looked in amazement at the blood on her fingers.

"I don't know. I think ... Micah, that was his name, I think the barrel of Micah's revolver scraped me when he fell back. Does that make sense?"

"It does."

———

I opened up the doors to my Ford Expedition, bundled her in as quickly and as best as I could, and retrieved my Beretta and holster. I wasn't sure if George had any other allies out there, working on his behalf, but I wanted to be safe. I slammed open my glovebox, grabbed a couple of napkins, pressed them into Carla's hand. She put them up to her bleeding head without hesitation. I started up the Ford and Carla said, "What ... what happened back there?"

"I'll let you know in a bit," I said, "but I've got just a few minutes to clear up things."

I quickly reversed and made a U-turn, and drove back up the access road, to the main road. I took a left, and then another left, and I went down the access road I had earlier told George to take. I went past the rear of the abandoned school and then came up on a black Cadillac Escalade. I pulled in right behind it.

"Carla, is there anybody else out there? Anybody else working with George?"

"No," she said, sitting in nearly a ball in the passenger's seat, her legs pulled up, her arms tight across her chest. "They were alone."

As I started to get out of the Expedition, she said, "My stuff ... some of my stuff was in the back ... why did they keep my stuff? Why?"

I had a number of readily available answers, none of which I wanted to share. "I'll be back, quick as I can."

The Cadillac was unlocked, which gave me a time bonus. Sure enough, in the rear seat were two bags I recognized as belonging to Carla. I tossed them out onto the road and with some more napkins—assisted by a water bottle—I wiped down the rear of the Navigator as best as I could.

As I worked, I spotted a smear of brown on the rear passenger seat. Dried blood.

Yeah, they had hurt her, all right.

When I was done trying to remove Carla's presence, the best I could, I had a thought. I removed my Ka-Bar knife, wiped that clean as well, and tossed it in the rear, where George's and Micah's belongings were stashed. If I was law enforcement, digging through that baggage might lead to some wonderful investigative opportunities, which is why I left it alone. And the knife might lead them in the direction of the murdered Kate Salzi, which sounded like a grand idea.

Then I closed the doors and got back to my Ford carrying Carla's bags, which I gently deposited in the rear seat.

"What now?" she asked.

"Going to get you to a hospital."

"But ... "

"Carla, I'm getting you to a hospital. Right now."

I retraced my drive back through Bellows Falls, got onto Route 103, and we were soon on Interstate 91, heading north. I goosed my speed up to eighty miles per hour.

Carla said, "I'm thirsty."

"Water in the cooler, right behind you."

She turned in the seat and clumsily retrieved a water bottle, blood-sodden napkin still on the side of her head. Her face was gray and smeared with dirt and old tears, but I liked the look in Carla's eyes. Unlike the dead look back at that schoolyard field, with a large man named Micah ready to kill her in a second, life was coming back to that face.

I guess it took killing George to do that. A fair and appropriate trade, it seemed to me.

Carla sat back down, put her seatbelt back on, unscrewed the top of the plastic water jug, took a long, long swallow. When she pulled the bottle away, she said, "What hospital are we going to?"

"The one in Springfield, about fifteen minutes away now."

"How do you know that?"

"I just do."

Carla took another healthy swig. The gray pallor of her face was beginning to change to a healthy pink. "You planned it, didn't you."

"Yep."

I checked my speed. Eighty was probably too fast. I backed down to seventy-five. Traffic was light, but then again, this was Vermont. Probably never had a traffic jam here in its entire history.

"You're something else, aren't you. You plan and plan and plan … but you were going to let George get away."

"At the time, I was," I said. "Your ex-sister-in-law, Wanda … she's in bad shape. With no body for her husband, it might take a number of years for any will to go to probate. Her and the boys, they won't be able to last that long."

"Are you pissed that I shot George?"

"No. Surprised."

Another sip again, more slow and gentile. "Glad to know I can surprise you."

I took Exit 7, started navigating my way to the Springfield Hospital, saw the pleasing blue signs with the white H in the center pointing the way. When I got to Ridgewood Road, it was straight ahead.

"I'll walk you in, but I can't stay," I said. "I've got a couple of other things to do. But I'll be back later today, I promise."

"What should I say to the ER personnel?"

I slowed down as I approached the two-story brick building, with its inviting blue signs.

"Surprise me," I said. "Come up with some sort of tale … but please leave me out of it."

Carla's eyes started tearing up as I pulled to the side of the main entrance. After I put the Ford in park, I walked around and opened her door, and then the rear door. "Give me a minute, all right?"

She swiveled so her legs were dangling outside. To the cooler in the rear I returned, and took out another water bottle.

"Your hands, Carla."

She stuck her hands out like an obedient schoolgirl, and I gave both hands a dousing, paying special attention to her right one. With napkins I scrubbed her wrists, her palms and her fingers, and dug a bit underneath each fingernail.

One more rinse and I dried her off.

"What was that all about?" she asked.

"Just in case some smart cop or state trooper decides to do a gunshot residue test on your hands. I want to make sure this gives you a chance."

Carla nodded and I said, "You okay to walk? I'm sure I can get a wheelchair from the hospital."

"To hell with that. I'm going in under my own power."

We both faced the main entrance, and she started slowing down. I took her left arm and looped it through mine, and she leaned into me as we got closer.

"Back there, in the field," she said. "What happened to Micah?"

"You know exactly what happened to him."

"Christ, yes, but who did it? It sure as hell wasn't you."

We made it to the entrance, and the main doors slid open with a whoosh.

"Remember our earlier conversation, on the way to Vermont? About national technical means of verification?"

"I do."

"That kind of spycraft is worthless without a robust Department of Defense behind it. That's it, here we go."

And inside we went, to the cool tile and warm colors and soft music that offered respite for at least one of us.

TWENTY

I GOT LOST TWICE going to my next destination, before finally locating it at a four-corner intersection in some remote corner of this part of Vermont. Based on how much driving and turning I did, I wouldn't have been surprised if I had ended up in New York, New Hampshire, or even Quebec, but the two battered pickup trucks and one dark blue Crown Victoria with a whip antenna all bore Vermont license plates, so I was certain I had finally arrived where I belonged.

My destination was a ramshackle collection of shacks and buildings grandly called the Four Corner Café, and I walked in and spotted Detective Mike Shaye at a far corner booth. Three other local guys were sitting on round stools at the counter, and after giving me bored glances, they went back to their lunches.

Shaye didn't get up as I approached and I didn't mind. I sat down across from him and his plate, which had a half-eaten omelet in the middle.

"How goes it?" he asked. He had on a dungaree jacket, black T-shirt, and dark green pants. He didn't look like a cop. He looked like the type of guy who'd stop by your house to grind a couple of stumps in your back yard, or who'd offer to plow your driveway when the snows arrived.

"I'm starved."

"Then order up," he said. "Guy named Hank Perry runs this place, used to sling hash for the Navy. Once he figured out how to reduce portions by 99 percent or so, he can scratch up a pretty good meal. Breakfast all day if that suits you."

"Thanks."

A teenage waitress sauntered by and I placed my order of pancakes, sausage, coffee, and a glass of milk. Shaye said, "Lots of challenges being a cop in a small town, you know?"

"I'm sure." I kept quiet, wanting to see where this was going.

He said, "There's the politics, of course, and the budget battles, and then the mindset of your citizens, who want you to do a fine and proper investigation if someone takes a baseball bat to his mailbox. I mean, dust for fingerprints, set up a surveillance, check for tire tracks, that sort of shit."

"You bet."

"Hunh." He ate for a couple of minutes, and then my order arrived, and I dug in and he finally said, "But what really can get to you is knowing that you've got no quiet time, no private time. Small town, small department, the good citizens feel like they own you, day and night. They watch you when you go to the bank, go to the supermarket ... and they time you at lunch, see how long you take."

The detective waved a fork at the place. "Here, they leave me alone."

"Why's that?"

"Most of the traffic here is from guys getting from one part of Vermont to another, not locals. And the owners here, they don't care what I order, or how long I stay."

"Sounds like a nice set of owners."

"Well, I did a favor for them. Something embarrassing involving a son, a couple of sheep, and a cellphone video."

"Seems like everyone has a favor to be fulfilled."

"True... like you?"

"Probably."

"Ha."

We both finished in silence and I said, "Thanks for this morning."

"I have no idea what you're talking about."

"Then I must be mistaken."

"Sounds like it."

I said, "Mind if I pay the bill?"

"Won't say no, that's for sure."

When the teen waitress came back, I paid the bill, left a hefty tip, and then Shaye said, "I think I'd like you to pay another bill."

"Not a problem. What do you have in mind?"

"Nothing for me, you understand."

"Sure."

I took one last sip from my coffee. "Here's the deal," Shaye said. "I have friends with a couple of charities. You ever hear of the Wounded Warrior Project?"

"Of course."

"I want to see a donation there, within the week."

"Not a problem. How much?"

A slight smile. "Make it a good number. And make sure it's good, or I'll track you down and make your life miserable, however secret it might be."

"A deal."

"Glad to hear it."

We both sat for a moment and I said, "Tell me, is this your day off?"

"Yeah, but not for long," he said. "I imagine I'll get a call here in a little bit. Actually, I'm surprised it hasn't come through yet."

"A call about what?"

"Oh, I have a vivid imagination. You know how it is, a detective lets his mind wander. Thinks about a good case to break up the day, keep him away from the usual vandalism, car thefts, burglaries."

"Fascinating. What's your imagination telling you today?"

"A double homicide, if you can believe it."

"The hell you say."

"Oh, yeah. Double homicide, probably a drug deal gone bad. It happens—not that often, but it happens. Especially if you find both guys shot, and with some cocaine sprinkled about. And if the two guys are from away, and have interesting ... backgrounds."

"Cocaine? For real?"

"Sure," he said. "Just enough left there to raise the right sort of questions."

I smiled. I was liking this detective.

"Feel like a poem before you leave?"

"Sure."

He fumbled into his shirt pocket for a moment, took out a folded sheet of paper. With a low voice he read the poem, written a lifetime and a world away:

> "'Twas only by favour of mine," quoth he, "ye rode so long alive:
> There was not a rock for twenty mile, there was not a clump of tree,
> But covered a man of my own men with his rifle cocked on his knee.
> If I had raised my bridle-hand, as I have held it low,
> The little jackals that flee so fast were feasting all in a row.
> If I had bowed my head on my breast, as I have held it high,
> The kite that whistles above us now were gorged till she could not fly."

He raised his head up from reading Kipling's poem. "Nice little bit, especially about raising one's hand to alert a rifleman to open fire."

"Kipling always had a way with words."

"True," Shaye said. "I've read it a few times, and always thought, man, that guy in the poem, Kamal, he was taking a chance. Just raising one hand. Leaves a lot to chance."

I nodded. "I guess if somebody was going to be inspired by this poem, he might raise two hands."

"Good idea."

A cellphone started ringing, and Shaye slipped it out of his coat pocket. "Detective Shaye here," he said. "Unh-hunh. Unh-hunh. Any witnesses so far? Unh-hunh. Okay, I'm rolling."

He clicked the phone shut, put it back into his coat. "Looks like my imagination just came through. Double homicide, in the old playing field of an abandoned school. I'm afraid our little chat is over."

"Not a problem."

We got up and walked out, and nobody bade us farewell. It's like we had never been there at all.

Outside he strode quickly to his unmarked cruiser. "Oh, I probably don't need to say this, but I'm going to do it, anyway. Leave my little corner of Vermont and never come back."

"I can agree to that," I said, "but can you give me the rest of the day? I need to make some arrangements, tie up the proverbial loose ends."

"Don't make a career out of it," he warned, opening the cruiser's door.

"I won't."

He got in, started the Crown Victoria's engine, and I motioned to him. "What's up?" he asked.

"Quick question."

"Better be quick, you know where I'm headed."

"When you were in Iraq, you were following that mullah, the one the Bigs decided you couldn't take out. What happened to him?"

Shaye shifted into reverse. "Oh, a number of weeks later, he was walking out of his favorite mosque when an unknown shooter splattered his head among a dozen of his followers. Amazing shot, I was told."

"Funny how that happened."

"Yeah," he said. "Never know what's going to happen when a lot of bullets are flying around. So long."

The unmarked cruiser went out to the road, the blue lights came on in the front radiator and above the windshield, and then he was off. I walked to my Ford, my long day almost over.

TWENTY-ONE

I HUNG AROUND DOWNTOWN Bellows Falls for a while that afternoon, conscious that time was sliding away and that I had promised Detective Shaye I would soon be departing. But my unfinished task rattled around in the back of my mind, like the thought of an unpaid bill to someone I owed a debt to. It had to be paid, had to be addressed.

As I drove, parked, and then drove again, I kept on thinking of Carla Pope and how vulnerable she had been, how light she had felt when I had escorted her into the Springfield Hospital.

There. Right across the street from O'Halloran & Son, Tracy Zahn strolled confidently down the sidewalk, heading to her place of work. She had on a short black skirt, short light tan jacket, and a confident bearing.

She was good to look at.

I got out and went across the street, joined her as she was walking to the front door, and if I startled her, she kept it under wraps.

"Oh! Look who's here ... my own personal man of mystery."

"Among other things, I hope," I said, sliding my arm into hers. "Can I bother you for a few moments?"

"That'd be great. I'd love to be bothered."

I escorted her into the office, where the handsome young lad manning the front—Patrick, I think his name was—gave Tracy a big grin as she came into view. He said, "Tracy, don't forget, you've got a viewing out at the Glynn property in fifteen minutes."

"Thanks, Pat," she said, and she tried to maneuver toward her desk, but I kept on propelling her to the rear, where the conference room was located.

I opened the conference room door and said, "Sounds like a busy afternoon. How much time do we have?"

"About two or three minutes," she said, smiling slyly at me. "Not enough time to do much."

"Oh, I'll see what we can do."

I closed the door behind me.

———

I think down in her cellular level, with the long-distant species memories of being out on the wide savannahs of Africa, she sensed some sort of danger. Like catching the scent of a far-off cheetah. But I kept my smile wide and inviting as I invited her to take a chair. I took one opposite her, making sure the door was behind me.

With the sound of the shutting door, Tracy's concern grew, and her legs and arms shifted, like unconsciously she was prepared to fight or flight. I wasn't worried about her fighting, and with me in front of the door, I also wasn't concerned about her flighting either.

"So," she said, trying to keep a cheerful tone in her voice. "What can we do in two or three minutes?"

"Depends," I said. "But I'm pretty sure I can kill you and Patrick, set the place afire, and then get out of here in about five minutes."

Her face paled right out, like the blood had decided to stop circulating right above her neckline. "Who the hell do you think you are?"

"I know exactly who I am," I said. "The question is, who are you?"

Eyes wide, Tracy glanced around and I said, "Sit right there. If you want to still be breathing by the time the sun sets, you just sit there."

"Please," she whispered.

"I ask the questions, you answer with no dancing around, and progress will be made. And I'm a big fan of progress."

A sudden nod. "Okay."

"How much were you paid? By George or whoever worked for him?"

There was a long second or two, when the rational part of her—how in God's name can I be under threat, here in my home town and my own office—was debating with the base part of her brain that was sensing extreme danger emanating from the man across from her, like infrared heat from an open oven door.

"A thousand dollars, to start," she whispered.

"As what, rental for the house on Timberswamp Road?"

"The cash … it was so easy, I mean … "

"I know. Business sucks. And a thousand dollars … you'd take that, no questions asked. I don't blame you."

Another nod. "He … he told me they were filming some sort of movie. All he needed it was for twenty-four hours, in perfect privacy. He promised the place would be left untouched when he was finished."

"I'm sure. But all that easy money coming your way … What a temptation. You called him right after I left that showing, true? And

286

you encouraged me to meet with that hulk … Eddie Century. I'm sure you thought Eddie would slow me down, hurt me so that George or his friend could catch up with me if I was dinged up at the hospital."

I didn't think it was possible that her face could grow more pale, but it surely did. I was almost convinced I could see the veins under her skin. "That's right."

"That gain you another paycheck?"

"Yes."

"Then you invited me to sneak into your condo at night when I was done meeting with Eddie Century. But I rang the front door. I didn't like the thought of sneaking in the back door. A single woman like yourself could shoot an intruder like me, and get away with it."

"I … I … why do you say that?"

"I saw you moving around after I rang the doorbell, like you were trying to conceal something. And when you led me upstairs, I smelled oil. A special kind of oil. Gun oil. That must have been one heck of a payout, to shoot me dead in your condo's rear entrance."

"I … I … "

"Things that tough?"

"Yes … but please, I tried to protect you. I really did."

"Without saying anything?"

"No … I couldn't dare say anything … but I did my best to protect you."

Something I hadn't thought about came to me. "I'll be … you told Detective Shaye I was at the Putney Homestead, didn't you. Pretty damn clever."

Tracy started rubbing her hands together, tight and tighter, like she was trying to break her own fingers. "I thought that if you were arrested, you'd be in custody. Until George left the area. I … hoped it would protect you."

"Some thinking."

"Please … "

Enough, I thought. Enough. I reached to my side, took out my Beretta, and she stared at it. I said, "Just to make my point, and one more question. You've done very good … so far."

Tracy couldn't speak anymore. She just nodded.

I said, "Did you only talk to George?"

"Yes, that's all," she managed to say.

"Anybody else?"

"No."

"Are you sure?"

"God, yes, please … "

I put the Beretta back under my coat. "Very good. We're done here."

Her eyes were filled with tears and I said, "I mean it. I'll be heading out and nothing will happen, just as long as you don't talk to anyone. Do you understand what I'm saying? Do I need to explain it any further?"

She shook her head. "No … no, you don't."

I got up from the chair. "Fine. Now put a smile on your face and walk me out the door. And if all goes well, we'll never see each other, ever again."

Tracy wiped at her eyes, nodded, and silently got up. I opened the door and went out into the office, and young Patrick turned and said, "Tracy, you've really got to get going to make that appointment."

"I'll be right along," she said, her voice a bit stronger.

I leaned over and extended my hand. "Patrick, am I right?"

He grinned, shook my hand. "That's right."

"Glad to meet you," I said. "Hey, if you get a moment, you know what you should do later today?"

Patrick was still smiling. "I don't know, what's that?"

"Buy a lottery ticket," I said. "Even if you don't know it, you've had one lucky day."

Outside Tracy grabbed my arm, pulled me back, tried to kiss me. Her lips brushed my cheek and in my left ear she whispered, "Please, can I make it up to you? Please? I-I'm so sorry ... so very, very sorry."

I kissed her cheek and disentangled myself from her touch. "No," I said.

"Please."

"No," I said. "And it's not negotiable."

TWENTY-TWO

DRIVING BACK TO SPRINGFIELD and its hospital, I was whistling with increasing happiness and satisfaction. Things were wrapping up nicely, and then after heading to Massachusetts and handing over the safety deposit key to the widow Wanda—all right, I had to smile at the expression, so sue me... if you can find me—I'd take a week off, and then get back to work. The past several days had drained my energy and bank account, and it was time to refill both. It had been quite a while since I had checked my special iPhone that presented job offers to me, negotiating complex and highly illegal deals. I was really looking forward to getting back to work.

I parked in the hospital's lot and hesitated.

Something wasn't right.

Something was wrong.

What was it?

I stepped out and slowly walked past the cars and saw a late model Chevrolet sedan, with US government plates.

The gendarmes had arrived.

Damn.

I thought about spinning on my heel and getting the hell out of Dodge—or Springfield, as it were—but I had promised Carla I was going to come back.

So let's do it, I thought, and I strolled into the Springfield Hospital's main entrance.

————

Up on the second floor, I made my way down a wide corridor, and spotted Room 213, where Carla was a patient. It was about five rooms away from a central nurse's station, and standing by the counter I saw two young and hard-looking men in fine suits, shoes, and an attitude that said they belonged to the unmarked government car down in the parking lot.

I tried to ignore them and slid into Room 213, whose door was wide open. Carla was sitting up in a bed, a bandage on her right temple, and she was wearing a flowered pajama top. An IV was in her right hand and there were sensors *blooping* and *bleeping* on a stand next to her hospital bed.

She smiled. "Ah, my savior has returned."

"I have," I said, "and probably not for long."

"Why, you have a bus to catch?"

"No, but I see a couple of strapping young men out by the nurse's station that look like they're teammates of yours. True?"

"Very observant," she said. "But I insist, really, that you pull up a chair."

"I really don't—"

She held a call button in her hand. "Sit. Or I press this switch, and a nurse and two well-armed and suspicious men will roll right in here. Now, you can try to bolt out, but I'll still press that button. And you'll still catch the eye of those two FBI agents. Or you can sit down and we can have a nice visit."

I pondered that and took an empty chair. "That's a compelling argument, Carla, so how can I say no?"

I sat down and she smiled, happy at roping me in. I hoped that was the only victory she was seeking this afternoon.

"How are you doing?" I asked.

"Oh, physically, I'm doing all right. I'll probably be released tomorrow, which is going to pose a problem for me."

"Why?"

She motioned her head to the open door. "Let's just say my two agents out there aren't very happy with me. They want to know how me, an Office Services Supervisor from the Boston field office, ended up here in Vermont, injured at about the same time police are investigating the death of two men in an empty field, about twenty minutes away. Seems like one hell of a coincidence."

"What did you tell them?"

"That I don't remember. All I can recall is that I was driving around in Manchester, minding my own business, doing some shopping, when somebody kidnapped me. I had a hood over my head, and couldn't hear, smell, or feel anything that would be worthwhile for an investigation, even while I was being … hurt. And the next thing I knew, some handsome stranger had picked me up, wandering on the road, and took me to the hospital."

"You really think I'm handsome?"

"You'll do," she said. "Now, I've answered your question. Here's mine. What do you intend to do with that safety deposit key that belonged to Clarence?"

I dug into my coat pocket, pulled it out. "This one?"

"Ha ha," she said, no humor in her voice. "That one."

"I intend to give it to Wanda," I said. "I'm pretty sure Clarence put her name on the access card so she could get to it."

"But how do you know what bank it belongs to?"

I held up the round Red Sox plastic badge attached to the keychain, rotated it so she could see. There was the logo of a bank—Seacoast Savings Bank of Devon, NH.

"Pretty apparent clue."

"Very apparent." I put the keys away and said, "Hey, you said your leaving tomorrow is going to pose a problem. What kind of problem?"

"The lack of employment kind," she said. "Those two FBI men have informed me that unless my story changes, they'll make sure my worn and tired ass will be fired by tomorrow. So I'll be out of a job."

"Oh," I said. "That's too bad."

"You know it," she said. "So tell me ... should I keep my mouth shut, or should I tell them a new story when they come back from their coffee break?"

"A new story ... "

The call button was in her hand again. Story. The one she had told, the one that had protected me, but which was going to put her out of work. Or it could be a new story, an accurate one, of who I was, how I worked, and where I lived. And more importantly, what I had done this morning in a school playing field. A new and accurate story that would save her job, her career.

"Well?" she asked.

"I'm not sure what I can do," I said.

"Then start thinking."

"Carla ... "

She jiggled the call button in her hand. "Fact is, I'll stop torturing you. It's not much fun. Look, I have a suggestion."

"Go for it."

"I want to work for you."

I spoke before I thought. "No. I work alone."

"You work alone now," Carla said. "Earlier you had my brother working for you. From what you've told me, it was a satisfactory arrangement, until the two of you ended up in Chester."

"Carla, no."

She went on and ignored what I had just said. "Think about how it'll work to your advantage. I know how to access, collate, and provide information. I have contacts in law enforcement all across the country. I can provide security, safety, and backup, and the people involved in your negotiations will think I'm just a pretty face that you have tagging along. Doesn't that sound inviting?"

"But Clarence, he had ... well, he had experience. In weapons, for example."

"So do I."

"Carla ... "

Her face narrowed and her voice lowered. "Do I need to remind you what I did to George this morning?"

"No," I said. "But in the past few days—please don't take offense—you weren't particularly stable and upfront about who you were and what you were up to."

"Offense not taken," she said. "Let's just say that was special circumstances, due to the death of my brother. A one-off that will never happen again. I promise."

Good point. And I hate to admit it, but she had maneuvered me right into a very tight spot, with no apparent way out. The window here was too small to make a crashing escape, like I did back in

Chester, and if I made a move to get the hell out of here, then Carla could press that call button and I'd have a handful of FBI trouble to deal with.

Maybe I could get away.

Maybe I couldn't.

And now I was used to working with a partner.

"Well?" she asked.

"Miss Pope?" I turned and the two FBI guys were at the door, looking in at me and her.

"Hey, can you give me a moment, please? I just want to wrap things up with my visitor."

The lead guy nodded, and they both went out into the hallway, but not far away.

Carla caught my eye. "Anything you'd like to say?"

"Sure," I said.

A pause.

"When can you start?"

ABOUT THE AUTHOR

Brendan DuBois is the award-winning author of twenty novels and more than 160 short stories. He's currently working on a series of novels with best-selling author James Patterson.

His short fiction has appeared in *Playboy, Ellery Queen's Mystery Magazine, Alfred Hitchcock's Mystery Magazine,* and numerous anthologies including *The Best American Mystery Stories of the Century,* published in 2000, as well as *The Best American Noir of the Century.*

His stories have thrice won him the Shamus Award from the Private Eye Writers of America, and have also earned him three MWA Edgar Allan Poe Award nominations. He is also a *Jeopardy!* game show champion. Visit him online at www.brendandubois.com.